Acclaim for Amish Novella Collections

"[T]riple the enjoyment here thanks to this gathering of novellas in one book. The trio of stories…create a tight braid of friendship and love as three young women follow their hearts despite bumps in the road."
—*Publishers Weekly* review of *An Amish Wedding*

"Three of the top authors in Christian literature collaborate on these three Amish-themed novellas. Characters overlap in the stories, which brings unity to the book. These heartwarming tales focus on finding oneself and finding love."
—*RT Book Reviews*, 4-star review of *An Amish Love*

"Perfect for the holiday season, this trilogy also makes good reading for fans of Amish fiction."
—*Library Journal* review of *An Amish Christmas*

"While the Amish maintain a plain lifestyle, that doesn't mean they're strangers to love or loss. In this captivating anthology, the characters keep readers engaged. The stories are authentic, inspiring and positive. Also included are some Amish recipes and a handy glossary of words and phrases."
—*RT Book Reviews* 4.5-star review of *An Amish Gathering*

"[T]hese three warm, entertaining stories are sure to please readers curious about the world of the Plain People as well as fans of Beverly Lewis, Cindy Woodsmall, and other authors of Amish fiction."
—*Library Journal* review of *An Amish Gathering*

An
Amish Wedding

BETH WISEMAN
KATHLEEN FULLER
& KELLY LONG

THOMAS NELSON
Since 1798

NASHVILLE DALLAS MEXICO CITY RIO DE JANEIRO

ISBN-13: 978-0-373-60318-3

An Amish Wedding

Published in Nashville, Tennessee, by Thomas Nelson.
Thomas Nelson is a registered trademark of Thomas Nelson, Inc.

Thomas Nelson, Inc., books may be purchased in bulk for educational, business, fund-raising, or sales promotional use. For information, please e-mail SpecialMarkets@ThomasNelson.com.

Scripture quotations taken from the King James Version.

Publisher's note: This novel is a work of fiction. Names, characters, places, and incidents are either products of the author's imagination or used fictitiously. All characters are fictional, and any similarity to people living or dead is purely coincidental.

Printed in U.S.A.

GLOSSARY

ab im kopp—off in the head, crazy

ach—oh

aenti—aunt

appeditlich—delicious

bensel—hard to handle; a handful

bruder—brother

daadi haus—a small house built onto or near the main house for grandparents to live in

daag—day

daed—dad

danki—thanks

Derr Herr—God

dochder—daughter

dumm—dumb

dummkopf—dummy

eck—special place for bride and groom at the corner of the wedding table

Englisch—non-Amish

Englischer—a non-Amish person

familye—family

frau—wife

freind—friend

geh—go

gut—good

haus—house

hiya—hello

kaffee—coffee

kapp—prayer covering or cap

kinn, kinner—child, children

kumme—come

lieb—love

maedel or *maed*—girl or girls

mamm—mom

mann—man, men

mei—my

milch—milk

mudder—mother

narrisch—crazy

nee—no

nix—nothing

onkel—uncle

roascht—bread stuffing and chicken baked in a casserole

rumschpringe—running-around period when a teenager turns sixteen years old

schee—handsome

schwester—sister

seltsam—weird

sohn—son

was in der welt—what in the world

wunderbaar—wonderful

ya—yes

Yankee—non-Amish person, term used in Middlefield, Ohio

CONTENTS

A PERFECT PLAN

BETH WISEMAN

To Pat Mackey, my fabulous mother-in-law

PROLOGUE

PRISCILLA GLANCED AROUND the yard at all the guests. Warm August temperatures allowed for an outside celebration, and it never rained on her special day. *Mamm* went all out for birthdays, but this year was the biggest yet. In addition to a beautiful pineapple layered cake that her oldest sister, Naomi, made, there was a ham, barbecued string beans, scalloped potatoes, creamed celery, homemade breads, jams, jellies, chowchow, and a variety of pies and cookies. She smiled as she turned away from the main food table.

Ten oblong tables spanned the front yard, topped with simple white coverings. On each table, *Mamm*'s blue Tupperware party bowls were filled with peanuts and chips, with a platter of pickles and olives in the center. Everything was perfect, right down to the decorations. Her sister Hannah had been put in charge of filling the balloons with helium, and yellow and blue bundles were tied to the head chair at each table. Priscilla's place setting had double the balloons from every color in the rainbow.

"I think everything turned out lovely." Naomi waved her arm around the yard. "And look how many guests showed up. There must be a hundred people here."

Priscilla took another look around the crowd and was happy to see that some of the folks were starting a game

of volleyball on the far side of the yard. Then her eyes landed on someone. "What is Chester Lapp doing here?"

Chester Lapp was handsome and well-respected in the community. He was a fine carpenter. Her father had purchased two rockers from Chester for the front porch. But he was nineteen. Why would he want to come to her sixteenth birthday party?

"Why shouldn't he be here?" Naomi folded her arms across her chest and grinned. "Our family has known his family forever. We even share a phone shanty."

"I know that." Priscilla rolled her eyes. "I'm just surprised he's here. I mean, I rarely see him socially. Just at worship, and he hardly ever goes to Sunday singings. I wonder who invited him."

Naomi scratched her cheek as she took a deep breath and looked away.

"You did, didn't you? *Why?*" Priscilla narrowed her eyebrows at her sister. Naomi was twenty-two and always playing matchmaker for someone. "I barely know him."

"Maybe you should get to know him better." Naomi breezed across the yard, turning back once to wink at her sister.

Priscilla sprinted a few steps to catch up with her. "Why do you say that? Has he said something? Tell me, Naomi."

Naomi stopped alongside Priscilla and whispered, "Let's just say he has asked about you more than once."

"When?" She tried not to get too excited as her eyes drifted in Chester's direction.

"Once when I saw him in town, a couple of months ago. Then I ran into him last week at the hardware store in Bird-in-Hand. He asked about you then too." Naomi shrugged. "So I invited him to your birthday party."

Priscilla twisted her mouth from side to side as she studied the tall, handsome man. "I'm still surprised that he came."

"I'm not." Naomi grinned, then walked away.

Priscilla kept her eyes on Chester, but jumped when he turned around and caught her staring. She quickly looked away and began straightening one of the paper tablecloths that had blown up in the wind, but she could see him moving toward her out of the corner of her eye.

"Happy birthday."

She looked up and smiled. *"Danki."* Then she began to line up the bowls and pickle tray so that everything was evenly spaced on the table. She could feel Chester's piercing blue eyes on her, and slowly she lifted her eyes to his again. An easy smile played at the corner of his mouth as he looped his thumbs beneath his suspenders. If it weren't for his traditional clothing, Chester wouldn't look much like an Amish man. Most men kept their hair in a bobbed haircut, bangs in the front, straight on the sides. Chester's hair was dark and curly above his brows and ears; his wavy locks didn't resemble much of a bob. Priscilla wondered if his beard would be curly as well someday, after he was married.

"It's a great party."

Priscilla pulled her eyes from his and went back to the task at hand. *"Ya*, it is. *Danki* for coming." She pushed one of the blue bowls an inch or so to the right, making sure it was the same distance from the pickle tray as the other bowl.

"What are you doing?" Chester folded his arms across his chest, still grinning.

"What?"

"You've been moving those bowls not even a quar-

ter-inch back and forth. I think they are perfectly spaced now."

Priscilla felt the heat rush from her neck to her cheeks. "I wasn't doing that."

"*Ya*, you were."

"No." She folded her arms across her chest, mirroring his stance. "I wasn't." She pulled her eyes from his and kicked at the grass with her bare foot.

He was right. She needed things to be in perfect order, but she wasn't going to apologize for it. She enjoyed organizing things. She'd recently alphabetized recipe cards for Naomi, and her mother was thrilled when Priscilla organized her sewing supplies, grouping her thread colors together and sorting material by color and fabric. Other people appreciated her need for things to be in order—but Chester was making fun of her for arranging a couple of bowls.

"Are you gonna be at the singing on Sunday?"

Priscilla found his eyes and wanted to look away, but couldn't. "Uh, *ya*. I usually go."

"How about going with me?"

She opened her mouth to speak, but nothing came out. Chester Lapp was older, handsome, and asking her to be his date for a Sunday singing. She'd be wound up like a top in preparation for it. Finally she took a breath and spoke. "I can't. But *danki* for asking me." She turned and darted off before he could say anything more.

CHESTER TIPPED BACK his hat and watched Priscilla hurry across the grass. Even in her haste, she was as graceful as a snowflake riding the breeze on a winter morning. He pulled off his hat, scratched his head, then replaced the hat, all the while keeping his eyes on her.

He didn't know that much about her. Beautiful, yes. She was petite with strawberry blond hair, and her blue eyes gleamed when she talked. It seemed like she'd blossomed into a young woman overnight, and she was old enough for him to ask out now. He'd accepted Naomi's invitation to the party hoping to get to know Priscilla a little better. Maybe asking her to a Sunday singing was too forward. But Chester knew that he had more in common with Priscilla than she realized.

While Chester was talking with Naomi, he'd casually mentioned that he planned to go skydiving before he was baptized into the faith. Naomi had burst into laughter. When she came up for air she said, "My sister has always wanted to do that. We think she's *ab im kopp*, but she says she will do it before she's baptized."

Chester didn't know any other young Amish woman who would consider such an endeavor, though it was perfectly allowable prior to baptism. This Priscilla King intrigued him.

PRISCILLA BALANCED HER youngest sister, Sarah Mae, on her hip as she chatted with her guests. Her best friend, Rose, walked up and whispered in her ear, "I need to talk to you."

Priscilla excused herself, and she and Rose eased away from the crowd.

"I just overheard Chester Lapp telling Naomi that he asked you to a Sunday singing." Rose thrust her hands onto her hips. "And you said no! Why?"

"I don't know him." She thought about the way Chester made her uncomfortable earlier, teasing her about the bowls.

Naomi walked up to them then, her lips pinched to-

gether in a frown. "Did you really decline an offer from Chester?"

"Why are you trying to fix me up with him? We barely know each other." Priscilla set Sarah Mae down in the grass beside her. "Good looks aren't everything." She raised her chin, not wanting to admit that Chester made her nervous.

"Too bad." Naomi tucked a strand of loose hair beneath her prayer covering. "Because the two of you have a common goal."

Priscilla rolled her eyes. "What might that be?"

"You both want to go skydiving. I don't know of any other two people in our district who share such a crazy goal." She shrugged. "I just thought it might be worth a mention." Naomi picked up Sarah Mae, grinned, and walked away.

Rose's eyes grew round. "You've wanted to go skydiving ever since Barbie and Elam's wedding."

"That doesn't mean that I should go on a date with Chester Lapp." Although she had to admit, he'd suddenly grown more interesting.

Priscilla had tried and tried to find someone who would jump out of a plane with her. Ever since she'd attended her *Englisch* friend's outdoor wedding, where a man jumped from a plane and right into the reception area, she'd dreamed of doing that herself. To free-fall through the air, soar like a bird...such freedom. Priscilla had talked to the man with the parachute for nearly an hour—and she'd left with a business card and phone number to call if she ever wanted to jump.

"I gotta go." Rose gave her a quick hug, wished her happy birthday again, and headed to her buggy. Priscilla stayed where she was, watching Chester talk with

her parents across the yard. When he walked away from them, Priscilla hurried toward him.

"Chester! Wait!"

CHAPTER ONE

Three years later

HICCUP...

Priscilla covered her mouth with her hand—not so much to stifle the intermittent spasms in her diaphragm, but to keep from exploding at her five-year-old sister. She took a deep breath as she studied the scene before her, then closed her eyes and blew the air from her lungs in an effort to calm herself. It didn't work.

"What have you *done*, Sarah Mae?" She stepped forward to where the little girl was sitting in the middle of the sewing room. *Hiccup...*

Sarah Mae's big brown eyes filled with tears. "What's wrong?" She blinked a few times, her bottom lip quivering. "Why are you using your mean voice?"

Priscilla took another deep breath, hiccuped again, then rubbed her tired eyes. "I'm not using a 'mean' voice, Sarah Mae."

"*Mamm* said I could have these scraps to make a dress for Lizzie Lou." Sarah Mae lifted up the finely sewn blue material for Priscilla to see.

It was the left arm of Priscilla's wedding dress, perfectly stitched and ready to attach to the body of the outfit she planned to be married in. In all her nineteen years, she'd never crafted a finer long sleeve.

"See, I made armholes for Lizzie Lou." Sarah Mae nodded toward her doll, which was propped up against a chair to the left. The rag doll with flowing brown hair went everywhere Sarah Mae went. And Lizzie Lou had many outfits—dresses for working in the fields and going to church service, along with brown, black, and white aprons. Lizzie Lou also had two *kapps* and a black jacket.

Priscilla cringed as Sarah Mae pushed her small fingers through slits on either side of the sleeve. "Sarah Mae..." *Hiccup...* She clutched her chest and tried to control her voice. Then she pointed with one hand toward a pile of scraps to her right. "Those are the scraps *Mamm* meant for you to use." She glanced about at the pieces of material scattered around Sarah Mae until she spotted her other sleeve. She squatted down next to her sister, picked it up, and poked her fingers through the holes on either side.

"That's Lizzie Lou's Sunday dress." Sarah Mae tucked her chin, then lifted her watery eyes to Priscilla's.

Priscilla handed what used to be the sleeves of her wedding dress back to her sister. She scanned the area around Sarah Mae, hoping and praying that the body of her dress was still intact.

"Sarah Mae," she said softly, following another hiccup, "there was another piece of sewn material, a much larger piece. Where is it?"

Sarah Mae stood up, tucked her chin again, then walked across the room. "Lizzie Lou wanted a hammock and a blanket."

"Sarah Mae! No!"

The dress was cut in half, one piece tied between two chairs, the other piece on the floor below the "hammock."

"How could you do this? That was my wedding dress, Sarah Mae! Not scraps!"

"I'm sorry, Sissy! I'm sorry!" Sarah Mae threw her little arms around Priscilla's legs and looked up, tears pouring down her face. "I'll make you a new dress for your wedding."

Priscilla patted Sarah Mae on the back as she thought about the time she'd spent on her wedding dress. "It's all right. I'll make an even better dress." She forced a smile for Sarah Mae. Four weeks until the wedding. It was doable. It might not be as finely stitched as the one that now served as two dresses, a hammock, and a blanket for Lizzie Lou, but it could be done. "Maybe Lizzie Lou needs to get married in her new dress," she mumbled under her breath.

"Sissy?" Sarah Mae pulled her arms from around Priscilla's legs and stared up at her sister. "I'm sorry."

"I know you are, Sarah Mae." She realized her hiccups were gone. She leaned down and kissed the little girl on the cheek. "You stay here and play. I'm going to go help *Mamm* with supper."

And after the meal and cleanup, Priscilla would go meet Chester at the phone shanty that bordered both their homesteads—as she always did on Tuesdays and Thursdays. She smiled. She was the luckiest girl in the world to be marrying Chester Lapp. If this was the worst thing that happened to disrupt the wedding she'd been planning for the past few months, she could live with it.

CHESTER ARRIVED AT the shanty about ten minutes early, anxious to hold Priscilla in his arms. In only a month she'd be his *frau*, and there'd be no more sneaking off to the shanty.

He leaned up against the structure, which resembled an old outhouse—a tall, wooden boxlike building that housed a telephone and a small stool. Most families had phones in the barns these days, but his father, along with Priscilla's father and the Dienners and the Petersheims, chose to keep with tradition, holding on to the shanty they had shared for years.

As he leaned against the weathered wood, he looped his thumbs beneath his suspenders and watched the sun setting in the west, leaving a warm glow atop the fields stretched before him as far as he could see. Tall green grass speckled with brown was evidence of the recent first frost and seemed a prelude for a hard winter.

Chester closed his eyes and imagined curling up on the couch beside Priscilla in front of a warm fire this winter. He was close to finishing the house he was building for them. The building inspector was coming tomorrow to check the electrical wiring. Installing electricity was required, even though they would never turn it on. And should they decide to sell, the resale value would be better if it was wired for electricity. But Chester was counting on spending the rest of his life in that house with Priscilla. He'd worked hard to make it everything they'd dreamed of. Four bedrooms would be enough room for the *kinner* they planned to have.

He heard movement and turned to his left to see Priscilla moving through the field like a beautiful butterfly, her arms swinging back and forth as she lifted her legs high through the pasture, a pallet of orange dusk behind her.

My sweet Priscilla.

Chester had loved Priscilla since she was sixteen. That was when he started courting her, carrying her home

from Sunday singings and making plans for their future. But since he was three years older than she, he waited until she was nineteen to propose. As he watched her hurrying toward him in a dark green dress and black apron, his heart skipped a beat, the way it always did when he first saw her.

She came to a stop right in front of him, breathless and beautiful. "How long have you been waiting?"

"Not long." He cupped her cheeks in his hands and gently kissed her on the mouth, lingering for much longer than he should.

She pulled back and smiled at him. "We'll be married soon enough, and you can kiss me like that all the time."

Chester would be lying to himself if he denied the fact that her looks had drawn him to her initially. She stood out among their people with her strawberry blond hair and stunning blue eyes. A natural blush filled her cheeks atop her ivory complexion.

Despite her comment, Chester kissed her again. She giggled and pushed him away. "Chester Lapp, you better behave yourself."

She was small and flowerlike, but Chester knew better than to be misled by her dainty appearance. Priscilla was as strong a woman as he'd ever met—inside and out. He recalled the day not long after her sixteenth birthday when they held hands and jumped out of a perfectly good airplane together.

His future wife could also swing a baseball bat like no woman he'd seen and outrun most of her teammates. She spoke her mind when necessary, yet was the most compassionate person he knew. She was organized and punctual, and expected others to be. She could obsess on

details sometimes, that was true, but in Chester's eyes... she was perfect.

"Have I told you lately how much I love you?"

She tapped her finger to her chin and twisted her mouth to one side. "Hmm...I can't recall."

He cupped her cheek in his hand. "I love you with all my heart. Forever."

Priscilla put her hand atop his, then pulled his hand to her mouth and kissed it tenderly. "I love you too, and I can't wait to be your *frau*." Then she let go of his hand, stepped back a bit, and frowned.

"What is it?"

"Something happened today. With my wedding dress." She let out a heavy sigh. "Sarah Mae used it to make doll clothes, along with a hammock and blanket for her doll's enjoyment."

It wasn't funny, but Chester stifled a grin just the same. Priscilla came from a family of girls. Naomi— the oldest at twenty-five and still unmarried—lived in the *daadi haus* on the family's property where she ran a bakery business. Then there was Priscilla's married sister, Hannah, who was twenty-two. Then Priscilla, and then Sarah Mae—her parents' little surprise.

Priscilla folded her arms across her chest. "Chester, are you laughing?" She tried to make her voice sound stern.

"No. Not laughing at all." He held his palms toward her. "Besides, you'll be beautiful on our wedding day no matter what you're wearing." He reached for her hand, then squeezed.

"I can make a new dress." She scowled a bit, then her eyes brightened. "The inspectors come tomorrow to look at the house, no?"

"*Ya*. I think everything will be fine, then I can move forward with the finishing touches for my bride-to-be." He hoped that everything would in fact be fine. With his father's help, they had done most of the wiring themselves. It would be a huge setback if something was wrong. He wanted to whisk Priscilla into their new home as soon as possible.

"Do your parents know you meet me here on Tuesdays and Thursdays?" Priscilla bit her bottom lip, then grinned.

"I think so. Do yours?"

She giggled. "*Ya*. We don't speak of it, but they know I'm not just going for a walk." She hugged herself and shivered. "I forgot my sweater."

Chester wasted no time taking off his black jacket, regretful he hadn't done it as soon as she arrived. He draped it around her shoulders.

"*Danki*." Priscilla settled into the jacket, smiling. "I hope the weather is nice for our wedding day. It might be a little cold, but I'm hoping there won't be any rain. I want everyone to be able to gather in the barn or outdoors following the ceremony."

"It will be a perfect day." Chester latched onto the collar on both sides of his jacket and pulled it snug around her. "You warm enough?"

"*Ya*. I'm *gut*."

Then she hiccuped, and he laughed. It was the cutest little sound he'd ever heard, and her eyes widened as she cupped her hand over her mouth.

"This is the second time this has happened today." Her cheeks flushed a bright pink. "How embarrassing."

"It's cute," he said as another hiccup escaped. "*Daed*

always tells us to eat a spoonful of sugar when we get the hiccups."

Chester's family was small by comparison to others in the district—only Chester and his brother, Abraham.

"Abe used to get the hiccups a lot."

"*Nee*, I don't know how cute it...*hiccup*...is."

They both laughed again, but jumped when the telephone in the shanty rang.

On the third ring, Chester stepped inside the booth and picked up the receiver. He said hello, then his smile faded and he tightened his grip on the receiver.

CHAPTER TWO

IT WAS ALMOST dark by the time Priscilla eased up the porch steps. She hung her head as she opened the door and moved inside. Naomi was peeling potatoes at the kitchen table.

"Why so sour?" Naomi wasn't wearing her *kapp*, and strands of her dark brown hair had fallen forward from the bun atop her head.

Priscilla and her sister didn't look anything alike. Naomi had dark hair, dark eyes, and an olive complexion, just like Sarah Mae and Hannah—and like their mother. Hannah used to tease her when they were young, telling her she was adopted.

Priscilla pulled out a chair across from Naomi at the large kitchen table. She sat down, propped her elbows on the table, and rested her chin in her hands. "I was with Chester at the phone shanty."

"Really? I'm *so* surprised." Naomi smiled. "I think we know where you go on Tuesday and Thursday nights, Priscilla." She set a peeled potato in the pot beside her, then her expression grew solemn. "Did something happen? You look sad, *maedel*."

"I'm okay, I guess." She bit her bottom lip. "Chester is pretty upset, though. The building inspector is coming tomorrow to check the wiring, and we've been nervous about that, praying everything would be up to code.

But tonight Zeke called and said there's a problem with the roof."

Chester's cousin Zeke was in town for the wedding, and he just happened to be a carpenter who specialized in roofing. Chester had asked him to check out the roof on the house.

"What's wrong with it?" Naomi sliced off a sliver of potato and handed it to Priscilla; she was the only one in the family who liked raw potato.

Priscilla waited to swallow before she answered. "The storm last week blew off some shingles. Zeke said he would help Chester repair it, but I know Chester wasn't expecting to have to fit that in. His job at the furniture store takes up most of his time, plus the chores around his house, and..." She sighed. "And now he has to fix the roof."

"God often challenges us, but I'm sure you and Chester will have a fine home." Naomi began cutting hard-boiled eggs on a chopping board.

"Potato salad?" Priscilla eyed the mayonnaise and jar of pickles on the table beside Naomi.

"*Ya. Daed* asked if I would make him some." Naomi carried the pot of potatoes to the sink, filled it with water, and put it on the stove.

Naomi took most of her meals with the family at the main house, even though she lived in the *daadi haus*. She also ran a baked goods business from her home, and she was a wonderful cook.

Priscilla let out a heavy sigh. "Did you hear what happened to my wedding dress?"

Naomi grinned as she sat down again and continued chopping hard-boiled eggs. "I did...something about clothes for Lizzie Lou?"

"Don't forget the hammock and blanket." Priscilla shook her head. "I was so upset with her, but when she started to cry, I thought…well, I guess I'll just have to make another dress. A better dress."

Priscilla reached for half a boiled egg, only to have Naomi playfully slap her hand. "*Ach*. No, *ya* don't. I have just enough." She pulled the plate of eggs closer. "I pulled a honey bun cake from the oven. Go get yourself a piece."

"We just ate supper."

"Then why are you trying to eat my eggs?"

Priscilla shrugged. "I don't know."

They were quiet for a few moments.

"I have a lot on my mind about this wedding. First my dress today, and then problems with the roof."

"Everything will be fine, Priscilla. You worry too much."

They sat quietly as Naomi chopped the eggs for the potato salad. Priscilla knew her sister was right. But when things didn't go as planned, she wondered if she was on the right path, the one God had planned for her.

Priscilla tapped her finger to her chin. "Remember how everything went wrong with Hannah's wedding?"

Naomi chuckled. "*Ya*. The church wagon showed up late with the supplies, we ran out of propane for the extra ovens *Daed* rented…" She shook her head. "And the poor groom was battling the flu."

"It's not funny, Naomi. I don't want those troubles at my wedding."

Naomi stopped chopping the eggs and locked eyes with Priscilla. "Hannah didn't let it bother her, Priscilla, because she loved Leroy and just wanted to be with him. You should be glad you found someone to spend your

life with and stop fretting about everything. You know worry is a sin."

"I know." Priscilla sighed again. "Why do you think I'm like that? I mean, I always pray that everything will go smoothly, even though I know we're not here on this earth to have an easy life."

Naomi handed her a piece of egg and a sympathetic smile. "Priscilla, where were you while we were growing up? Did you not listen at all? We cannot understand God's plan for us. Everything is His will. It might seem like things are falling apart sometimes, but often God has something better in store for us down the line." She sat taller and smiled. "You will enjoy life much more if you will just relax."

CHESTER CLIMBED UP the ladder and joined Zeke on top of the roof. Zeke had come from Ohio to serve as one of Chester's attendants for the wedding, and Chester was sure thankful that his cousin was in the construction business.

"I'm surprised more of these shingles didn't blow off during the storm." Zeke pointed to the section of the roof over the kitchen. "Look. See how different some of them are? You need to talk to the person who sold these to you."

Chester rubbed his forehead, wondering how neither he, his father, nor his brother had noticed the difference in the shingles. "*Ya.* You're right."

"Don't worry, cousin. I can help you with this."

"*Danki*, Zeke. Since Abe broke his wrist, he hasn't been able to be of much help." Abe had fallen from the roof a few weeks earlier, and they were grateful that his injuries had been no worse.

They climbed down the ladder, and Zeke followed Chester to the front door. He turned the knob and motioned Zeke ahead of him and into the living room so Zeke could see the progress he'd made the past week.

Zeke scanned the room, then raised a brow toward Chester. "Mighty fine." He ran his hand along a built-in bookcase on the far wall. "And a bit fancy."

"Priscilla's idea." Chester stepped next to Zeke and eyed the floor-to-ceiling bookcase. "She likes to read, and she said she hopes that our *kinner* will too."

Zeke grinned. "Planning to start a family right away?"

"As soon as possible." Chester smiled back at his cousin, thoughts of Priscilla and their wedding night swirling in his head. He allowed himself the vision for a couple of seconds, then added, "We want lots of *kinner*. Priscilla will be a fine *mamm*."

Zeke put his hand on Chester's shoulder. "I'm happy for you."

Chester showed Zeke the rest of the house. The kitchen was large and spacious with plenty of room for the table and chairs Priscilla's parents gave them as a wedding present. As he waited for Zeke to have a good look, he pictured Priscilla cooking their meals and tending to their *kinner*. Their wedding couldn't come soon enough.

FOLLOWING SUPPER CLEANUP on Thursday, Priscilla brushed past her mother in the kitchen, anxious to meet Chester at the phone shanty. She pulled her black sweater from the rack by the door, and she'd almost made a clean getaway when her mother cleared her throat. After holding her breath for a moment, Priscilla eased around and faced her.

"Priscilla, before you go on your *walk*…"

Mamm folded her arms across her chest and held her

chin high in such a way that Priscilla knew she was trying to be firm—but Priscilla saw the slight twinkle in her eyes.

"I'd like for you to stop by the Zooks' house. I have something for you to take to Rachel."

Priscilla glanced at the clock hanging on the wall in the kitchen. She loved Rachel Zook and enjoyed visiting with her, but Chester would be waiting.

"That boy will wait, Priscilla." *Mamm* grinned as she left the kitchen, leaving no doubt that she did indeed know about the meetings at the shanty. She returned a moment later with a small lap quilt.

Priscilla had seen *Mamm* working on a pink quilt— of course it was for Rachel. Everything in Rachel's life was bright pink, even her clothing, shoes, and socks. The walls of Rachel's room were also painted pink, and everyone in the community contributed to the pink décor.

Bishop Ebersol allowed Rachel to dress in the untraditional color, and he often referred to her as one of God's special blessings, which she truly was. Rachel was the same age as Priscilla, but in her mind she was only about five years old.

Priscilla took the quilt from her mother and studied it for a moment. She couldn't believe how many different shades of pink formed the stars and border. "It's beautiful, *Mamm*. I'm sure Rachel will love it."

Her mother smiled. "I loved making it for her."

Priscilla headed out the door, wondering how she could keep her visit brief. She wasn't sure she'd ever had a short visit with Rachel.

She'd barely cleared the porch steps when she took off in a run. The Zook place wasn't far down the road, but

it was in the opposite direction from the phone shanty. She'd have to hurry.

Five minutes later she arrived on the Zook porch and tried to catch her breath. She folded the quilt over one arm and patted her cheeks for a moment, trying to ease the sting from the cool wind. She knocked on the door.

Mary and John Zook had fourteen children—more than anyone else in their district. Priscilla figured John Zook was happy that nine out of fourteen of those *kinner* were boys. Lots of help in the fields.

Priscilla wanted a large family too, but she thought six or seven *kinner* would be enough. She wasn't sure how Mary kept up with fourteen, especially since they all still lived at home. Priscilla was pretty sure that Annie had just turned two, and the oldest boy, Ben, was twenty-one.

Priscilla tucked a strand of loose hair beneath her *kapp* as the wooden door opened. Mary Zook looked through the screen, with Annie on one hip and two slightly older girls standing beside her. A smile lit the woman's tired face.

"Priscilla, come in." Mary eyed the quilt draped over Priscilla's arm as she shifted Annie on her hip. "What've you got there?"

"*Mamm* made it for Rachel," Priscilla said as she stepped into the large living room. She offered the quilt to Mary, hoping to make a quick exit. But Mary shook her head.

"Let me have one of the girls go get her. She'd be so disappointed if she knew you came calling and she didn't get to see you." Mary set Annie down as she spoke to one of the older girls—either Frieda or Elizabeth. Priscilla couldn't remember who was who. They weren't twins, but they looked a lot alike.

"I don't want to disrupt your household so soon after the supper hour." But Priscilla knew it was too late. Rachel would be downstairs soon. *Wait on me, Chester.*

Mary picked up Annie again, then eased her into a playpen filled with toys. "Are you excited about your wedding?"

"*Ya.* Very excited." Priscilla felt her cheeks warm a bit, the way they did every time someone asked about her upcoming nuptials. She couldn't wait to be Chester's *frau.*

"I remember our wedding day like it was yesterday." Mary's brown eyes took on a faraway look, then she met eyes with Priscilla and laughed. "But we've stayed busy since then."

Priscilla felt even more heat in her cheeks, unsure if Mary was referring to all the children they'd had or something else. Before she had time to decide for sure, she heard a familiar voice. And even though she knew she'd be late to meet Chester, the sound of Rachel's sweet voice warmed her heart.

"Pre-Ceelia!" Rachel ran to Priscilla the way she always did and threw her arms around her. Rachel was several inches taller than Priscilla, and overall a large girl. As always, she was dressed in a bright pink dress with matching pink shoes and socks. Her prayer covering was white, but there were two pink flowers sewn on either side. Priscilla couldn't breathe for a moment as Rachel engulfed her in a big hug.

She'd grown up with Rachel, but she couldn't recall when her friend became so obsessed with the color pink. It must have been when they were both very young, because for as long as Priscilla could remember, Rachel required pink—on her person, in her room, and basically everywhere she went. Priscilla had comforted Rachel

many times when they were places that weren't pink. About five years ago, when Mary was sick, Priscilla and her mother took Rachel to the doctor for a cold. Rachel pulled a pink crayon from the pocket of her apron and colored on the *Englisch* doctor's pretty white wall. She carried a pink crayon everywhere she went.

Mary tapped Rachel on the shoulder and spoke to her tenderly. "Careful, Rachel. You don't want to hurt Priscilla."

"I love Pre-Ceelia!" Rachel finally released Priscilla from the embrace.

"I love you too, Rachel." She held the quilt out to her. "*Mei mamm* made this for you."

Rachel brought both hands to her mouth and gasped, then she slowly took the quilt from Priscilla and brought it to her face. She inhaled as she pressed her face into it and mumbled something Priscilla didn't understand.

"Move the quilt, Rachel, so we can understand you." Mary tapped Rachel on the shoulder again, and Rachel brought the quilt away from her face.

"*Danki* to Pre-Ceelia's *mamm* for my present." Rachel buried her face in the quilt again.

Priscilla glanced at the clock on the fireplace mantel. "You're welcome, Rachel. I'll tell *Mamm* how much you like it." She smiled at Mary. "I guess I better go."

Mary nodded, but Rachel pulled the blanket from her face like it was on fire. Her eyes grew round as she spoke. "I have something for you too!" She bounced on her toes. "I have a present for Pre-Ceelia!" She turned to Mary. "It's in *mei* room, *Mamm*. I go get it!"

Rachel ran to the stairs and bolted up them two at a time. Priscilla bit her bottom lip and looked at the clock again.

"You've always been one of Rachel's favorite people," Mary said.

Priscilla smiled as guilt pinched at her heart. She shouldn't be in such a hurry to leave, but Chester…he was surely at the phone shanty wondering where she was. "Rachel is one of my favorite people too."

Rachel returned and handed Priscilla a letter-sized envelope. *To Priscilla* was written across it with pink crayon. "For your marriage day. Not to open until your marriage day!" She raised her shoulders, then dropped them slowly as she smiled. "It's from God."

"*Danki*, Rachel. This is very special." Priscilla pressed the envelope to her chest. "Are you sure you don't want me to open it now?"

Rachel shook her head so hard that Priscilla worried she would have a headache. When she finally stopped, she pressed her lips together and frowned. "No! God said only to open on your marriage day!"

Priscilla touched Rachel on the arm. "Okay. I promise to open it on my marriage—wedding day." She looked at the clock again.

Rachel let out a heavy breath and nodded, and Priscilla put the envelope into her pocket. "I'll see you soon." She turned to leave, but Mary snapped her fingers.

"*Ach!* I almost forgot. I have two of your *mamm*'s bowls from our last gathering. She sent home the leftovers with me. Let me just run and get them." Mary eased around the playpen and scooted past Priscilla, Rachel, and the other girls toward the kitchen.

Priscilla forced a smile before her eyes landed on the clock.

Wait for me, Chester…

CHAPTER THREE

PRISCILLA RAN AS fast as she could, lifting her legs high as she made her way across the hay field to the phone shanty. And for the third time this week, she had a case of the hiccups. Yards before she reached the meeting place, she could hear the phone ringing, but there was no sign of Chester. She picked up the pace as she wondered if maybe Chester stopped somewhere to try to call the shanty. Lots of folks in their community had cell phones, but neither Priscilla nor Chester did. Mostly it was out of respect for their parents, who were against any type of phone near the house. The families sharing the shanty also chose not to have an answering machine, even though Bishop Ebersol didn't have a problem with it.

She stepped into the shanty and reached for the phone hanging on the wall just as another hiccup echoed within the small space. *Please be Chester.*

"Hello."

"I'm looking for Chester Lapp."

She stifled a sigh. "He's not here right now. Can I take a message for him?" Priscilla picked up the pencil that was beside a small pad of paper they kept on a shelf underneath the phone.

"Yes, if you don't mind. This is Joel Cunningham. I'm the building inspector, and we met yesterday."

Priscilla took a deep breath, then blew it out slowly,

afraid to ask…but needing to know. "Is everything okay? Did the house pass the inspection?" To her embarrassment, she hiccuped into the phone, then squeezed her eyes closed as she spoke. "I'm so sorry."

There was a slight chuckle on the other end of the line. "No problem. Eat a spoonful of sugar."

That was the second time she'd heard that. Before she could respond, the man continued.

"There are a few things I need to go over with Chester. Can you take my number and have him give me a call?"

Priscilla wrote down the phone number, promised to have Chester call him tomorrow, and hiccuped as she hung up. She tucked the number in the pocket of her apron with Rachel's envelope before she headed for home, sorry she had missed Chester and fighting worry about what problems the building inspector may have found. Instead, she thought about what Naomi had said.

FRIDAY MORNING CHESTER finished sanding a bench he'd been working on all week. It was a special order, and Mr. Turner said it needed to be finished today so that the customer could pick it up Saturday morning. He knew it might mean staying late tonight, and he had hoped to get off early to go check on Priscilla. She'd never missed one of their Tuesday or Thursday meetings at the shanty. But Mr. Turner's snappy tone didn't leave much room for an argument. His boss hadn't seemed himself lately. The elderly man had even barked at a customer for slamming the door when he entered the store. Chester wasn't surprised that the patron left without buying anything.

He heard the bell chime on the front door, but he knew Mr. Turner was there, along with two other employees, so he didn't get up, but instead started staining the bench

with a light walnut color. He heard a woman's voice talking to Mr. Turner...and then recognized it as Priscilla's. He wiped his hands on a towel and turned around to see her entering the work area in the back of the store.

"I'm so sorry I missed you at the shanty." She glanced over her shoulder and waited until the door shut behind her, then threw her arms around his neck. He squeezed her tightly before gently easing her away.

"Is everything okay?" He kissed her softly on the lips before she answered.

"*Ya*. I'm sorry. *Mamm* wanted me to take something to Rachel Zook, and it was hard to get away." She grinned as her cheeks flushed a light pink. "I missed you."

Chester kissed her again, keeping one eye on the door. "I missed you too."

She bit her bottom lip. "The phone at the shanty was ringing when I finally got there. It was the building inspector."

Chester tipped back the rim of his hat and rubbed his forehead. "*Ya*. He called me here at the shop this morning."

Priscilla stared at him. "How bad is it?"

"It could have been worse, but *Daed* and me are gonna have to do some rewiring upstairs." He shook his head. "Seems like a lot of work when we won't be using electricity."

"I know." She frowned. "I can't imagine us not living there forever."

After everything he'd put into building this house for them, he sure hoped that they would live there forever. But now he could add wiring repair to the roof repair. It was going to be a challenge to have everything done by mid-November.

It was tradition for the bride and groom to spend as long as three months living with the bride's parents. During that time, they would visit family and friends—sometimes stopping at several homes in one day. It was also when they would collect the bulk of their wedding presents. But both Chester and Priscilla were hoping to move into their new home two weeks after the wedding.

He cupped her cheek in his hand and gazed into her beautiful blue eyes. He didn't want to think of the problems he'd had with the house—beginning with the foundation, which didn't set right. Then the lumber for the frame was delayed, putting him behind schedule on the entire project. And now, these latest issues.

He pushed the thoughts from his mind, resolved to focus on the future and his new life with Priscilla. After a tender kiss, he said, "Do you know how much I love you?"

She smiled. "With all your heart."

He reached down and squeezed her hand. "I guess I better get back to work. But I'll see you at your *haus* on Sunday." He gave her a quick wink.

As was customary, the church deacon would announce to church members on Sunday that Priscilla and Chester were getting married. Then her father would stand up and announce the date and time. Communion was held in October, and wedding publications were always announced during worship service within a few weeks after that. Most of the community already knew about the upcoming wedding, but publication was a long-standing tradition, and those who didn't already know would clear their calendars for the first Tuesday in November. On the day of publication, Priscilla and Chester were allowed to skip church service and spend time alone at Priscilla's

house, and Priscilla would cook them a fine meal. He was looking forward to spending some time alone with her.

PRISCILLA STAYED IN the sewing room for most of the afternoon and tried to work on a new wedding dress, but the treadle sewing machine kept locking up. After a while, she gave the foot pedal a swift kick and moseyed to her room. She plopped down on the bed, her head filled with wedding plans. She was thankful that she'd already made her bridal attendants' dresses. Naomi's and Rose's dresses were safely put away, with no chance of becoming doll clothes for Lizzie Lou. She was also thankful that Hannah had decided early on that she didn't want to be an attendant because her baby was due the same week as the wedding. That had made it much easier on Priscilla. Otherwise, she would have been forced to exclude either one of her sisters or her lifelong best friend, since only two attendants were allowed.

After leaving Chester earlier in the day, she'd spent the morning helping her mother and Naomi clean the basement. With the wedding now three and a half weeks away, *Mamm* wanted every nook and cranny in the house clean. But Priscilla knew she needed to finish her wedding dress too.

She ran her hand along the intricate stitching of her red-and-white Lone Star quilt, knowing that she wouldn't be sleeping alone beneath it for much longer. She couldn't wait to be in Chester's loving arms for the rest of her life.

Once they were in their own home, they would share Chester's king-size bed, one he'd made just for them. Her furniture would nicely fill one of the extra bedrooms in their new home. Leaning back on her hands, she studied her bedroom. Everything was in the proper place, and

not much had changed over the course of her nineteen years. But as she took inventory of the life she'd lived in this room, somehow everything looked different to her today, each piece of furniture and keepsake reflective of her life up until now.

Daed had made her full-size bed when she seven years old, replacing Hannah's hand-me-down twin bed. She could still remember the first time she slept in the "big girl bed," tucked beneath a new set of sheets and quilt. She glanced at the matching oak dresser that came a few months after the bed; the top three drawers were stuffed with undergarments, extra *kapps*, socks, tights for the winter, and sweaters. The bottom drawer was filled with letters from relatives, Christmas cards she'd received, and books. The rocking chair in the corner of the room once belonged to her grandmother, and the clock hanging on her wall was a gift from her mother just last year. Her family and friends knew how much she loved clocks, especially handmade ones like the one from *Mamm*— enclosed in cedar with delicate gold hands, keeping the world on schedule. Priscilla loved to fall asleep at night to the gentle ticking.

It would all be going with her to her new home, and she was thankful for the familiarity her possessions would provide. She glanced to her left. Rachel's envelope was on her nightstand. She thought about opening it, but recalled the promise she had made. *Sweet Rachel*.

It would be time to go help with supper soon, but for just a moment, she decided to indulge herself. She lay back on her bed and closed her eyes, visions of her wedding day swirling in her mind. Naomi and Rose would be by her side. Zeke and Abe would serve as Chester's attendants. *Mamm* would cry, of course—just as she had

when Hannah got married. Her friends and family would all bring lavishly decorated cakes and keepsake containers filled with candies, cookies, and all kinds of special goodies to be passed around the *eck*. There would be a meal of *roascht* and all the fixings bountiful enough to feed the family and friends in attendance. It was a perfect plan, and it was going to be a great day.

Hiccup. Not again! Her chest rose and fell with each spasm. She'd never had the hiccups so much in her life.

She heard the murmur of voices across the hall, but she didn't budge as she continued to envision her wedding day. Then the voices became clearer.

"I hope we're not going to have a repeat of Hannah's wedding."

Priscilla's eyes flew open at the sound of her mother's voice. She didn't move, just listened as Naomi answered.

"I'm sure everything will be fine, *Mamm*."

"I hope so. Poor Chester is having all kinds of trouble with the *haus*." Her mother paused, and Priscilla cupped her hand over her mouth and hiccuped again. "You know what happened with the wedding dress. And now this."

What? Priscilla bolted off the bed and held her breath as her heart raced. She could tell from the sounds coming from across the hall that *Mamm* and Naomi were straightening Sarah Mae's room.

"I don't know if we should even tell Priscilla just yet that her favorite *aenti* and *onkel* won't be able to come." *Mamm* sighed deeply. "You know how much your sister worries."

No! Not only were *Aenti* Rebecca and *Onkel* John her favorite kinfolks, but her aunt was supposed to be making Priscilla a special cake topped with candied yellow

roses. Priscilla stood quietly, her hand firmly across her mouth, and listened. Her body jerked with another spasm.

"No problem, *Mamm*. I'll make Priscilla a special cake."

Priscilla pulled her hand away and smiled at Naomi's offer. *Hiccup!* Her eyes widened as she realized how loud it was this time. In seconds her mother and Naomi were standing in her doorway.

"I thought you were downstairs in the sewing room working on your dress." *Mamm* put her hands on her hips and frowned.

"I was…" She paused as her chest heaved in and out. "But the sewing machine kept locking up on me. Now, please tell me why *Aenti* Rebecca and *Onkel* John aren't going to be at my wedding." Priscilla put her palms on her chest and held her breath, but it didn't go any good. *Hiccup.*

Mamm walked to the bed and smoothed the quilt where Priscilla had been sitting, then she turned around and folded her hands in front of her. "Rebecca is going to have a baby, and the doctor in Middlefield told her she shouldn't travel."

Priscilla cringed. "What? *Aenti* Rebecca is pregnant? She's…she's nearly *your* age, *Mamm*. How can that be?"

Mamm slammed her hands back to her hips as she cleared her throat. "I assure you, Priscilla, women can get pregnant at the age of forty." She stared at Priscilla, raised her eyebrows, and stood taller.

Priscilla sat back down as she quickly calculated her mother's age. Forty-five. "*Ach, ya.* Sarah Mae." She grinned.

Naomi stepped forward and put a hand on Priscilla's arm. "No worries, Priscilla. I'll make sure there are candied yellow roses on one of your cakes."

"*Danki*, Naomi."

There was no doubt in Priscilla's mind that her sister would make a great cake. *Hiccup!*

"That's a terrible case of the hiccups," Naomi said as she sat down in Priscilla's rocking chair.

"Please don't tell me to eat a spoonful of sugar. I've already heard that twice." *Hiccup.*

Naomi kicked the floor with her bare feet until the oak rocker swung into motion. "I can't even remember the last time I had the hiccups."

Her mother sat down beside Priscilla on the bed and crossed one leg over the other.

Priscilla hiccuped again, and they all chuckled. "Until lately I can't remember the last time I've had them either. But I got them when I was at the phone shanty with…" She shifted her eyes toward her mother, who was grinning. "…with Chester. He got the call that there were problems with the roof. Oh…and before that I got them when I found Sarah Mae cutting up my wedding dress." She tapped her finger to her chin. "And when I answered the phone at the shanty when the building inspector called with bad news." Her expression dropped. She glanced back and forth between her mother and sister. "And now I have them again when I hear this sad news about *Aenti* Rebecca and *Onkel* John." She sat up taller and gasped. "Every time I get the hiccups, something bad happens with the wedding."

Mamm slapped her playfully on the leg. "*Ach*, Priscilla. You're being superstitious. That's nonsense."

Maybe.

But just the same…she was going downstairs to eat a spoonful of sugar. And she would pray for no more embarrassing eruptions.

CHAPTER FOUR

SATURDAY MORNING PRISCILLA pulled her black jacket snug around her as she walked down the road toward Rose's house. She needed to talk to her best friend—specifically, she needed Rose to convince her that she'd lost sleep last night for no reason. Priscilla had prayed hard for God to take away her anxiety about the wedding, but sleep eluded her anyway.

She kicked a pebble in the road, but quickly picked up her pace when she noticed the clouds darkening above her and felt the sting of the wind's chill on her cheeks. Leaves on either side of the road started to swirl in small brown and orange tornadoes around her, and within seconds she felt raindrops splashing her face. Rose's house was in view, so she sprinted toward the porch. By the time she reached the steps, she was soaked.

"Priscilla King, what in the world are you doing?" Rose pulled Priscilla into the living room. "Wait here. I'll get you a towel."

Priscilla stood dripping on the hardwood floor until Rose returned. "Sorry, I got water on the floor."

"That's okay. Let's move into the kitchen and sit at the table." Rose pulled out a chair for Priscilla, who then sat down on top of the towel. Droplets of water spilled onto the top of the table, and Rose handed her a kitchen

towel for her face. "Didn't you know we were in for rain this afternoon?"

Priscilla shrugged as she patted her face. "Where is everyone?"

Rose sat down across from her. "*Mamm* and *Daed* went to Strasburg Tractor Supply to get a part for the plow, James and Ben are in the barn, and *Aenti* Tabby is visiting a friend. So this is a *gut* time to talk." She put her elbows on the table and dropped her chin into her hands. "What's wrong, Priscilla? You look like something's bothering you."

Priscilla shrugged again. "I—I don't know." She scratched her nose, then fumbled with the damp towel on the table. "Just so much to do before the wedding."

Rose put her palms flat on the table and sat taller. She lifted her chin. "Priscilla, you've had everything for this wedding planned out for months. What's *really* bothering you?"

Priscilla smiled. Rose knew her better than anyone, so her prodding wasn't surprising. Still, she felt silly. She rubbed her eyes for a moment, then looked up at her friend. Leaving out no details, she told how she had been getting the hiccups as a forewarning of unwelcomed events. When she was done, she waited for Rose to comment. But Rose just stared at her.

"I know you think I'm *ab im kopp*, but isn't it strange?"

Rose folded her arms across her chest and grinned. "*Ya*, I do think you're off in the head. That's just plain silly, Priscilla. Those things can happen to anyone." She leaned forward to reach for Priscilla's hand and squeezed it. "Don't worry, *mei maedel*. Everything is going to be fine. Trust the Lord's will."

Priscilla forced a smile. "You're right." She eased her

hand from underneath Rose's and stood up. She pointed a finger at her friend, whose nuptials were set for December. "I just hope you don't have all the problems we're having, come time for your wedding."

Rose raised her shoulders, then dropped them slowly. "If we do, we will put our faith in God and work through it. Which is what you should do."

Priscilla walked to the window and took a peek outside. The sun was slowly lifting above blue-gray clouds. "I guess I better head home before it makes wet again." She turned to Rose, gave her a hug, and darted down the porch steps.

She was determined to put her trust in God's will and not fret about silly superstitions.

CHESTER PULLED THE stool up close to the workbench in the barn and sat down. He took off his hat and reached for the clock he'd been working on, picturing it on the mantel in his and Priscilla's home. His future *frau* loved clocks, and he wanted her to cherish this wedding gift. He ran his hand over it gingerly, pleased that the last coat of stain was dry. Now he just had to apply the glossy finish and install the clockworks.

He took great care applying the lacquer, making sure it was smooth and didn't leave any bubbles. He'd spent most of the day working on the roof with Zeke, and he hoped to finish the clock in time to take it to Priscilla tomorrow when she cooked for him at her house. He tried to picture the deacon announcing to the congregation that he and Priscilla would be married. They'd been formally engaged since July, and traditionally the publication of their engagement would have been a surprise to most of the community. But both he and Priscilla had

been guilty of spreading the word from the moment she had agreed to become his *frau*. Chester reckoned a few folks weren't sure of the date, but Priscilla's father would announce the day and time after the deacon spoke. He couldn't wait until November when they would take their vows before God, friends, and family.

As much as he would like to hear the deacon and Priscilla's father speak about their upcoming wedding, he wouldn't give up tomorrow afternoon with Priscilla for anything. It was rare that they were allowed to spend time alone, and Chester wanted it to be a day to remember.

He set the clock off to one side so that it could dry. By morning, it would be dry enough to install the parts.

"Done with the clock?"

Chester turned to see Abe walking into the barn, his wrist still in a cast. "*Ya*, almost."

"Sorry I haven't been able to help you more with the *haus*."

Chester started to answer, but then he noticed something holstered to his brother's hip. "You know Bishop Ebersol doesn't like us using cell phones unless it's for business. And neither do *Mamm* and *Daed*."

Abe put his good hand on his hip. "*Ach, ya*. But I'm in *mei rumschpringe*. Besides, everyone has one."

"I never had one before I was baptized, and I still don't." Chester frowned. "I'd put that in my pocket if I were you. No need to rub it in *Mamm*'s and *Daed*'s faces."

"They've already seen it, and they didn't say nothing." He reached down and touched the phone. "I wouldn't need one if *Mamm* and *Daed* would allow an answering machine in the shanty. We miss calls all the time, and I never know what's going on."

Chester elbowed Abe as he brushed past. "Don't play

trickery with me. You just want to be able to call Linda. Bet she has a phone too, no?"

Abe grinned. "How'd you know about Linda?"

Chester turned to face him. "Everyone knows about you and Linda. You've been carting her home from singings for weeks, and you get a goofy look every time you're around her."

"I do not." Abe stood taller and raised his chin.

"*Ya*, you do." Chester chuckled as he walked out of the barn.

Abe was on his heels. "What do you mean, goofy look?"

Chester kept walking but did his best to imitate the look Abe got when he was around Linda. He lifted his nose and squinted his eyes. "Like this."

"You look like a pig."

Chester laughed. "Exactly! So do you when you give Linda that *dumm* look."

They were walking up the porch steps to the house when Chester heard the vibration coming from Abe's hip. Abe unlatched the phone and brought it to his ear.

"At least you got the good sense to keep it on vibrate," Chester mumbled, shaking his head.

As he reached for the screen door, Abe nudged him with his elbow. "It's for you."

"What? Who is it?"

"Mr. Turner."

"Huh?" How on earth had his boss tracked down his brother's cell number? For that matter, how did he even know Abe had a phone? Chester dismissed the thoughts as he brought the phone to his ear.

Mr. Turner was up in years, but generally he was a likable fellow, even though he'd been acting a bit out of

character lately. But Chester had never heard him scream the way he was hollering into the phone at this moment. He held the phone out a few inches from his ear, shocked at what Mr. Turner was saying.

CHAPTER FIVE

PRISCILLA LIT THE bayberry-scented candle that she'd saved for this occasion. Then she arranged some chrysanthemums in a vase, ones she'd picked that morning. If she had any regret about the ways of the Old Order Amish, it would be that flowers were not allowed at weddings. She wished her special day could be filled with them.

She breathed in their scent as she eyed the two place settings she'd carefully laid out for her dinner. *Mamm* insisted she use the good china, white plates with ivy delicately etched around the edges, and she put them atop lace place mats that were more for looks than anything else. Cream-colored napkins, silverware, and company tea glasses finished off the setting.

She and Chester would have about two hours alone while everyone else was sharing a meal after church service. After spending the morning preparing, everything was ready. Chester had requested "underground ham" for the main meal, a recipe her mother often carted to social events. Chester loved the cheesy ham and potato dish that was baked and topped with crumbled bacon. Earlier that morning, Priscilla had baked two loaves of bread and a butter pecan cake. Chester liked the cream cheese filling and rich, flavorful icing. She planned to spend the rest of her life tending to him, their house, and eventually their *kinner*.

Now, as the fragrance of the candle mingled with the rewarding smell of her cooking, she stepped back and smiled. And no hiccups. She'd convinced herself that her superstitions were unfounded, and she refused to let worry block her heart from the voice of God. He was in control. She pushed loose strands of hair up underneath her prayer covering and smoothed the wrinkles from her black apron. Chester liked her burgundy-colored dress the best, so she was happy to wear it. She closed her eyes and thanked God for all He'd blessed her with.

As she heard the *clippity-clop* of hooves coming up the driveway, she took another look around the kitchen. Joy bubbled inside her as she moved through the living room. She pulled the wooden door open, but when she looked through the screen at Chester, her elated spirit floundered. She knew when his smile was forced. She pushed the screen door open, and he handed her a box wrapped in yellow and tied with a white bow.

"Danki," she said as she accepted the present. She bit her bottom lip. *No kiss?*

"You're welcome." Chester took a deep breath. "It smells *gut* in here." He took his hat off and hung it on the rack by the door. His blue shirt brought out his eyes, which met with hers as he finally leaned down and kissed her.

"Is everything okay?" Priscilla held her breath, praying nothing else was wrong with the house.

"Sure."

They stood there for an awkward moment, and Priscilla was certain that everything was not all right.

"I made your favorite, underground ham." She reached for his hand and pulled him into the kitchen, cradling

the package in her other arm. "It's keeping warm in the oven."

"You're the best, Priscilla. I love you."

As he kissed her again, Priscilla slowly eased away and placed the present on the table. "What's wrong, Chester? I can tell something's not right." Her stomach rolled as she watched his face fall. "Please tell me." She pulled out her father's chair at the head of the table. "Here, sit. I'll pour you some tea."

After she poured them each some tea, she sat down beside him on one of the long wooden benches and waited.

"I know how much you've been looking forward to this day." He smiled, looking at the flowers and the candle flickering in the jar on the table. "I don't want you to be concerned or sad about anything."

She cupped one hand over her mouth. She *did* want this to be a special day, but it wouldn't be if something was bothering him.

"I talked to Mr. Turner today." Chester ran a hand across his forehead as he sighed.

Priscilla lowered her hand and placed it on her chest, trying to speculate why this would upset Chester.

"Abe got a cell phone, and Mr. Turner went to a lot of trouble to find Abe's phone number. He evidently called all over town until someone said to try Linda's parents' phone in the barn. So, long story short…he found me."

"What did he want?"

Chester locked eyes with her, and she wanted to look away. She couldn't stand to see him so sad.

"He accused me of stealing money." Chester stared at the wall to their left. "Two hundred dollars."

Priscilla's eyes grew round. "What?"

Chester put his elbows on the table and dropped his

forehead into his hands. "How could he think I would do that?" He kept his head down as he spoke. "Then he fired me."

"What? That's not fair!" Priscilla jumped up from her bench, hands on her hips. "Did you tell him that you would never do such a thing?"

Chester leaned back in his chair and reached up for her hand. Gently, he pulled her back down until she was seated again. "Of course I did. But he said I was the one who closed the store on Friday, which I was, and that the money didn't just walk away. He said he had two hundred dollars cash from a customer in an envelope inside his desk. And it was gone Saturday morning when he opened the store." He let out another heavy sigh. "I'm upset about losing my job, but I'm even more bothered that he thinks I stole from him."

Priscilla folded her arms across her chest and tipped her head to one side. "This just doesn't make sense. Mr. Turner has always liked you…and trusted you. He obviously misplaced the money."

"*Ya*, he did."

"Was anyone else around? Maybe someone else took it."

Chester shook his head, and Priscilla sat quietly for a moment. Mr. Turner had been good to Chester since he started working there almost two years ago. The elderly man had always been kind and fair. He said it was a big step for him to hire help after thirty years of running the business by himself. Turner's Furniture was a small store with a variety of furniture, but Mr. Turner often commented about how well Chester's pieces—especially his rocking chairs—sold. And Chester did a lot

of other things for Mr. Turner…inventory, stocking, and even some ordering.

"Don't you think it's strange that he would track you down on Abe's phone instead of talking to you in person?" She shook her head. "I just can't believe he accused you of stealing."

"Mr. Turner hasn't been himself lately. I don't know what to make of it." Chester paused with a faraway look in his eyes before turning back to her. "I'm sorry to dump this on you today, but it really has me down." He eased his hand over to hers and squeezed. "But let's don't talk about this anymore. I want you to open your present."

She tried to clear her mind and focus on their special time. "Why am I getting a present? It's not my birthday."

"It's my wedding present to you. I couldn't wait."

She gasped. "But I don't have your present ready yet." She'd been sewing Chester a Sunday vest and matching pants, but they weren't finished.

He stood up, pulled her into a hug, and whispered in her ear, "I love you, Priscilla. Let's don't let worry plague our hearts today." He kissed her on the cheek. "Will you open your present?"

"Ya!" She eyed the box on the table.

Chester picked up the package, reached for her hand again, and they walked into the living room. Once they were settled on the couch, Priscilla delicately worked the white bow from around the package and carefully peeled back the yellow paper. She pried open the top of the box. Tears welled in her eyes as she lifted the beautiful clock from the box, and when the scent of freshly stained wood filled her nostrils, she knew right away that Chester had made it for her.

"It's the most beautiful thing I've ever seen." She ran her hand gingerly along the smooth casing of the clock.

"Not from where I'm sitting." Chester cupped her cheek and kissed her on the mouth, lingering for long enough to give her a glimpse of what their time as husband and wife would bring, and she kissed him back.

She forced herself to ease away from him and looked down at the clock again. "This will look beautiful on our mantel."

Chester smiled—a real smile. And she was glad that he seemed to be forgetting about Mr. Turner.

"Are you ready to eat?" She stood up from her spot on the couch.

"*Ya*. It smells mighty *gut*."

They strolled hand in hand into the kitchen, and once Chester was seated, she refilled both their tea glasses, placed a jar of chowchow on the table, and put out a loaf of butter bread and two kinds of jam. Then she carefully pulled out the underground ham from the oven and placed it on the table.

They bowed their heads in silent prayer before Chester dived in, eating like a man who hadn't had a meal in a month.

"Chester Lapp, you act like you've never had underground ham before." Priscilla's insides warmed as she watched him devour her cooking. She pushed the bread and jam closer to him. "Don't forget some butter bread and jam. It's rhubarb."

CHESTER NODDED, HIS mouth stuffed. He was doing his best to show Priscilla how much he appreciated the fine meal she'd laid before him, but he didn't have much of an appetite, and his mind was filled with worry despite

his best attempts to clear his head. The roof and wiring on the house needed repairing, he was getting married in just over three weeks, and now he would start his married life without a job. Even though he planned to grow hay on his sixty acres, it wouldn't provide enough income to live. Mr. Turner had paid him more than a fair wage for the thirty hours per week he put in at the store.

Still chewing, he glanced up. Priscilla was pushing her food around on her plate. He knew that this news was weighing heavily on her. He swallowed, then said, "Priscilla, I can see the concern on your face. Please don't worry."

She offered him the hint of a smile. "I know everything's going to be fine."

She sat taller, scooped up a forkful of ham, and he watched her take the bite. Surely, her appetite must have left her when he shared his news, but Chester knew how important this time was to Priscilla. And to him.

After the main meal, Priscilla served them each a slice of cake, and Chester was pretty sure it was the best cake he'd ever had, but he continued to fight the anxiety that roiled in his stomach. It seemed like he and Priscilla just couldn't catch a break. Everything leading up to the wedding was going wrong—the house, Abe breaking his wrist, Priscilla's dress, her favorite aunt and uncle not being able to attend, and now…he didn't have a job. If he didn't love Priscilla as much as he did and know that she was the one for him, he might question the challenges the Lord had laid before them. His father said that too much opposition meant that you weren't on the path God intended for you. But Chester trusted God's will, and lots of good things in life came with opposition.

Then why did *Daed*'s words keep lingering in his mind?

He was jarred from his thoughts when Priscilla hiccuped.

CHAPTER SIX

No. Not now.

Priscilla clamped her hand over her mouth. Slightly embarrassed, she reminded herself that superstitions were not to be heeded. Chester raised his brows a bit as he bit into a slice of cake. She hiccuped again. "Oops," she said, and raised her eyes to Chester's. "I don't know why this keeps happening."

"I think it's cute."

"It's not cute, Chester." She hiccuped again, and he grinned, which caused her to smile back at him. "It's bothersome."

Chester laid his fork on the small plate in front of him, not even a crumb of cake left. "I have to go to the bathroom. Be right back."

She watched him walk through the living room and down the hallway. She held her breath, but when that didn't help, she stood up and began clearing the dishes from the table, hiccuping off and on. As she filled the sink with soapy warm water, she tried to focus on something other than her hiccups. Her wedding. She envisioned the scene for the hundredth time this week, and pictured herself and Chester promising to love each other for the rest of their lives.

After she slipped their dishes into the water, she returned to the table and carefully picked up the casserole

dish with the leftover ham. Her father would eat it the next day for lunch. With great care, she covered the dish with foil. It had belonged to her grandmother and was her mother's favorite, oblong and white with three-inch sides, and a farm scene around the sides that had faded over the decades. Priscilla pulled the door of the refrigerator wide, bent down, and scanned inside for a place to store the dish.

"Boo!"

Chester's fingers poked her in the ribs, and the dish crashed to the floor. Priscilla stared at the broken dish as the sauce from the underground ham flowed slowly onto the wooden floorboards. She slowly raised her eyes to Chester's.

"Priscilla, I'm sorry." He squatted down and picked up the broken dish, which continued to drip as he lifted it. "I was trying to scare away your hiccups."

She put the broken dish on the counter and covered her face with her hands to hide her tears.

"Priscilla, I'm so, so sorry." Chester put his arms around her and pulled her close, but she jerked away.

"Everything is going wrong, Chester! Everything!" She swiped at her eyes and kept her head down.

Chester let out a heavy sigh. "I thought you were just looking in the refrigerator. I didn't see that you were holding the food."

She sniffled as she looked back up at him. "It's not just this. It's everything. If I didn't know better, I'd think God was sending us a message that we're just not meant to get married." When Chester's jaw dropped, she knew she shouldn't have voiced her thoughts. "I shouldn't have said that," she said as she reached out to him.

He backed away, his expression strained. "Maybe you're right."

"No, Chester. I love you." A tear slipped down her cheek as she realized that her hiccups were gone. "I'm sorry I said that." Her stomach knotted as she watched him take another step back.

"I love you too, Priscilla. But maybe you're right. Everything is going wrong. I don't even have a job now. It's been one thing after the other, and..." He took a deep breath as he thrust his hands on his hips and stared at the floor. After what seemed like an eternity, he looked up at her, and his eyes softened like the sound of his voice. "I love you," he repeated.

She ran to him and threw her arms around his waist. "I love you too, Chester. And no matter the challenges, I want to be your *frau*." She lifted her eyes to his. "The most important thing is our love for each other."

His lips met with hers, and Priscilla closed her eyes, melding into his arms and refusing to let pre-wedding stress come between them.

ALL THE WAY HOME, Chester thought about Priscilla's fears, a mirror of his own. It was hard not to question if he and Priscilla were on the right path. But how could their love for each other be a mistake?

By the time he got home, his thoughts were resolved. No more fretting about the wedding, the house, or a job. God would provide in His own time. Right now, he wanted to get home before his folks and Abe returned from church, climb into bed, and take a rare nap—even if only for an hour. He hadn't slept much the night before, and by the time he kicked off his shoes and hit the bed, he fell fast asleep.

Less than thirty minutes later he opened his eyes and saw Abe standing at the end of his bed. He rubbed his eyes, then leaned up on his elbows. "How long have you been standing there?"

"Long enough." Abe shifted his weight and grinned. "I hope Priscilla can put up with your snoring." He nodded his head toward the door. "*Daed* wants you to come downstairs. He said he needs both of us to help him carry something in the barn."

Chester groaned as he swung his legs to the side of the bed. "It's Sunday. No work on Sunday." He ran a hand through his hair, blinking until he felt alert. Then he noticed an envelope in Abe's hand. "What's that?"

Abe pushed the envelope toward him. "Something from Rachel Zook."

Chester took it, smiling at the pink drawings all over the envelope. Rachel was a special girl.

"*Ach*, and she told me at least a hundred times to tell you not to open it until your wedding day." Abe grimaced as he rubbed at the edge of his cast with his good hand.

"Hurting, *bruder*?" Chester stood up and laid Rachel's gift on his nightstand.

Abe shrugged as he dropped his hand to his side. "A little. But it mostly just itches under the cast."

Chester grabbed his hat from the bedpost. "Well, let's get downstairs and help *Daed* with whatever project we shouldn't be doing on the Sabbath." He patted Abe on the shoulder as they left the room.

PRISCILLA'S EYES GLASSED over as she showed her mother the broken casserole dish. "I'm sorry, *Mamm*."

"It was an accident, *dochder*." Her mother cupped her face in her hands and smiled. "Don't be sad, *mei mae-*

del." She kissed her on the forehead, then opened the refrigerator and pulled out a pitcher of tea. As she poured them each a glass, she told Priscilla about church service, how the deacon announced their engagement, and how her father informed everyone about the date and time. She handed Priscilla a glass. "It might be wrong to be prideful, but today..." A smile lit her mother's face. "Your *daed* was a proud man as he announced your wedding. It was very touching."

They both sat down at the kitchen table.

"Hannah and Leroy weren't at worship today. We stopped by there on the way to church, and Hannah is just miserably huge, so I talked them into keeping her off her feet today." *Mamm* took a long drink of tea. "But your sister said there is no way she is missing your wedding."

Priscilla forced a smile, figuring that Hannah would probably go into labor right in the middle of the ceremony. "Where is everyone else?"

"Your father and Sarah Mae are outside in the barn, and Naomi's in the *daadi haus*." Sarah Mae skipped into the kitchen from outside, swinging Lizzie Lou at her side—wearing, of course, her new blue dress. Priscilla tried to calm her heartbeat as she thought about how she still had to finish sewing her new wedding dress.

"*Mamm*, I'm going to give Lizzie Lou a bath." Sarah Mae held up her rag doll with smudges of black underneath her hand-painted blue eyes. The days of faceless dolls were long gone, except for the tourists, and Sarah Mae's doll was handmade by a woman in town. A Christmas present last year.

"I think we better just give Lizzie Lou a sponge bath." *Mamm* walked to the counter and came back to the table with a damp kitchen towel. She dabbed underneath Lizzie

Lou's eyes until Sarah Mae was happy and skipped back outside. A few moments later her mother snapped her fingers together. "*Ach*, I almost forgot to tell you. Rachel Zook talked to me after worship, and she told me over and over again to make sure you open the envelope she gave you on your wedding day, and not one day before." *Mamm* paused. "What did she give you?"

"I'm sure it's a picture. You know how Rachel is always drawing everyone pictures."

Mamm nodded. "She's such a sweetheart…and she looked so pretty today dressed in a new pink dress."

They were quiet for a few moments, but Priscilla couldn't hold it in any longer. "Today wasn't as *gut* a day as I'd hoped, *Mamm*." She ran her finger along the rim of her tea glass. "Chester lost his job."

"Honey, I'm so sorry." *Mamm*'s voice was soft and comforting. "But marriage will be filled with *gut* and bad days, to be sure." She shook her head and blinked her eyes a few times. "But wait a minute. Why did Chester lose his job?"

Priscilla felt her face flush. She knew Mr. Turner's accusation wasn't true, but she didn't even like to say the words out loud. "He said Chester stole two hundred dollars."

"Well, that's hogwash. We know Chester wouldn't do that." She shook her head. "Poor boy. I know it comes at a bad time."

"We've had a lot of bad timing lately." Priscilla searched her mother's eyes. "You don't think we're going against God's plan for us, do you? I mean, so many things keep going wrong, and—"

"Priscilla…" *Mamm* placed her hand on top of her daughter's. "I don't think that at all. Sometimes we can't

understand the life lessons that God sets before us. But everything that happens puts His overall plan in motion." She gave Priscilla's hand a squeeze. "And it is normal to be nervous this close to your wedding."

"I'm not nervous about marrying Chester. I'm nervous about the fact that things keep going wrong."

"Focus on the love in your heart for Chester and your future together." *Mamm* eased her hand away and stood up. "And think about Sisters Day Thursday." She smiled before she left the room.

Priscilla stayed at the table for a while. She was excited about Sisters Day. Normally, it was a time for the women to get together for baking, quilting, canning, or another planned activity. It was always a fun day, but Priscilla suspected that there was something entirely different planned for this Sisters Day.

Something for her.

CHAPTER SEVEN

PRISCILLA SAT UP front with her mother in the buggy while Naomi and Sarah Mae huddled together in the back. A cold front had blown in this week, and temperatures were low enough to require a jacket over their dresses, as opposed to the capes they had been wearing so far this fall. Priscilla rubbed her hands together, wishing she'd brought her gloves. But the chill in the air couldn't thwart her excitement about Sisters Day.

She knew what was coming, and she couldn't wait.

Please, dear Lord, I pray that everything goes well today. Please keep any worry from my heart. And...I pray I don't get the hiccups.

Anna Ruth Smoker was today's hostess, and although everyone who attended brought a dish, Anna Ruth always made extra desserts when the event was held at her house. Priscilla smiled as she counted the number of buggies parked out front.

The Smoker residence was beautiful inside and out. It was a new home built to resemble an old farmhouse, but every time Priscilla visited, she could still smell a hint of fresh paint, even though there was always a lingering aroma of freshly baked cookies in the air.

Her stomach tickled with butterflies as *Mamm* knocked on the door. Her heart raced as they stepped inside the roomy living room.

"Surprise!"

Priscilla threw her hands to her mouth and pretended to be surprised, the way all brides-to-be did when Sisters Day was transformed into a party before someone's wedding. Bridal showers like the *Englisch* have weren't part of the Old Order Amish ways, but instead someone hosted a Tupperware or Home Interior Party, and the hostess credit went to the bride-to-be so that she could pick out whatever she wanted for free. Priscilla had been to dozens of these parties over the years, dreaming of one day being the guest of honor. Everyone always bought lots of items to ensure a plentiful shopping spree for the bride. She was anxious to see what type of party they'd planned for her.

"Danki, danki," she said as she made her way through the crowd, which included Chester's mother, Irma. Mary Zook and her girls were there too, including Rachel.

"Pre-Ceelia! Pre-Ceelia!" Rachel pushed her way to Priscilla and threw her arms around her. Once Rachel's mother finally coaxed Rachel to step aside, Priscilla saw Rose, all her friends, and… "Hannah!"

She walked briskly to her sister, who looked incredibly uncomfortable in a recliner in the corner. But a smile stretched across Hannah's face. "I wouldn't have missed this, Priscilla."

Priscilla leaned down and hugged her very pregnant sister, then glanced around the room, still anxious to see what type of party had been planned for her. *Yes! Tupperware!* She eyed the food containers and fancy gadgets lining a table against the wall in the living room.

"Let's go have a look." Her mother tucked her arm in Priscilla's, and together they walked to the table while the other women chatted amongst themselves. *Mamm* picked

up a Whip 'N Prep, and Priscilla filled with excitement at the thought of owning the nonelectric appliance that could whip egg whites, creams, and all kinds of sauces.

"Ach, Mamm." Priscilla accepted the item from her mother and inspected it. "I've always wanted one of these, ever since I saw Linda Petersheim get one at her party." She slowly placed it back on the table, knowing it was expensive.

"That's why I'm buying it for you." *Mamm* stood taller and grinned. "The *Englisch* don't have anything on us, my dear. That is a fine kitchen tool, and no electricity needed."

Priscilla smiled. *"Danki, Mamm."*

Her mother nodded as they walked back to the living room, making sure they greeted everyone. Priscilla didn't notice the smell of fresh paint today, only the wonderful aromas of freshly baked goods. She couldn't wait to see what was in store for her in the kitchen, that her friends and family had prepared for this special day. For her.

Thank You, God.

CHESTER AND HIS father sat on the back of the plow eating sandwiches Chester's mother had made that morning. Abe was in town getting supplies since he wasn't much help on the plow with his broken wrist. Chester was glad that the last of the harvest was in, and as he ate his ham and cheese sandwich, he hoped Priscilla was having a good time at her party. He was pretty sure she'd known about the event, but it would have been improper for her to have mentioned it, and Priscilla played by the rules. He knew that the mishaps lately were causing her grief.

Please, Lord, I pray that things go gut *at Priscilla's party today.*

"Chester, I'm planning to help you as much as I can with your *haus*, but…" His father ran his hand the length of his beard. "I just don't see how we are going to be able to finish everything in time for you to move in by mid-November as you and Priscilla were hoping. You might need to stay with her folks for a couple of months, at least."

Chester's heart sank, but he knew his father was right. There was just too much work to do. "*Ya*, I know."

They were quiet for a few moments.

His father stored his trash in the same black tin lunch box he'd been carting around for as long as Chester could remember. Chester stuffed his garbage in something a bit more modern, a small vinyl ice chest no bigger than his father's lunch box, but with a cooling block. He'd offered to buy his father one—Abe had one too. But *Daed* insisted his old box was just fine.

"You going to talk to Mr. Turner about getting your job back?" *Daed* tipped back the rim of his straw hat. "Just don't make no sense, him firing you like that."

Chester jumped off the plow. "He thinks I stole that money, *Daed*. I think that bothers me more than anything else." He turned to face his father. "How can he think I would do that?"

His father eased his way off the plow as he pulled his jacket snug around him. "I don't know, *sohn*. That's why I think you should go talk to him."

Chester thought about the hurtful words Mr. Turner spewed at him on the phone. *"That money was there! Now it's gone, and I know you took it! I don't want you back in my store. Ever! Do you understand me? I will mail you your final check…minus the two hundred dollars!"*

"I don't know, *Daed*."

They were quiet again as they readied the plow and mules to resume work.

"Guess you'll be going to meet Priscilla at the shanty tonight?" *Daed* grinned. It was the first time his father had openly admitted that he knew where Chester went on Tuesdays and Thursdays. "Soon enough, you'll have your own home."

Chester forced a smile, but he sure did wish things were different. He wasn't looking forward to living with Priscilla's family for longer than the two weeks they'd originally planned, plus he didn't have a job. It wasn't the way he wanted to start their married life.

Daed put his hands on his hips and scowled. "Did you know your *bruder* got a cell phone?"

Chester twisted his mouth to one side. "*Ya*. I'm not sure exactly how long he's had it."

"He knows we don't like that." *Daed* shook his head as he stepped onto the plow. "I would say he came to his senses and decided to get rid of it because it's just not our way, but..." *Daed* grinned. "He found out what it was going to cost him every month. I overheard him tell Linda that he was getting rid of it." His father chuckled. "But turns out it ain't cheap to get rid of those things either. Something about a cancellation fee."

Chester smiled. Abe was always the first one to be interested in a new gadget, but he didn't like to spend his hard-earned cash unless he had to. Abe only worked about fifteen hours per week in Bird-in-Hand behind the counter at an Amish-owned deli.

"I know that the temptations of the outside world are many. And I know that more and more folks are putting phones in their barns and even carrying mobile ones."

Daed shook his head. "But if we're not careful, we'll become just like the *Englisch*—never a peaceful moment."

Chester nodded. Almost everyone they knew had a phone in the barn, some with ringers in the house. And even though Bishop Ebersol frowned on cell phones, lots of folks in the district had them. He and Priscilla had talked about the convenience of having a phone in the barn, but in the end they decided they wanted their *kinner* to experience Old Order life as it should be: detachment from the rest of the world. Chester knew that times were changing and more and more of their people were converting to the ways of the *Englisch*, but even if just for a while, he and Priscilla wanted to share the same phone shanty with their folks, the Dienners, and Petersheims. The same phone shanty that they'd shared for so many Tuesday and Thursday evenings.

He smiled as he thought about holding Priscilla in his arms tonight.

PRISCILLA LEFT SISTERS DAY elated. There was so much going on that she didn't have time to worry about everything that had been going wrong lately. Her friends and family had spent lavishly on Tupperware items for their own homes, increasing the hostess credits. Priscilla used her gift credits to purchase a vast assortment of kitchen utensils, tools, and containers, although her mother had insisted on buying the Whip 'N Prep.

She spent the afternoon working on her wedding dress, which was coming along nicely, and she was pretty sure she could finish it this week. With the wedding only two and a half weeks away, she'd be busy with final preparations. For the first time in days, her heart was free of

worry, and she silently thanked God for the many blessings in her life.

After supper and cleanup, she pulled her black coat on and topped her prayer covering with her black bonnet to protect her ears from the early evening winds.

She ran across the field, anxious to tell Chester about her day. Blue-gray skies with only a hint of orange signified that the day's end was near. She could see Chester waiting for her in the distance.

"I take it you had a *gut* day," he said as she flung herself into his arms.

"*Ya*, I did. It was *wunderbaar*!" She eased away from him, feeling light and peaceful. "Sisters Day was my bridal party, and I got so many wonderful things for our new home. I can't wait to be your *frau*, Chester, and I refuse to let worry fill my heart. Our wedding will be beautiful. We will get the *haus* done, and you will find a new job." She exhaled a long sigh. "Everything will work out according to God's plan."

She stepped back from him, met his eyes, and smiled. "So! No more fretting!" She'd let no shadows cross her heart today.

Her husband-to-be smiled down at her, and she could see joy and approval in his blue eyes.

"*Gut*. I'm glad to hear that you will let go of worry. And you're right. Everything is according to His plan. We'll be fine."

Chester leaned down, and as the cool wind breezed against her cheeks, his kiss warmed her all over. She kissed him back, ready to be Mrs. Chester Lapp.

Then the phone rang.

CHAPTER EIGHT

CHESTER WASN'T SURE he'd ever seen a person transform so suddenly. As the phone in the shanty rang over and over again, Priscilla's face had changed to something—frightening.

"Chester Lapp, don't you *dare* answer that phone. Don't pick it up! Pretend it's not ringing." She squeezed her eyes closed and pinched her lips together.

Chester gently took her by both shoulders until she opened her eyes. She glared at the ringing phone as if it were evil. "Priscilla...what is wrong with you?"

She let out a heavy sigh. "Every time that phone rings, there's a problem." She cut her eyes at him, and he tried not to grin. "Don't answer it, Chester."

"Okay, okay," he finally said, holding his palms up. "I won't answer it. But I think you're being a little crazy. It could be for someone else."

"Or it could be someone calling to tell us something else is wrong with the house! Or some other catastrophe relating to our wedding." She hiccuped. "Oh no! Oh no!"

She slapped her hand over her mouth so hard that Chester was sure it must have stung.

"See! This is what happens! Bad news and hiccups always go together!" She took two steps back. "I have to go."

Chester glanced back and forth between his some-

what *ab im kopp* fiancée and the phone. "Listen." He held up one finger. "It isn't ringing anymore. You don't have to go."

"*Ach! Ya*, I do!"

She hiccuped again, and Chester couldn't keep from grinning.

"This is not funny, Chester. I have to go before something happens to mess up this day." She turned and ran, but looked over her shoulder. "I love you!"

Still grinning, he watched her run across the field. "I love you too, Priscilla!"

She didn't turn around, but waved a hand in the air.

Life with his Priscilla would never be boring.

PRISCILLA BOLTED UP the porch steps, ran through the living room, and hit the stairs two at a time. She bumped into her mother on the way up.

"Priscilla, what are you in such a hurry for? Come back downstairs. I have some things to talk to you about, things about the wedding, the food, and—"

"No! Not today. I can't, *Mamm*. We'll talk tomorrow."

"But, Priscilla—"

She slammed her bedroom door and didn't hear the rest of what her mother said. Flinging her bonnet and jacket on her bed, she placed both hands on her chest and took a deep breath. The hiccups were gone.

She sat down on the bed and thought about how ridiculous—and childlike—Chester must have thought her behavior. The bedroom door flew open.

"Priscilla Marie King…" *Mamm* stood in the doorway with her hands on her hips. "What in the world is wrong with you?"

Priscilla cringed, knowing she shouldn't have been so

snappy with her mother…or slammed the door. "Sorry, *Mamm*."

"I thought you'd be excited to hear what I have to say about plans for your wedding." She dropped her hands to her side. "Not rush to your room and slam the door."

"Sorry." She hung her head for a moment, but then superstition flooded over her. Even though she didn't have the hiccups anymore, she was still afraid to ruin this day. "Can we talk about it tomorrow?"

"What's wrong with right now?" *Mamm* edged closer to the bed and scowled. "This isn't like you, Priscilla."

"It's been such a nice day, and I don't want anything to spoil it, and…" She glanced at her mother for only a moment before she hung her head again. "Every time I get the hiccups something goes wrong. Something to do with the wedding." She looked up. "I know it sounds silly, but I just don't want to talk about anything to do with the wedding."

Her mother just stared at her for a moment. "You don't really believe that, do you? Silly superstitions, that's all."

"I guess not." She silently prayed that if she was lying, God would forgive her.

Mamm jumped up and clapped her hands together. "Well, my news was not bad news, but it can wait until tomorrow. And tomorrow, young lady, you and I are going to take a little trip to town."

"For what?"

"You'll see. The public library opens at ten o'clock. So plan to leave here around nine."

Priscilla stood up. "Why are we going to the library?"

"Because I suspect I know what is causing your hiccups, and I want to see if I'm right. And it might help you."

FRIDAY MORNING MAMM parked the buggy in front of the Pequea Valley Library in Intercourse. After she tied the horse to the hitching post, they walked briskly to the building, their heads tucked to avoid the nip in the air. On the way to the library, Priscilla's mother had given her the wedding updates she'd tried to give her the night before—mostly about the food and the cake Naomi was planning to make, very close to the one her aunt would have baked.

"We're looking for a book about hiccups," *Mamm* said to a library clerk when they entered the large room filled with rows and rows of bookshelves.

"Okay…" The young woman, about Priscilla's age, motioned with her hand for them to follow, but then stopped. "What exactly are you looking for?"

Mamm stood taller and repeated herself. "A book about hiccups."

"Like how to get rid of them?" The woman's mouth tipped up at one corner, and Priscilla was embarrassed. But *Mamm* was undeterred.

"No. What causes them."

"Oh. Okay. Follow me to the computers. I'll see what I can find."

"Thank you." *Mamm* smiled, and she and Priscilla followed the woman to a row of computers on the far wall. After a few minutes, they were given the names of three books.

"That's a general health book." The librarian pointed to the second book on the list. "That's probably the best one. I'll show you where to find it."

Once *Mamm* had the book in her hand, she thanked the woman and walked to a long table and sat down.

Priscilla sat next to her and folded her arms. This was a waste of time.

"*Mamm*, everyone gets the hiccups. I don't know why we're doing this."

Her mother didn't look up as she flipped a page. "But not everyone believes that their hiccups are a warning of something bad to happen." She glanced at Priscilla and narrowed her eyebrows. "I don't think God would like that."

Priscilla sighed. "I'm not trying to make God mad. It just seems like more than a coincidence that—"

"There are no coincidences in life, Priscilla." *Mamm* glared at her for a moment. "Everything is His will. You know that."

She knew her mother was right, and there was no point in arguing, so she sat quietly while her mother flipped through the pages. She glanced around the room at the few patrons whose heads were buried in a book. Occasionally, one of the *Englisch* would nod in her direction and whisper to someone, but overall folks in Lancaster County were used to seeing Plain People.

Mamm tapped her finger to one of the pages in the book. "Here you go. Read this." She slid the hardcover book in front of Priscilla. She scanned the page, but followed her mother's finger when she leaned over. "Right here. Read."

Priscilla leaned her face closer to the page. *The most common triggers for short-term hiccups are: eating too much, drinking carbonated beverages, excessive consumption of alcohol, sudden temperature change, worry or emotional stress.*

Mamm started talking before Priscilla could process the information. "You eat like a bird, so that's not it. You

don't drink sodas or alcohol, so rule that out. And there's been no sudden change in temperature. So! There you have it." *Mamm* slammed a pointed finger down on the page. "Stop *worrying*, and your hiccups will go away." She stood up. "Ready to go home?"

Priscilla sat in the chair and stared up at her mother. "That's it? Just stop worrying, and no more hiccups?" It couldn't be that easy.

Mamm frowned as she slid back into her chair. "Priscilla, worry is a sin, and it blocks the voice of God."

"So He's punishing me by giving me the hiccups." She regretted her sarcastic tone and knew right away from the scowl on her mother's face that she didn't appreciate it.

"You know that's not true. But you have worried about this wedding of yours since you were a little girl. Do you remember the large weddings your dolls used to have? You would place them in their proper positions all over your bedroom. Then you would go through the ceremony. And you've always had the perfect plan for your own wedding."

Priscilla smiled as she remembered.

"But, Priscilla, only God's plan is perfect. So worrying about what might or might not go wrong before, during, or after this wedding is doing you no good. Everything is in His hands." She squeezed Priscilla's hand. "Do you love Chester and want to be with him the rest of your life?"

"Of course."

"Then stop worrying. Not only will your hiccups stop, but you will hear God's plan for you more clearly. Just follow Him, Priscilla." *Mamm* stood up smiling, as if she had conquered the evils of the world. "Now, let's go."

Priscilla, still skeptical, followed her mother out of the library. *God, is she right? Is worry troubling my heart and keeping me from trusting Your will?*

CHAPTER NINE

Priscilla sat at the kitchen table as her mother paced in the kitchen. She was still seeing Chester at the phone shanty on Tuesdays and Thursdays, but they'd only spent a short amount of time together. Chester looked exhausted each time, but insisted he was fine. She knew he was still upset about losing his job and frustrated by the slow progress of their house.

"Naomi has everything ready to make your cake on Monday." *Mamm* read from a list and checked as she went along.

"Where is Naomi? She seems to go missing a lot."

Mamm tapped her finger to her chin. "Zeke Lapp was here the other day. I didn't think too much about it, but now it wonders me if maybe they haven't taken a fancy to each other. But now, of course, he's back in Middlefield looking after his *daed*. You know his father cut his leg while chopping wood."

"*Ya*, Chester was disappointed that Zeke had to leave, so he's planning to ask his friend John to fill in as an attendant."

Mamm was back to her list. "And everyone knows their duties as far as the food preparation. It will be a busy day on Monday with everyone coming here to get things ready. The extra propane ovens will be delivered on Monday also." *Check*. "Your father and several other

men are finishing up the temporary structure next to the house for the reception." *Check*.

Priscilla nodded. Her family had a large farmhouse with an especially big living room to host the service, but like most Amish homes, theirs wasn't nearly large enough to accommodate almost four hundred guests. So her father, cousins, and friends of the family had built a framed structure right next to the house, and today they would cover the top and the sides with heavy blue plastic to keep it warm for guests. Additional tables and benches would be set up underneath. It was a common practice in their district, and Priscilla was glad to see that the temporary shelter hadn't blown away. She shook her head to clear the negative thought as her mother went on.

"You said you finished your wedding dress, *ya*?"

Priscilla nodded.

"And Naomi and Rose have both tried on their dresses?"

"Naomi has. Rose is coming over this afternoon to pick hers up."

"Make sure she tries it on."

"I will." Priscilla fidgeted with the ties on her prayer covering. She was thankful that she hadn't had a case of the hiccups since their trip to the library, but things still weren't coming together as she'd hoped. Chester said there was no way the house would be finished in time for them to move in two weeks after the wedding. She'd cringed when he told her it could be a couple of months, or longer. She knew that many newly married couples spent the first few months with the bride's parents, but Chester had built them a lovely new home, and she was anxious to begin their life together in their own house.

Chester, his father, and even Abe with his broken wrist

had been working late into the night on the new home. But Chester said to be prepared for an extended stay with her parents. Another thing that wasn't in her plan.

She took a deep breath. *God, I know that everything is in Your hands, and I will not question You.* It was a prayer she had repeated daily, but she sometimes still felt disappointed. But she figured disappointment was better than worry. Worry had gotten her nowhere, it was a sin, and she knew her mother was right—it blocked the voice of God. She was resolved in knowing that her wedding and her life were in God's hands.

"Your father, Chester, and Abe will oversee the group arranging the benches, tables, and chairs." *Mamm* walked into their large living room, then returned to the kitchen. "Naomi, Rose, and I will make sure the *eck* is positioned correctly for you, Chester, and your attendants."

Members of the church district would spend most of the day on Monday cooking, getting things ready, and also show up at six o'clock the morning of the wedding to help.

"Oh. I also wanted to ask you if you want *Aenti* Mary Katherine to bake her special red velvet whoopee pies? I know Naomi will be making a special cake, and there will be lots of other cakes and desserts, but..."

"Everyone loves *Aenti* Mary Katherine's whoopee pies. I think that would be *gut*."

"Great. Let's see..." *Mamm* tapped her pen to the pad, but they both looked up when they heard a buggy coming up the driveway. Priscilla walked to the kitchen window and peered outside.

"It's Rose." Priscilla pulled the wooden door open and watched through the screen as Rose walked across the grass—clawing at her arms with both hands. She

pushed the screen open and stepped aside so that Rose could come in.

"Why are you scratching yourself like that?" Priscilla cringed as she watched her friend rubbing both arms atop her green dress.

Rose shook her head as she continued to scratch. "I've got this horrible rash all over my arms." She lifted one sleeve of her dress to show Priscilla the red bumps covering her arm from the elbow down. "It's on both arms."

Mamm walked over. "How did you get this, Rose?" She eased Rose's sleeve up farther and inspected.

"It's a long story, but let's just say that a bouquet of flowers unexpectedly had some poison ivy in it."

"Are you putting anything on it?" *Mamm* asked as she lowered Rose's sleeve.

"*Ya. Mamm* got me something at the drugstore." She pinched her eyes together as she began to claw at her arms again.

"Wait right here, Rose." *Mamm* turned to leave the room, but glanced over her shoulder. "I have something that will help."

"I have been itching all morning." Rose's face twisted into a deep frown.

Priscilla watched as Rose scratched, and a minute later both turned as Priscilla's mother came back into the room.

"This is from the natural doctor, a blend of herbs and ointment." She handed Rose a small plastic container. "Take this with you. Sarah Mae wandered into some poison ivy last year. This helped her a lot."

Priscilla remembered how miserable her sister had been. "How long will the itching last?"

"I don't know." Rose lifted her sleeve again. "See how bad it looks." She shook her head.

Mamm patted Rose on the shoulder. "I'm so sorry, Rose. I hope it's better by the wedding so you can enjoy yourself." She smiled. "Use the salve. It should help."

After her mother excused herself, Priscilla went to get Rose's dress. She returned a minute later and handed it to her friend. "*Mamm* said you should try it on."

Rose scratched at her arms. "I'm sure it's fine, Priscilla. Do you mind if I don't try it on right now? I am itching so much, and I want to go home and try this ointment."

Priscilla shrugged. "Sure. I understand." *It probably won't fit because that just seems to be how things are going.* She struggled to push the negative thought out of her mind.

After Rose left, Priscilla pulled a loaf of bread from the oven, then tinkered about the kitchen. She put two glasses in the sink, wiped down the counter, and thought about what the next few weeks would be like.

As was traditional, she and Chester would help with cleanup the next morning, and it was always the new bride and groom's duty to wash all the clothes and linens. Her mother had laughed and said it was usually the only time an Amish man would do the laundry during his lifetime.

She turned around when the screen door in the kitchen slammed and Naomi entered. Her sister walked straight to the refrigerator and pulled out a pitcher of tea. She poured herself a glass and sat down at the table with a sigh.

"Too bad Zeke had to go back to Middlefield," Priscilla said. "Have you heard from him?"

Naomi took a drink. "Why would I have heard from him?"

"Oh, I just thought you might have." She grinned at her sister.

"I'm not going to talk to you about this, Priscilla." Naomi hurried toward the living room, but there was a new bounce in her sister's step. Priscilla smiled. Naomi had been playing matchmaker for everyone else for as long as Priscilla could remember. She hoped that Naomi had found someone special.

FRIDAY EVENING CHESTER was tired after working on the house all day. He'd spent the early morning hours looking for a new job in town, but he wasn't having much luck. He didn't know how to explain to potential employers that he was fired for stealing money, so he just didn't mention working for Mr. Turner, which left him with little work experience to take under consideration, other than farming.

He'd just pulled his suspenders off his shoulders when Abe walked into his bedroom. He quickly asked his brother if he was done in the bathroom. A hot shower was going to feel mighty good.

"*Ya*, I'm done." Abe ran a comb through his wet hair. "*Mamm* wanted me to remind you to put your marriage license in a place where you won't forget it on Tuesday." He shrugged. "I guess you could give it to me."

Chester stood perfectly still as he scanned his bedroom. *Where did I put it?* He and Priscilla had gotten their marriage license almost two months ago. He pulled open the drawer of his nightstand and rummaged through some papers, then quickly moved to the top drawer of his chest.

"You lose your license, *bruder*?" Abe chuckled, but stopped right away when Chester glared at him.

"It's here somewhere." He yanked open the second drawer, pretty sure he didn't store it where he kept his underwear. Closing it, he turned to face Abe. He could feel the color draining from his face. "Priscilla will have my hide if I've lost our marriage license." He shook his head. "I know it's here somewhere."

"It wonders me if *Mamm* won't have your hide too." Abe grinned as he backed out of the room and shut the door.

Chester sat down on the bed and scratched his forehead. *Think, think. Where did I put it?* He looked around his small room again and spotted Rachel's envelope atop his nightstand. He'd managed to keep track of a picture from Rachel, yet he'd lost the one document necessary for him to marry Priscilla in four days.

God, why is everything going wrong? He knew how important it was for Priscilla to have everything in order. It was just part of who she was, and this wedding was definitely an event that she wanted to run smoothly. He might not have questioned whether or not they were on the right path if she hadn't, but with so much opposition…

He let out a heavy sigh, knowing that he loved Priscilla with all his heart. She was everything he'd ever wanted in a wife and mother, and they balanced each other, with her necessity to have things organized while Chester so often focused on the moment to moment. And sometimes Chester was able to push back a little and let Priscilla know that the world would not come crashing down if everything didn't run smoothly all the time. He knew that Priscilla trusted God's plan for their lives, as he did.

There'd been the problems with the house, her wedding dress disaster, change of plans for the cake, Chester losing his job, and now this. What else could possibly go wrong?

CHAPTER TEN

PRISCILLA TRIED TO stay focused on church service this brisk Sunday morning, but her mind kept drifting. They were gathered in the Petersheims' barn because Elizabeth and Elam's house was small and couldn't accommodate over a hundred people. Priscilla wasn't sure how it housed Elizabeth, Elam, and their five children.

This would be her last time to attend church as a single woman, and tonight would be her last time to attend a Sunday singing with Chester. Soon they'd start their own family, and someday their teenagers would gather on Sunday evenings.

She glanced around the barn. As usual, the women were sitting on long wooden benches facing the men on the other side, and the bishop and deacons were in the middle. Priscilla smiled at Chester, and he returned the smile—sort of. Priscilla sensed by his expression that something was wrong. She hadn't had time to talk to him before the service, but after lunch she'd see if something was bothering him.

Naomi sat next to *Mamm*. Priscilla was disappointed that Zeke had been called back to Middlefield to tend to his *daed*, but she certainly understood. She had hoped Naomi the matchmaker might have found a match of her own. Rose sat two rows in front of Priscilla. She felt sorry for her friend, who scratched her arms through most of

the service, but despite her poison ivy, Priscilla caught her and Luke exchanging smiles.

She stifled a yawn and refocused on the service… though visions of her wedding in two days challenged her attention span, and within a few minutes her mind trailed. Chances were good that things were not going to go as she'd planned. She tried to recall when she'd become such a perfectionist, needing things to run smoothly all the time. Yes, she'd always dreamed that her wedding day would be special, but it was more than that, and Priscilla knew it. She thought back to what Naomi had said to her.

When there was order in her life, she felt like she was on the right path, God's path. When things fell apart, she questioned her actions, inactions, and everything that did or didn't happen to cause the upheaval. As she pondered her past up to now, Bishop Ebersol's voice suddenly boomed, and her eyes rounded as she held on to his words.

"To question the Lord's will is to not believe in His perfect plan."

Priscilla locked eyes with the bishop, then hung her head, knowing that his words were the essence of everything she'd been taught her entire life. *Why haven't I been living by that?* Her perfection was not God's perfection. She closed her eyes.

I'm sorry.

CHESTER HELPED THE men rearrange the benches and set up tables after the church service ended. It was chilly in the barn despite the propane heaters placed throughout, but Chester's forehead dripped with sweat. How was he going to tell Priscilla that he couldn't find their marriage license? There was a three-day waiting period in

Pennsylvania, so even if they went tomorrow to get a new one, there was no way they could get married the following day.

He helped Abe set out some additional folding chairs in preparation for the meal, although he didn't have much appetite.

"You find your license?" Abe grinned, and Chester felt his blood start to boil. He reminded himself that smacking Abe went against their ways.

"No. I didn't." He shoved the last of the chairs up against the table. But when he turned back toward his brother, Abe wasn't smiling.

"Seriously? You didn't find it?" Abe stroked his clean-shaven chin as his eyebrows drew inward.

"No."

"What are you going to do? The wedding is in two days, and that ain't long enough to go get another one."

"I don't know, Abe!"

"No need to holler, *bruder*." Abe put a hand on Chester's shoulder as he glanced around the barn at the other men. "I'll help you look some more tonight."

Chester lowered his head, rubbing his forehead. "I don't know where else *to* look."

"Will you tell Priscilla?" Abe lowered his hand and sighed. "Maybe you should wait."

"I've looked everywhere, Abe. It just isn't there. I'm going to have to tell her." He dropped his chin. "So much has already gone wrong, and now this." He looked up at Abe. "We can't even get married without that license, and everyone is already coming on Tuesday, tomorrow everyone will prepare the food, and…" He stopped when he caught movement out of the corner of his eye. *Pris-*

cilla. She eased her way through all the men setting up tables and benches.

"How's my favorite husband-to-be?"

Abe made a dash for the barn door. "See you later."

"They're getting ready to bring out the food, so I was sent to make sure the tables were ready."

Chester looked around. "I think so." He forced a smile and wondered how he was going to tell Priscilla that the wedding would have to be postponed.

Fifteen minutes later he was seated next to Abe and his father, picking at his food while Priscilla and the other women scurried about, making sure everyone was taken care of.

After the meal, he had the perfect opportunity to tell her. They were standing off to the side of the house, but when Priscilla started detailing the plans for Tuesday, he just didn't have the heart to interrupt. She seemed to have made some sort of peace with the fact that so much had gone wrong.

"It's God's will for us to be challenged," she said. "But I love you so much, Chester. I can't wait to be your *frau*."

Now as he rode alongside Abe in the buggy on the way home, he knew that he would have to tell her the truth tonight at the singing. It would only make things worse if he kept putting it off.

PRISCILLA BATHED HERSELF in lavender bubble bath that she and her mother had made recently, and the sweet smell reminded her of spring. By then, she would be Mrs. Chester Lapp.

As she towel-dried her hair, she thought again about how this would be her last official Sunday singing. Lots

of older folks still attended from time to time, but mainly it was the younger people, those who were of dating age.

She'd prayed hard about the challenges that she and Chester had faced as the wedding drew closer, but she hadn't had any more hiccups, and she was doing her best not to worry. She'd felt much more open and able to hear God's guidance. Nothing was going to stop her from becoming Chester's *frau*.

After she dressed, she gathered up the Sunday vest and pants she'd made for him. If anything had gone right along the way toward the wedding, it was the clothes she made for Chester. Each seam was lovingly sewn and straight, and she couldn't wait to give them to him.

"I'm going, *Mamm*," she said when she walked into the living room downstairs. She reached for her heavy black coat on the rack, then pulled her arms through the sleeves. "I saw Chester pulling in from my window."

"Enjoy yourself." Her father looked above his gold-rimmed glasses and smiled. Her mother got up from the couch and gave Priscilla a hug.

"*Ya*, have fun, dear." She kissed Priscilla on the cheek. "Sarah Mae is with Naomi at the *daadi haus*, so your father and I are going to enjoy this nice fire and some quiet time."

Priscilla smiled. Her parents were still so much in love. "I won't be too late." She pulled on her black bonnet and headed outside, glad that the Petersheims' house was close by. Close enough to walk if it hadn't been so cold.

"You look beautiful," Chester said when she climbed into the buggy.

"*Danki*." She handed him the vest and pants. "They're not wrapped, but I couldn't wait to give them to you."

She grinned. "I hope they fit." She'd asked Abe about sizes, so hopefully he'd given her the right measurements.

Chester ran his hand gingerly over the vest, then the pants. "I'm sure they'll fit perfectly," he said, but just like this morning, she sensed something was wrong. He clicked his tongue, and they started toward the Petersheims'.

When they arrived at the singing a few minutes later, Chester leaned down and kissed her as soon as they were out of the buggy. "I love you."

"I love you too." She gazed into his eyes. "Chester, is everything okay?"

"*Ya.* Why?"

"I don't know." She shrugged. "You just seem… like…" She reminded herself not to fret. "Never mind. Let's go into the *haus*. Looks like lots of folks are here." She squeezed his hand as they made their way up to the front porch. "Our last Sunday singing before we're married."

Chester smiled, but Priscilla's stomach was beginning to churn.

I trust God's will. I will not worry…

CHESTER STAYED BY Priscilla's side, smiling when it was required amidst the talk of their upcoming wedding, but for the most part he kept quiet. How was he going to tell Priscilla that her special day was not going to happen? At least not this Tuesday. He took a deep breath as he listened to his fiancée describe the cake her sister was planning to make the following day.

"*Ach*, Rose. Wait until you see it. Naomi makes such beautiful cakes." Priscilla's smile was radiant, and Chester didn't think he'd ever seen her look so happy. Rose

didn't look quite as happy as she scratched her arms continuously. He'd heard about her run-in with some poison ivy.

There was a plentiful spread of food on the table in the Petersheims' kitchen. Under different circumstances, Chester wouldn't have been able to stay away from the many snack trays and desserts, but his stomach churned with anticipation. And dread.

About an hour into the singing, he couldn't take all the wedding talk anymore.

"Priscilla, I need to talk to you." He gently coaxed her away from Rose and whispered, "Privately."

Her face registered the appropriate amount of concern. *If she only knew.*

"What's wrong?"

"Can we please go? I really need to talk to you." He edged through the crowd in the kitchen.

"Chester, you're scaring me." Priscilla blinked her eyes several times.

Please don't start crying.

He brushed past Lena Petersheim and gave her a quick thank-you for hosting the singing.

"See you on Tuesday," she responded with a wink.

Chester hurried out the door and down the porch steps toward his buggy. He could hear Priscilla calling behind him. Once he got to his buggy, he opened the passenger door for her to get in. Even in the moonlight, he could see her beautiful blue eyes filling with tears. *I'm so sorry, Priscilla.*

"Chester?" Her eyes were wide and glassy as she stared up at him. "Please tell me what's wrong."

He gently grasped her shoulders. "Everything is going

to be fine, Priscilla. Here, just get in, warm yourself with the heater, and we'll go talk."

She sniffled a bit, but climbed inside the buggy. He waited until they were on the road before he said anything.

"I'm going to pull over up here off the main road."

Priscilla was quiet as he edged off of Blacksmith Road and onto an unmarked dirt road that he knew was a dead end. An almost full moon lit the area around them, and he twisted in his seat to face her. He reached for her trembling hand.

"Are you cold?"

She shook her head. "Just concerned. What's going on, Chester?" She blinked her eyes a few times, and her lip trembled.

"I'm so sorry for what I'm about to tell you." He pulled his eyes from hers and hung his head. "We can't get married on Tuesday."

She jerked her hand out of his grasp. "What? Why?" Her voice shook as she spoke. "It's because everything is going wrong, isn't it? God must not want us to get married!" Her voice rose an octave as a tear slipped down her cheek. "I've tried not to worry." *Hiccup.* "Oh no! I should have known…"

"Priscilla—"

"Stop!" She held up one palm toward him. "I know what you're going to say. You love me, but there is just too much going against us. We're not on the right path." She lowered her face into her hands and sobbed.

"Priscilla, that's not what—" He reached for her, but she pulled back.

"All my life, I've needed everything perfect, even though we're taught to trust His will when things don't

go as we've planned. Just when I realized that everything happens on God's time frame and in His way, you"—her voice grew angry as she swung her hand in his direction—"decide the challenges are too much for you." She shook her head, crying hard. "It just wasn't meant to be."

"Maybe not." He regretted the words the moment they hastily slipped from his tongue, but it hurt him that Priscilla would feel this way. Yes, they'd had obstacles, but he never thought that it was enough for her to not want to marry him.

"Take me home." Her body shook as she cried.

"Priscilla, wait. You're not understanding me. I'm trying to tell you that we can't get married on *Tuesday*. That doesn't mean that I don't want to marry you."

She sniffled. "What?"

Chester reached for her hand again, and this time she didn't pull away. "I love you, Priscilla. I want to marry you more than anything." He took a deep breath. "But I've lost our marriage license. I can't find it anywhere." He shook his head as he talked. "I'm so sorry. We don't have time to get another one by Tuesday."

Priscilla stared at him with her mouth hung open. "That's it?"

"That's enough, isn't it? We'll have to postpone the wedding, and I'm not sure how we're going to let everyone know, and I can't believe I've blundered so badly."

"Chester." Priscilla's voice was firm as she said his name. Her brows rose, and a slight grin formed at the corner of her mouth. "*You* never had the marriage license. I have it safely put away at my house."

He didn't move as Priscilla's comment soaked in. *How could I have forgotten that?* He thought back to their trip to the courthouse to get the license. "You put it in your

purse that day, didn't you?" He slapped his forehead with his hand as she nodded. "I can't believe I didn't remember that until now."

Relief washed over him. About the marriage license, anyway.

They'd said some hurtful things to each other. Was Priscilla really just about to give up on them?

CHAPTER ELEVEN

PRISCILLA SAT QUIETLY as they rode to her house. Her heart was heavy. She'd reacted much too quickly and said things she didn't mean—once again forgoing what she knew to be true and falling back to her old ways. Chester was the man she wanted to marry, and that was much more important than the challenges they'd faced up to this point. But he was quiet. Too quiet.

When he stopped the buggy, she turned to face him. "I'm sorry."

"Me too."

"Do you still want to marry me, Chester?" She fought back tears.

"Do you still want to marry me?"

That was not the answer she'd hoped for. She quickly swiped at a tear that rolled down her cheek. "Of course."

"I want to marry you too, Priscilla. There's just been…"

She braced herself and didn't breathe as she waited for him to go on. When he didn't, she finished his sentence. "There have just been a lot of things going wrong."

"*Ya.*"

Chester got out of the buggy, and walked around to where Priscilla was standing. He leaned down and kissed her, but despite his words earlier, his lips betrayed him.

She could feel it in his touch. Something had changed. He was having doubts.

"I love you." She wrapped her arms around his waist.

"I love you too."

She pulled back and stared into his eyes for a long while. "See you Tuesday?"

He smiled a little. *"Ya."*

Priscilla walked across the yard to the house, turning back twice to look at Chester and wondering if he would actually show up.

MONDAY MORNING PRISCILLA watched as Naomi put the yellow candied roses on the cake she was making. Within the hour, their house would be bustling with church members who would set up for the wedding tomorrow.

"It's beautiful." She sat down at the kitchen table across from her sister.

Naomi adjusted the tiny roses along the edge of the cake and looked up. "What's bothering you? For someone who is getting married tomorrow, you seem down in the dumps."

Priscilla shrugged. "I don't know. I guess it's because Chester and I had harsh words last night." She took in a deep breath and looked up at the ceiling for a moment, then blew it out. "I mean, I think everything is fine, but…" She touched the corner of the cake and pulled back a tiny dab of cream cheese and pineapple icing.

Naomi slapped her hand. "Priscilla, that is something I would expect of Sarah Mae. Stop that." She grinned and went back to work. "Now tell me…but what?"

She tried to organize her thoughts. "We've had so much go wrong. You don't think it's God's way of telling us not to get married, do you?"

Naomi didn't look up. "What do you think?"

"Don't do that, Naomi." Priscilla gently tapped the table with her hand. "I want to know what *you* think."

Naomi stopped what she was doing and walked around to sit down beside her. "Here's what I think." She put her hand on top of Priscilla's. "Life is not perfect. And sometimes in your world, Priscilla, you need things to go exactly as you've planned, even though you know it is our belief that life should not be easy. But you forget... we are here living God's plan. Sometimes things might seem like they are falling apart or going wrong because God has something better planned for us around the corner." She tipped her head and smiled. "Life is a learning journey, Priscilla. But sometimes I think you forget the lessons being taught."

Priscilla knew that Naomi was right. *Please, God. Let me trust Your plan for my life.* She knew that it was just a wedding and that the meaning behind the event was far more important than the affair itself. She hoped Chester could forgive her outburst, and she hoped that God would calm her heart as she fought the fear that Chester was now having doubts about their future.

CHESTER HAD A surprise for Priscilla, even though he wouldn't be able to tell her until two weeks after they were married. But even though he was excited about it, worry threatened to weigh him down. He loved Priscilla more than anything in the world, and her desire to have things organized and orderly was one of the things that drew him to her. But if the past month was any indication of how their wedding might go tomorrow, he worried that she would be disappointed. He'd prayed long and hard last night after he dropped her off at home, and through

communion with God, he asked the Lord to fill his heart with faith. Surely love was the right path, even if it was paved with challenges. And today, Priscilla seemed to be working things out in her heart and mind. The day before they'd both reacted out of fear and worry, both emotions that they knew kept God's wisdom just out of reach. He hadn't been able to talk to her much with so many people around getting things ready, but she had smiled most of the day. And things were looking up in other areas too. Zeke had made it back from Middlefield tonight, saying his father was doing better. Even though John had been ready to step in as an attendant, Chester was glad that his cousin was back.

Chester finished towel-drying his hair, tossed the towel into the hamper, and sat on the bed. He noticed Rachel's envelope on the nightstand. As he picked it up and ran his finger along the seam, he remembered how he promised Rachel that he wouldn't open it until the day of his wedding. Smiling, he put it back down, then fluffed his pillows and got comfortable in bed. A subtle breeze blew through the opened window, enough for him to crawl underneath the covers. He slept so well when the nights were brisk. He wondered if Priscilla liked to sleep with the window cracked this time of year.

He snuffed out the lantern, pulled the covers up to his neck, and stared at the ceiling. A glimmer of moonlight spilled through the window and into his room, producing tiny specks of light on the ceiling. He connected the dots in his mind as he thought about how this was the last night he would sleep in this house as a single man. That was the plan anyway. He sure hoped Priscilla wasn't having doubts. Despite his determined attitude that he wouldn't let worry plague his thoughts, the nasty emo-

tion kept creeping up on him just the same. He squeezed his eyes tight as if to will it away.

I trust You, Lord. I'm not going to worry.

But an hour later he was still awake, and still playing connect-the-dots above his head. They were supposed to be at Priscilla's house at six o'clock to help with last-minute setup, and the wedding would begin at eight o'clock. He finally dozed off around eleven, but awoke with a startle at three. His eyes bolted open as he tried to recall the dream he'd just had. As he sat up in bed, he remembered. They were at the wedding, and Priscilla was crying. It was raining on her special day, and the food was cold because they ran out of propane. Naomi dropped the special cake she'd made for Priscilla. His heart raced.

Please, dear Lord, don't let all that happen.

He lit the lantern and ran a hand through his shorter curls, glad his mother had cut his hair the day before, then edged his legs over the side of the bed. Rubbing his arms to warm himself, he shook his head. He didn't believe in premonitions or predictions of doom and gloom, but the dream felt so real that it shook him up. Was this what he had to look forward to in a few hours?

Deciding that sleep was out of the question, he got dressed in his wedding clothes. A new crisp white shirt his mother made, black slacks, and…he picked up the black vest he'd planned to wear, but hung it back on the rack and chose the clothes Priscilla had made. He slipped on his black suit jacket and walked to the mirror carrying the lantern. He placed it on his chest of drawers while he looked in the mirror and carefully fastened his bow tie. Today he and his attendants would don the bow ties, as was tradition. He finished off his outfit by putting on a brand-new black hat with a three-and-a-half-inch brim.

Dressed and ready to go, he still had two hours before he needed to leave. Abe had already said that he would take care of the morning chores today. Chester sat down on his bed, his stomach churning with anticipation, excitement—and a tinge of worry. Then he remembered Rachel's envelope. He picked it up and slid out a single sheet of paper, expecting one of the pink-colored pictures Rachel was known for. He pulled the lantern closer. It was pink all right. But it wasn't a picture. And Chester's eyes filled with water as he read the words scribbled on the page.

PRISCILLA AWOKE TO the sound of Rusty the Rooster crowing. Sarah Mae had named the rooster, who was clueless about when he was supposed to crow. Every other rooster they'd had announced a new day when the sun came up. Not Rusty. He sang when he saw light. Any light. And that meant that someone was already up downstairs with lanterns lit. She glanced at her clock, which showed four a.m. She was much too anxious to try to sleep for another hour or so.

After she cleaned up and brushed her teeth in the bathroom, she dressed for her wedding. As she slipped her dress on, she was pleased. Every stitch might not be as perfect as her first dress, but the navy blue dress fit well. She pulled her hair into a tight bun, then pinned it beneath a new black *kapp*, a gift from Hannah. She eased to the mirror in her room with the lantern in her hand. She looked at herself in the mirror in her black prayer covering, which was to differentiate between the white *kapp* she normally wore.

I am a bride. Today is my wedding day.

She smiled, walked back to her bed, and sat down. As

she pulled on a new pair of black socks and new high-topped black shoes, she sighed, knowing she was dressed way too early. Folks wouldn't start arriving to help for another couple of hours. She carried the lantern out into the upstairs hall, glad that Rusty must have gone back to sleep, but she wondered if anyone was up downstairs. She eased down the stairs, careful to skip the creaky third step on the way down. There was a lantern lit in the kitchen, but no one was downstairs at the moment, so she walked back upstairs and sat down on her bed, unsure what to do with herself.

Her muscles tensed. Despite her prayers and communion with God, she couldn't seem to shake the apprehension that festered within her heart. She bowed her head. *I know in my heart that You have a plan for me and that I shouldn't worry so much about what this day might bring, so please, God, wrap Your arms around me and Chester today, and let us not lose sight of what is most important.*

Priscilla lifted her head as she recalled the times in her life she'd heard the voice of God. In those instances, she had known that she was right with God in her heart and mind, fearful of her Lord, but without fear in her heart of human actions and reactions. She knew the difference, and she knew that human fear and worry had overcome her as of late, as hard as she'd fought it. She lowered her head again and prayed for renewed faith and total trust in God and His plan for her. When she was done, she stood up and decided to go back downstairs. There still wasn't anyone in the kitchen, but maybe she'd try to eat a bowl of cereal. She didn't think she could stomach a big breakfast this morning.

When she got to the doorway, she turned around and looked back at her bedroom, knowing that tonight Ches-

ter would share her room. She walked toward the bed, placed the lantern on the nightstand, then pulled up her covers on the bed and smoothed the wrinkles. She loved her Lone Star quilt with its brilliant red, but her mother had made her a new quilt to take to her new home— a lovely white wedding quilt with the traditional intertwined rings. She only wished she didn't have to wait months to start keeping house in her new home.

Her head swirled with thoughts. She was excited and nervous about spending her wedding night with Chester, but she loved him with all her heart. No sooner did she have the thought when she wondered if Chester would for sure show up today.

Of course he will.

She took a deep breath. Then she noticed Rachel's envelope on her nightstand. *Sweet Rachel.* And Priscilla had kept her promise. She picked up Rachel's envelope, slid her finger along the seam, and gazed at the white piece of paper with large pink lettering. Then she began to cry. How could Rachel have possibly known that this was exactly what she needed to hear at this very moment?

CHESTER READ RACHEL'S special gift three more times.

> God say you shoud not be scard Chestr. True *lieb* stop scaredness. You *lieb* wont be perfect if you scared Chestr.

Following the written words were two pink hearts, and underneath Rachel signed it, *I lieb you, Chester.*

Chester smiled as he blinked back tears. He knew the Scripture well. *There is no fear in love; but perfect*

love casteth out fear: because fear hath torment. He that feareth is not made perfect in love.

At that moment, worry and fear fled his heart and mind, and all he wanted to do was get to Priscilla. Even if it was four o'clock in the morning.

CHAPTER TWELVE

PRISCILLA BROUGHT RACHEL'S letter to her heart as a tear rolled down her cheek. God used someone so simple and pure as Rachel to speak to Priscilla through Scripture. She read it again.

> To Pre-Ceelia, I *lieb* you. Today is you happy marreage day. I happy two. God go befor you and withs you and He not gonna let u down. So dont be scard Pre-Ceelia. I think it Gods perfect plan. ☺☺☺

Priscilla swiped at another tear as she translated Rachel's message.

And the Lord, he it is that doth go before thee; he will be with thee, he will not fail thee; neither forsake thee: fear not, neither be dismayed.

She closed her eyes and wept, knowing she was going to marry Chester Lapp come rain or shine, and no case of the hiccups or any other unplanned occurrence would make her wedding any more perfect than the love that she and Chester shared. She wanted to tell him she was sorry, that this day would be perfect no matter what, because it was a union to be blessed by God. Her heart filled with gratitude as she pressed Rachel's letter back to her chest.

Then she heard a noise outside, and next thing she knew, her windowpane broke. Tiny pieces of glass spilled

onto the hardwood floor. She stepped back and wondered if a bird hit her window, but then she saw...*a rock*?

Easing slowly toward the window, she heard someone calling her name. She edged around the broken glass, then heard her name again. *Chester?*

"Priscilla, are you up there? I have to talk to you. It's important."

She peered out the window. "Chester, what are you doing?" It was a loud whisper, but she wasn't sure he heard her, so she spoke a little louder. "You broke the window. What are you doing?"

"I have to talk to you, Priscilla."

A few hours ago she might have wondered if Chester was here to call off the wedding, or she would have worried about what he had to say. "I have to talk to you too."

Her bedroom door flung open, and she spun around to see her father standing in the doorway, barefoot and in his long pants and pajama shirt. His hair was sticking up on the top of his head, and he had a scowl on his face.

"Tell that boy to come into the house like a normal person." He turned to leave, scratching his head, but turned back. "And tell him I expect him to replace that window." He narrowed his brows, but a grin shone on his face. "You two only have a few more hours before you're married and together all the time. He had to break *mei* window?" He shook his head and left.

"Chester! I'll meet you downstairs."

Priscilla sprinted down the stairs, out the front door, and across the yard to where Chester was waiting in the darkness. In the moonlight, she could see his blue eyes calling to her, and she jumped into his arms. He cupped her face in his hands, kissed her on the mouth, the cheek, the forehead, then back on the mouth again.

"Priscilla, I love you with all my heart. It doesn't matter what happens today or—"

She gently put her finger against his lips. "I love you too, Chester, and I'm not concerned about anything." Her breath clouded in front of her from the cool night air, but inside she was warm and peaceful. "Today will be a wonderful day even if it rains, nothing goes as planned, and I get the hiccups… It doesn't matter. It's perfect because I love you!"

"Priscilla," he whispered as he drew her close again. "In a few hours you will be *mei frau*."

"*Ya*. I will." She gazed into his eyes and touched his cheek. "And I can't wait."

They both turned around when they heard footsteps on the front porch. *Mamm*.

"Chester Lapp, I don't know what you're doing here at this hour on your wedding day, but both of you get in here out of the cold. I'm heating up a breakfast casserole, then there is much work to be done." *Mamm* shook her head as she turned and went back into the house.

Priscilla and Chester both chuckled as they made their way slowly across the yard hand in hand.

THREE HOURS LATER Priscilla watched as almost four hundred friends and family gathered inside the living room area, spilling into the temporary addition her father, friends, and family had built. *Mamm* had opened all the window blinds early that morning. An orange glow filled the horizon and lit the fields with golden hues as rays of light filtered through the house. Priscilla could feel God's presence all around her.

The ceremony began right at eight o'clock, and the congregation sang several songs in German. From her

place on a backless bench in the front row, Priscilla sat almost directly across from Chester, and he'd never looked more handsome. She searched his face for any sense of hesitancy, but he sat tall and confident, and he looked as at peace as Priscilla felt. Forty benches filled their large living room, and more benches and chairs were in the extra space connected to the house, with the double doors from the living room open so everyone could hear the ceremony. A fire roared in the fireplace, and the smell of *roascht* filled the house. Her attendants, Rose and Naomi, sat to her left. Chester's attendants, Zeke and Abe, sat to his right.

The bishop presented stories about the Old Testament, followed by several Scripture readings, and then a lengthy sermon that focused on the bond and commitment of marriage. It was over two hours later when the deacon asked Priscilla and Chester to step forth and join him.

Priscilla choked back tears as she listened to Chester. "I, Chester, take you, Priscilla…"

Then with a shaky voice, she vowed to love Chester for the rest of her life, and Bishop Ebersol blessed their union. He took Chester's right hand and Priscilla's right hand and joined them together, placing his hand on theirs. After he pronounced them husband and wife, he asked if either of the fathers would like to speak or offer words of wisdom for the new bride and groom.

Chester's father stood up and reminded them that the man is the head of the household and that Priscilla is his helpmate, but as he looked at Chester, he also emphasized to his son that he is responsible for providing for his family. For a brief moment, Priscilla thought about

how Mr. Turner had fired Chester, but she quickly tossed the thought aside.

Priscilla's father spoke to Priscilla and Chester next. A knot formed in Priscilla's throat as she listened to words from her *daed*.

"*Mei dochder*, I pray you will find much happiness in your life with Chester, and that you will keep God in your heart as challenges arise, as they most certainly will." Her father swallowed hard as he turned to Chester. "A man will leave his father and mother and be united to his wife; and the two will become one flesh. So they are no longer two, but one. Therefore, what God has joined together, let man not separate." *Daed* looked back and forth between Priscilla and Chester, and she could see her mother and both attendants dabbing at their eyes. "Be *gut* to each other. Follow the ways of the Lord in all you do."

With tears in her eyes, Priscilla nodded at her father before her eyes met with Chester's, and she knew that God's love was shining on them.

A final prayer by the bishop drew the ceremony to a close. Priscilla smiled as she glanced at Rose—whose dress fit perfectly, and who wasn't scratching her arms. She looked at Hannah, still pregnant and with no signs of labor today. What a party they would have now.

A rush of women headed toward the kitchen, and the men wasted no time as they began transforming benches into tables and setting up a table in a U-shape under the temporary shelter. The corner of one table, the *eck*, was for Priscilla and Chester, along with their wedding party. As was customary, they would be served first. Priscilla's attendants sat to her left, along with other young unmarried women. Chester's attendants sat to his right, next to

more unmarried women. Young married men sat on the remaining side of the formation.

Soon they were served the traditional *roascht*, mashed potatoes, gravy, creamed celery, pepper cabbage, applesauce, rolls, and homemade bread and jam. Women bustled about, and after everyone at the *eck* was served, the women tended to the first group seated. As a courtesy, folks ate as quickly as they could so that setup could begin for the next group, then the next. Usually, it took three shifts to feed the wedding guests.

After everyone had eaten, Priscilla and Chester, along with their attendants, returned to the *eck*. Priscilla was excited to see all the desserts and sweets that her friends and relatives brought. And, of course, there were "wedding nothings"—the cookies always served at weddings. After she and Chester inspected the items, they passed them around the table for the others to see. Many of the cakes had something written on top specifically for Priscilla and Chester, often an inside joke of some sort. She laughed when she saw that Naomi had added something to her cake—in between the candied yellow roses she'd written *Skydivers Forever*.

Chester reached over and squeezed her hand under the table as he smiled. "I love you, Priscilla Lapp."

Her heart warmed as she squeezed back, but suddenly Chester's smile faded and was replaced with a scowl.

CHESTER STARED ACROSS the room at the man who had caused him so much heartache and wondered what he was doing here. Then he remembered. Chester had invited him a long time ago.

"What's wrong?" Priscilla's voice was tight.

He forced a smile. "Mr. Turner is here." He rubbed his

chin for a moment. "It just wonders me why he would come after the way he talked to me."

"I'm surprised too." Priscilla paused as she squinted in Mr. Turner's direction. "And isn't that Mrs. Turner with him?"

Chester sat taller. "*Ya*. It is." He watched the older man and his wife take a seat across the room as he pushed aside the conversation they'd had awhile back. "But that's okay. Don't give it another thought." He focused on his food, his new bride, and the blessings God had bestowed on him, but he could feel Mr. Turner's eyes on him. He avoided holding eye contact with the man, but as soon as they were through looking at all the cakes and candies, he was going to go talk to him.

About thirty minutes later he excused himself after he saw Mr. Turner walk outside with his wife. He wasn't sure if they were leaving or just getting some fresh air. Outside, a cluster of people gathered on the porch, and it took him a minute to locate Mr. and Mrs. Turner sitting in the double porch swing, eating dessert. He moved through the crowd, past a portable heater on the porch, and approached them slowly, unsure what he would say.

"Chester!" Mr. Turner set his plate down on a table beside him. "I'm glad you found me. I have much to say to you."

Mrs. Turner also put her plate down. "Chester, it was a beautiful ceremony. Just lovely."

Chester's mind spun with confusion as Mr. Turner stood up and extended his hand. Hesitantly, Chester shook his hand. Then Mrs. Turner stood up.

"I owe you a huge apology, son." Mr. Turner lowered his head for a moment, then looked back up at Chester. "I—I..." He shook his head as Mrs. Turner put her arm

around her husband. She rubbed Mr. Turner's back as she spoke.

"Chester, what my husband is trying to say is that he made a terrible mistake by accusing you of taking that money." She turned toward her husband, frowning, although she continued to rub his back. Then she turned back to Chester. "I told him that there had to be some kind of mistake."

"I've been trying to call you." Mr. Turner met eyes with Chester as his brows drew downward into a frown. "No one ever answers at the phone shanty, and your brother's phone says it's been disconnected." He lowered his gaze. "I should have gone out to your house, but…" Mr. Turner looked up again, his eyes soft and glassy. "I was ashamed."

Chester thought about the couple of times that he and Priscilla just let the phone ring at the shanty, fearing bad news. He waited while Mrs. Turner went on.

"Mr. Turner is having some—some medical issues." Her expression fell, and Chester hoped she wasn't going to cry. "He didn't remember putting the money in a jar at home. I found it when I was cleaning."

"Chester, I'm so sorry." Mr. Turner stepped forward a bit. "I'm an old man, and I reckon I'm forgetting things left and right." He paused as he let out a heavy sigh. "And I'm only going to get worse."

Mrs. Turner blinked back tears. "We're hoping the medication will help, but we both know that we can't run the store anymore."

"I'm so sorry, Mr. Turner, that you're sick." Chester took a deep breath as he thought of an uncle he had who suffered from Alzheimer's. "Is there anything that I can do to help?"

"As a matter of fact there is," Mr. Turner said, standing taller. "We'd like for you to run the store."

Chester's voice echoed the hope he felt in his heart. "Really?"

"We understand if you can't forgive me, Chester." Mr. Turner shook his head. "I reacted so hastily. Just not like me to do that." He sighed again. "Anyway, we were wondering if you might want to buy Turner's Furniture Store. You're such a fine carpenter, and we'll be glad to finance it for you."

"Buy it?" Chester's eyes grew round as saucers, and he wondered if this day could get any better. "I'd be honored, sir." He held out his hand.

"Wonderful!" Mrs. Turner hugged Chester. "And as a wedding present and apology, we'd like for you to take over the store right away and not worry about any payments for the next six months until you and Priscilla get settled."

"Thank you both." Chester smiled as he silently thanked God as well for his good fortune and offered a prayer for the Turners.

BY LATE AFTERNOON plans were already underway for another meal. Following a day of socializing and fellowship, some guests had slipped out to attend other wedding receptions. Since everyone in their community married in November or December, it was almost impossible to have a date exclusive to one bride and groom. As was customary, Priscilla was the one to choose what they would have for the evening meal. She'd chosen chicken and wafers and steamed peas.

Finally the day came to a close around nine o'clock,

and Priscilla and Chester said good-bye to the rest of the guests. Priscilla hugged Hannah.

"I made it through your wedding, Priscilla." Hannah smiled as she patted her large belly. "Now, I'm going to go home and coax this baby into having his birthday on your anniversary."

"I can't wait!" Priscilla said as Hannah slipped past her with her husband. Rose and Luke were behind Hannah. Priscilla was glad to see that the dress fit and that Rose didn't seem to be scratching anymore. She hugged her friend good-bye. Out of the corner of her eye she could see Naomi and Zeke standing outside talking, and she smiled to herself.

"It's been a perfect day," she whispered to Chester as they watched the last of their guests leave.

"*Ya*. It has."

Now it was time to go upstairs with her new husband.

FOR THE NEXT two weeks Priscilla and Chester visited family and friends, sometimes hitting four or five houses in one day. They ate dinner and supper with someone different each day, and they received some wonderful wedding gifts. One of her favorites was a small red suitcase that was filled with towels, washrags, and homemade lavender soap—a gift from one of Chester's cousins.

In the evenings, Chester worked on their new house while Priscilla continued to help her mother with the regular chores. He was scheduled to start back to work at the furniture store the following day, but this evening he was home from working on the house earlier than usual.

"I want you to come see the *haus*." Chester kissed her after he looked around and saw that they were alone.

Priscilla hadn't seen the house since the wedding, at

Chester's insistence. He had been very tight-lipped about it, which made her wonder if they'd be staying even longer than the anticipated two months with her family.

"I thought you didn't want me to see it until everything was ready for us to move in."

He shrugged. "I changed my mind."

"Okay." She was anxious to see how much progress had been made.

A short while later Chester pulled into the dirt driveway. He jumped out, then went around and opened the buggy door for Priscilla. She glanced up at the roof and wondered if they'd made all the repairs. And what about the electrical issues and touch-up work that still needed to be done?

Chester scooped her into his arms and laughed.

"What are you doing?" She laughed along with him as she clung to his neck.

"The *Englisch* aren't the only ones who can carry a new bride over the threshold."

Chester eased his hand to the doorknob and turned. Then he pushed the door open with his foot and set Priscilla down in the entryway.

She blinked her eyes a few times to make sure what she was seeing was real. "Chester..." She cupped her hands to her mouth as her eyes scanned the living room. On the floor, on the built-in shelves, and on the fireplace mantel were vases full of flowers. She swiped at a tear as she fell into Chester's arms. "*Danki! Danki!* They're beautiful!"

"All for you, my sweet Priscilla." He hugged her tight and kissed her lips.

Priscilla took a closer look. There was a rocking chair from Chester's house in the living room. She eased away

from him and moved toward the kitchen. There was a pitcher on the counter, two canisters, and some kitchen towels laid out. Around the corner, she could see their bedroom. She hurried that way. Chester's bed and all his furniture was in the room.

"Why did you move some of your things in when the house isn't finished?" She met his eyes, but he just smiled. Priscilla took a closer look. The fireplace mantel was sanded and finished, and it hadn't been before. The floor wasn't covered in sawdust anymore, but instead shone with a fresh layer of wax. All the little things that hadn't been completed were done.

"The roof and the electrical issues are fixed too."

Priscilla ran from room to room. Not one thing was left unfinished. "How did you do this?"

"Several nights last week, about two dozen members of the community met me here, and we finished everything." He winked. "Kind of like a mini barn-raising." Then he walked to Priscilla and pushed back a strand of hair that had fallen across her cheek. "Tomorrow we will get your things. It's completely ready to live in."

Priscilla swiped at a tear. "I love you, Chester."

It was all a part of God's perfect plan.

* * * * *

ACKNOWLEDGMENTS

Thank You, dear Lord, for putting these stories in my head and for blessing me beyond my wildest dreams. To my friends and family, I couldn't do this without you, especially my husband, Patrick.

Much thanks goes to my editors, Natalie Hanemann and L.B. Norton, for their fantastic insight. To my publishing family at Thomas Nelson, I'm blessed to have you on my team. To my agent, Mary Sue Seymour, glad to have you on board, my friend. Kelly Long and Kathy Fuller, as always…it's been a pleasure working with you. You're both awesome! To Barbie Beiler, thank you SO much. Sending blessings your way. Reneé Bissmeyer, my best friend and kindred spirit, thank you for painting with me on Sunday afternoons, a new hobby that soothes my soul. And last but not least, to my sons, Eric and Cory. I love you both very much. Cory, congratulations on your marriage. May God bless you and Kaitlyn always.

ABOUT THE AUTHOR

Award-winning, bestselling author **Beth Wiseman** is best known for her Amish novels, but her most recent novels, *Need You Now* and *The House That Love Built*, are contemporaries set in small Texas towns.

Both have received glowing reviews. Beth's latest release, *The Promise*, is inspired by a true story. Visit Beth on the web at bethwiseman.com, look for her on Facebook (Fans of Beth Wiseman), www.Facebook.com/pages/Fans-of-Beth-Wiseman/47576397539?pnref=story, or follow her on Twitter: @bethwiseman.

A PERFECT MATCH

Kathleen Fuller

To my family

CHAPTER ONE

"THOSE COOKIES SMELL *APPEDITLICH*." Naomi King smiled at Margaret as the young woman pulled a tray of chocolate chip cookies out of the oven. She brushed a bit of excess flour from her hands. "Chunks or chips?"

"Chunks, this time." Margaret put the cookie sheet on top of the stove and turned to Naomi. "I noticed the chunky ones sell faster than the chips."

Using a knife, Naomi cut the freshly rolled bread dough into narrow strips, which she then manipulated into twists. "I'm surprised we ran out of the bread twists so soon."

"They've been pretty popular too." Margaret picked up a metal cooling rack and put it on the counter next to the stove. A knock sounded on the front door. "I'll get it." She left the kitchen.

With quick, practiced motions Naomi put the pale twists on a baking sheet and popped them into the oven. She wound the timer and walked over to the sink to wash her hands. The window above the sink was open halfway, letting a refreshing cool breeze into her small kitchen. Not for the first time she said a prayer of thanks for Margaret's help with her bakery business. For the past three months, since Naomi started selling baked goods from the *daadi haus* where she lived behind her parents' home,

business had been brisk. She wouldn't have been able to keep up, not without Margaret's help.

A few moments later Margaret returned and handed Naomi thirty dollars. "Three loaves of bread, a gooseberry pie, and two pumpkin rolls. The *Englisch* woman was a repeat customer, by the way."

"That's what I like to hear." Naomi looked at the money. "*Geh* ahead and keep it."

"But you already paid me."

"I know. You've been working hard these past two weeks. You deserve a little extra."

Margaret smiled and tucked the money into her purse, which was hanging on a peg near the back door. "Did you know you have a leak in your front room?"

"What?"

"A small drip in the corner, by the couch. I noticed it as the woman was leaving."

"Nee." Naomi hurried out of the kitchen, down the narrow hallway to the small sitting room. She saw several drips of water slip from a sag in the ceiling. Last night an intense storm had hit Paradise. Being a deep sleeper, she'd slept through the whole thing. But this morning Margaret had mentioned seeing several large branches littering the yards along the road, ripped from the trees by the harsh winds. The winds must have damaged the roof somehow.

Quickly she went to the back porch and retrieved a bucket. She moved the couch out of the way and put the bucket under the drip. After getting a towel from the linen closet she wiped up the water from the hardwood floor.

"How bad is the damage?" Margaret moved to stand next to her.

"I think the floor is all right." Naomi looked up at the ceiling again. "I don't know about the roof."

"Isn't the *haus* pretty old?"

"At least fifty years. My *grossvatter* built it for his parents." She rubbed her fingers against her temple. "I hate to tell *Daed* about this, but I'll have to. He's so busy with wedding preparations; he doesn't need another thing to worry about." She also didn't think her father needed to be repairing a roof, not at his age. "So many things have been going wrong lately. Like the house Chester is building for Priscilla and him to live in. The foundation didn't set right, the lumber they ordered for the frame was delayed, and Chester's brother, Abraham, broke his wrist when he fell off the roof. Now this." She frowned.

"It's only a small leak, Naomi. It shouldn't be any trouble to fix. Do you want to tell your *daed* now? I can handle any customers that come by, and I'll whip up another batch of cookies too."

Naomi shook her head. "He's not home. I'll wait until tonight." She looked at Margaret, her eyes suddenly going wide. "The bread twists!"

"I took them out already," Margaret said.

Naomi breathed a sigh of relief. "I don't know what I'd do without you."

Her friend's cheeks pinked. "You'd do just fine." She smiled. "All this baking has made me hungry."

"Let's break for lunch."

A short while later Margaret joined Naomi on the back porch underneath the extended roof, a shiny red apple in one hand, a turkey and Swiss cheese sandwich in the other. With the toe of her black lace-up shoe, Naomi pushed a chair toward Margaret and took a bite of her tuna fish sandwich.

It had rained most of the morning. Heavy drops fell from the edge of the roof, but there was enough shelter to keep the women dry.

"We won't be able to sit out here much longer." Margaret sat down and let out a small shiver. "Winter isn't far around the corner."

Naomi pulled her sweater closer to her body. "I'm surprised it's so chilly. Must be because of the storm last night."

Margaret polished the apple on the edge of her white apron. A few grease spots dotted the thin fabric. "How are the wedding plans going?"

"Other than what I've already told you, *gut* so far." Naomi set her sandwich down on her napkin and took a sip of water from her glass.

"And to think those two wouldn't be getting married if you hadn't helped them find each other."

"Oh, I didn't do much."

"You must have, because Priscilla said you convinced her to give Chester a chance. And I remember seeing you talking to Chester a few times. The next thing I hear, the two of them are courting." Margaret sighed. "It's all so romantic."

Naomi smiled. "They are a perfect match, *ya*? My sister has never been so happy."

"I know I shouldn't say this, but I'm a little jealous." Margaret rolled her apple around in her hand. "I wish I could find someone to love."

"You will."

"Sometimes I really doubt that. I'm almost twenty-four, Naomi."

"What about Ben Hooley?"

"Him?" Margaret waved her hand as if she were batting away a pesky fly.

"But he's picked you up a couple of times." Naomi thought of the quiet, stolid man who had moved to their district a few years ago. "I thought you two liked each other."

"He only gives me rides home as a favor to *Daed*. He doesn't even talk on the ride home. Ben Hooley isn't the *mann* for me, that's for sure." She leaned forward, her cheeks turning pink, her voice lowering to a whisper. "I'm kind of embarrassed to ask you this."

"We're friends, Margaret. You can ask me anything."

Margaret's light blond eyebrows formed a V over her pale blue eyes. "Could you...could you help me find someone?"

Naomi gave her an encouraging smile. "You don't need my help to find a beau. Any *mann* would be interested in you. You're smart and sweet and lovely."

"I'm old." Margaret's frown deepened. "And I can't be that sweet and lovely, because no one has been interested in me for a long time."

"You just haven't found the right *mann*. He'll come along."

"Do you really believe that?"

"I do. God has set apart someone special for you, Margaret. You'll meet him in the Lord's timing."

"I wish the Lord would hurry up, then." Margaret leaned back in her chair and put the apple on the desk. "I also wish I could be patient about this, like you are. I'm not at peace with being an old maid."

Naomi flinched a little inwardly. She'd never considered herself an old maid, and at twenty-five, she was older than Margaret. But she'd never felt any pressure

from her family to get married, and her life was busy and satisfying. She'd had little time to think about dating. *Except for David…*

She put her former boyfriend out of her mind. She'd come to terms with what he did three years ago. She even counted herself blessed that she hadn't married him.

"It scares me," Margaret said.

"What does?"

"That I'll never know what it's like to fall in love. To have a *kinn*." Her gaze met Naomi's. "I don't want to be alone."

Naomi reached out and patted her hand. "You won't be."

Margaret's face brightened. "Does that mean you'll help me? Like you helped Priscilla?"

"Ya," Naomi said, glad to see the strain seep away from her friend's expression. She didn't know exactly what she could do to help Margaret find a beau, but she'd figure that out later.

Margaret smiled. "I knew I could trust you to understand." She reached into the pocket of her apron and took out two cookies, offering one to Naomi.

"Are these the ones you just made?"

"Ya. They're still a little warm."

Naomi bit into the soft cookie. Chocolate and sugar flavors flooded her mouth. "Mmmm. I think these are the best batch you've made so far."

"I could barely make a peanut butter and jelly sandwich when I first started here."

"Now that's an exaggeration." Naomi ate the rest of the cookie. "Truly delicious."

"I have a *gut* teacher. Do you still like teaching your cooking classes?"

"I love it. I teach my last one this Saturday. I suspended the class for the rest of the month because of the wedding."

"Have any men signed up?" Margaret wiggled her delicate eyebrows. "Amish *mann* don't like to cook, but I've heard there are a lot of *Englisch mann* that do."

"*Nee.* I never had a man sign up. Although it could happen someday."

"Make sure you let me know when it does. I may drop in on the class." Margaret grinned, popped the last bit of cookie into her mouth, and stood. "I'll get started on the next batch."

"All right. I'll be inside in a minute." Naomi sat in the chair for a few moments, thinking about Margaret's request. *I don't want to be alone.* Naomi had never thought about spending her life alone. She'd always been surrounded by family, friends, and students. But her sister Hannah was married, and Priscilla would be shortly. Naomi frowned, feeling a tiny twinge in her heart. What if she had to spend the rest of her life alone?

"WE'RE SO GLAD you were able to come for the wedding, Zeke."

Zeke Lapp looked at his aunt, seated beside him at the table. He selected a roll from the basket to his right. "Me too. I'm overdue for a visit. Sorry it took so long for me to come."

"That doesn't matter. You're here now, and that's all that counts." She picked up a white dish and handed it to him. "Butter?"

"Danki." He smeared a pat on the still-steaming roll.

"I hope you don't mind eating so early." Irma cut the last chunk of tender roast beef on her plate into four

tiny pieces. "Normally we have supper around five, but I thought you might be hungry." She glanced at her husband and son. "These *mann* are always hungry."

Zeke grinned. "I don't mind eating early at all. Especially an *appeditlich* meal like this."

His aunt blushed, her gaze cast downward.

He glanced around the table at his uncle Emmanuel and his cousin Chester, whose upcoming wedding was the reason for Zeke's extended vacation in Paradise. He hadn't seen his Pennsylvania relatives since his family had moved to Middlefield, Ohio, more than fifteen years ago. Where had the time gone?

"How was the trip?" Emmanuel asked. "It's been years since I rode on a bus."

"Not bad. Took a little nap. A bit of a bumpy ride, though. Lots of construction in Ohio." Zeke swirled the roll in the last of the thick brown gravy covering his plate. He had to stop himself from shoving the soaked bread into his mouth. He appreciated a good cook, and his aunt was one of the best.

"Don't see how you could sleep on a bus." Chester looked up from his plate, fork in hand. "Those seats aren't comfortable."

Zeke started to say something, but just looked at his cousin.

Chester's brow lifted. "What? Do I have food on my face or something?" He grabbed a napkin and rubbed his mouth and chin, which already showed a shadow of a beard.

"*Nee.* Just can't believe my little cousin is getting married." It sounded corny, but it was how he felt.

Emmanuel laughed. "He's not exactly little, Zeke."

"I know." He'd been surprised to see that Chester was

a couple inches taller than his own five-foot-nine height, and at least twenty pounds heavier. "I can still remember you following me around when you were a *kinn*."

"Pestering you, I'm sure."

"*Ya*, but not too bad."

"I remember the time I nearly fell out of the tree in your backyard, trying to catch you." Chester set down his napkin. "You were a climbing fool."

"Still am." Zeke grinned again.

"Guess you have to be when you're a roofer. Business going well?"

"Very well. But I'm glad I could take some time off. I needed the vacation." He'd spent the last ten years working almost nonstop as a roofer, mostly for *Englisch*—or Yankee, as they referred to them back home—construction companies. Chester's wedding was the perfect opportunity to get away from Middlefield for a while. It wasn't the city of Middlefield he was escaping, but the women in his community. He definitely needed a break from their constant matchmaking.

Emmanuel pushed away from the table. "Now that the rain's stopped, we should check on the *haus*. After the storm last night and the rain today, I'm hoping it's still in one piece."

Chester scowled. "The way our luck's been, I'd be surprised if it is."

"Having problems with the construction?" Zeke asked.

His cousin filled him in, and Zeke nodded. "I'll come with you, if you don't mind."

"Are you sure you're not too tired from your trip?" his *aenti* asked.

"Thanks to that nap, I'm not." Zeke put his fork and

knife on his empty plate. He'd practically scraped the dish clean. "I'd like to see how the *haus* is coming along."

Emmanuel nodded. "I'd appreciate your input, especially on how we did the roof."

Chester stood. "I'll hitch up the buggy. The *haus* is just down the road. We can stop by the Kings' on the way. I need to drop something off at Priscilla's." He took his yellow straw hat from the peg near the back door of the kitchen and plopped it on his head before leaving the room.

Zeke carried his plate and empty tea glass to the sink.

"You don't have to do that," his aunt said, jumping up from her chair. She took the dishes from him. "I'll clear the table."

Zeke started to protest, then caught himself. Living as a bachelor, he was used to cleaning up after himself. And making his own meals. And doing his own laundry. But he didn't want to overstep his bounds in his aunt and uncle's house, especially after he'd just arrived.

Thirty minutes later he and Chester arrived at the Kings'. There was still enough light in the dusky sky that Zeke could see the large white house and small *daadi haus* behind it. At the end of the driveway a plain wooden sign hung from two hooks suspended from a wooden frame: Kings' Baked Goods. Underneath the name, in smaller letters, were the words In the Back.

"The Kings have a bakery?" Zeke asked.

"Naomi, Priscilla's oldest sister, does. Does *gut* business too." Chester pulled the buggy to a stop next to the house. He reached into the buggy and pulled out a pie plate.

"That's what you have to drop off?"

"Um, *ya.*" He rubbed the back of his neck. "She, ah, needs this pie plate."

Zeke didn't say anything, not wanting to tease his cousin about the flimsy excuse to see his future bride. He imagined he'd be the same way if he were getting married.

"We won't be but a minute," Chester added as they got out of the buggy.

"Take your time. I'm in no hurry."

They walked up on the porch, and Chester knocked on the door. A woman opened it.

"Hey, Naomi."

Zeke didn't move. He'd seen plenty of pretty *maed* in his time, but this was the loveliest woman he'd come across. Her chestnut-colored hair peeked out from beneath her white prayer *kapp*, the deep brown color matching her wide, round eyes.

"Hi, Chester. Come on in. Priscilla's in the kitchen with *Mamm.*"

The men stepped into the living room. Chester headed for the back of the house. Zeke cleared his throat, stopping his cousin in his tracks.

Chester turned around. "Oh, sorry. Naomi, this is my cousin Zeke Lapp. He's visiting from Middlefield." With that he disappeared.

Zeke grinned. "I think he's in a hurry."

"I think so too." Her lips curved into a smile. "When did you get into town?"

"Earlier today."

"Then you missed the storm. That's a *gut* thing. I wouldn't want you to get a bad impression of Paradise."

"Actually, I'm originally from here. I'm remembering now how much I missed it when we first moved away."

An older man walked into the room, shaking his head. "Naomi, I wish you would have told me about the roof sooner." He stopped and looked at Zeke.

Naomi introduced the two men.

Mr. King glanced at Zeke. "Sorry. Having problems with the *daadi haus*."

"The roof just started leaking today," Naomi explained. "Otherwise it's been fine."

"That sag in the ceiling isn't fine," her father said. "It needs to be repaired before the next rain." He tugged on his beard. "I guess I can get someone out here tomorrow to take a *gut* look at it, since I had to promise your *mamm* I wouldn't get up there. She said I don't need to throw my back out before the wedding." He looked directly at Zeke. "Just so you know, my back is fine."

"I'm sure it is." Zeke took a step forward. "If it's all right with you, I could take a look at it."

"Wouldn't want to put you to the trouble." But there was a glimmer of hope in the man's eyes.

"No trouble at all. I fix roofs for a living."

"Then I'm glad you're here." He looked at his daughter. "Naomi, show him the leak."

For the first time Zeke saw uncertainty in her eyes. It disappeared as she nodded. *"Ya."*

Her father moved to leave the room. "Appreciate your help," he added, glancing at Zeke.

Zeke glanced at Naomi and saw the hesitation return. While her father might be appreciative, he wasn't sure she was.

CHAPTER TWO

"So your *schwester* is marrying my cousin." Zeke examined the sag in the ceiling. "How did that come about?"

Naomi told him how Chester and Priscilla had begun courting. "She wasn't too keen on him at first, but I knew he was a *gut mann*, and encouraged her to give him a chance. I'm glad she did."

"So am I. He seems really happy."

"I should hope so. If he wasn't, they'd have a big problem on their hands."

His low, throaty chuckle sounded in the room. "*Ya*, they definitely would. Speaking of problems." He pointed at the ceiling.

Naomi stood beside the partially full bucket while Zeke inspected the damage. Since the rain had ceased, the drip had dried up. The only evidence of the leak was the water in the bucket and the dark, sagging spot above.

"Probably a few shingles blew off in the storm last night. Maybe the tar paper underneath them too."

"Can it be fixed?"

He turned to her. His yellow straw hat was frayed at the edges and pushed back from his face, revealing a mottled port-wine birthmark above his left eyebrow. "Easily. Won't take me long at all." He strode toward the front door.

"Where are you going?"

"Up on the roof." He looked at her over his shoulder. "I need to see where the shingles and tar paper are missing."

"It's getting dark outside." She tossed a quick glance at the window. "You don't have to do this tonight."

"There's enough light to see by. It will only take a minute."

"All right. I'll get the ladder from the barn."

He shook his head and walked to her. "*I'll* get the ladder from the barn. Just tell me where it is."

She did, and soon they were both outside. The ladder didn't quite reach the eave of the roof.

"I'm sorry. I wish I had a taller ladder."

"Doesn't bother me any." Zeke dashed up the rungs and, planting his palms on the edge of the roof, hoisted himself up with little effort.

Watching him traverse the roof as if it were a playground made her stomach flip. "Be careful," she called, the words out before she could stop them.

"I always am." He smiled down at her, his teeth bright in the dusky light.

Naomi watched as he continued his inspection. His birthmark was unusual; she'd never seen one like it before. Yet it didn't detract from his looks at all; instead it drew her attention to his hazel eyes and the wrinkles that appeared in the corners when he smiled.

Which made her pause. Obviously he wasn't in his early or midtwenties. But by his clean-shaven face, she knew he wasn't married. Widowed, perhaps? She doubted he was a lifelong bachelor. Someone as kind and appealing as he would have easily found a wife.

Zeke shimmied down the ladder even faster than he'd climbed up and strode toward her. "The *gut* news is it's an easy fix. Bad news is I'll have to do it in the morning.

By the time we'd get back to my *onkel*'s to get tools and supplies, it would be too dark to work today."

Naomi nodded. "I agree. What should we do in the meantime?"

He looked up at the roof again. "You don't have any plastic sheeting by any chance?"

"*Nee*. I don't have much use for it."

"Is it supposed to rain anymore tonight?"

"I don't think so. The forecast in the paper this morning said the rain would discontinue in the evening, which it has. Tomorrow is supposed to be cloudy."

"Okay. I'll wait until morning to fix it. Keep the pail underneath the leak. If it does rain, that should contain it."

Naomi nodded. "For *gut* measure, I'll pray there won't be any rain."

"I'll add my prayers to yours, then." He put his hands on his narrow hips, his fingers lightly resting on the waistband of his dark blue broadfall pants. "I'll see if Chester has any leftover shingles and paper at the new *haus*. If not, I'll pick some up on my way here tomorrow."

"Would you like to come in for some coffee?" Despite the chilly weather, he wore short sleeves. Just looking at him made Naomi hug her own arms.

He shook his head. "Chester is probably ready to *geh* by now. He's supposed to show me the new *haus* tonight."

"All right." She felt a tiny bit disappointed he had to leave so soon, and she hid a frown. *Where did that feeling come from?*

"I'll see you tomorrow, then." Zeke started to leave. But then he turned and faced her. "It's been a real pleasure meeting you, Naomi."

She stilled at his unexpected words. He shoved his

hands in his pockets and walked away. She stood in the middle of the doorway as he made his way to her parents' house. Was he...whistling? A little off-key, but definitely whistling. As she watched him go, she murmured, "Likewise, Zeke Lapp."

DESPITE NAOMI'S PRAYERS, it started raining shortly after Zeke left. Showers continued the next morning. Waking up well before sunrise, Naomi groaned when she heard the rain pummeling the *daadi haus*. She threw on a pale gray dress and white apron, thrust bobby pins into her hair and *kapp*, and shoved her feet into her black stockings and shoes. A knot formed in her stomach. Had it rained all night? She said a quick prayer that the leak in the roof hadn't expanded.

She hurried to the living room, glancing out the front window at the curtain of rain and wind pelting the glass. She turned on the battery-operated lantern on the small end table by her chair and held her breath as she looked at the ceiling. As she feared, the ceiling was sagging even more, and now a steady stream of water flowed from it.

A chill hung in the room. Naomi shivered, glancing at the coal stove in the opposite corner of the room. She'd hoped to put off lighting it until mid-October. So much for that idea.

But first she had to tend to the leak. She glanced down at the pail underneath the drip. Water splashed against the rim with every falling drop. She bent down to pick up the bucket.

Whoosh! The ceiling suddenly gave way.

ZEKE HAD JUST tied up Chester's horse and buggy next to Naomi's barn when he heard a faint cry come from inside the *daadi haus*. He quickly tied a loose but strong

knot in the reins and ran to the building, leaping over puddles and hurdling the three steps leading to the inside. He threw open the door. As he had feared when he woke up to the pounding rain that morning, more water had leaked into the house. Naomi stood right underneath the leak, her dress soaked through, a steady stream of rain falling on her.

"Z-Zeke?"

His shin rammed into the side of the couch as he hurried to her. When he reached her, he heard her teeth chattering. Without thinking he pulled her out from under the leak. Quickly he whipped off his jacket and wrapped it around her damp shoulders.

"Y-your j-jacket," she said. "I-it's g-getting wet."

"Don't worry about it. What happened?"

"Th-the ceiling."

He looked up and saw a hole the size of a soup can in the center of the sag. He groaned.

"Here." She started to take off his jacket.

His hands covered hers, stopping her. "*Nee*. You need it more than I do."

The storms over the past two days must have been part of a cold front. He'd noticed the drop in temperature when he'd left his uncle's house a little while ago. Zeke looked around the living room, dimly lit by the weak light of the lantern. The sun had risen, but the heavy cloud cover prevented much light from coming through the window. He spied a coal stove in the corner of the room. "I'm going to light the stove, okay?"

"*Ya.*" She pulled his jacket closer to her, still looking a little shocked. Her white *kapp* hung limp and askew on her head.

Zeke saw a basket of newspapers beside the stove.

He picked up a sheet and lit it with the handheld lighter he found on a small shelf near the stove. Holding the lit paper high in the flue, he checked to make sure there was an updraft in the chimney. If not, the house would soon be filled with choking smoke. Satisfied when the wisp of smoke wafted up the flue, he put the paper in the stove, added several more layers on top, and waited for them to catch.

"I can finish that."

He turned around at the sound of Naomi's voice. He hadn't heard her leave the room, but she had changed into a dry, long-sleeved dress and a light blue kerchief. At least she wasn't shivering anymore.

"It's okay. It will only take a minute." The newspapers lit quickly. He laid a bed of coal over the glowing embers, then shut the front of the stove and faced Naomi. "I'm so sorry. I should have fixed the roof last night."

She shook her head. "It would have been dangerous to do that in the dark, with just a flashlight."

"Still, I could have put some plastic over the ceiling. That would have held the water back."

"Considering we didn't have any, I don't see how you could have." Naomi walked over to the leak and wiped a droplet of water off the end of her nose.

Still feeling guilty, he moved beside her and picked up the pail. "I'll take care of this." Making sure not to spill any water on the dry part of her wood floor, Zeke carefully carried the pail to the door and tossed the water onto the grass just beyond the front porch. He went back inside and put the pail back under the leak. The rain had started to let up a bit, and the water was now coming down in a thin stream.

He looked at her. If she was angry, he didn't blame her. Although he had to admit she looked cute in her kerchief. If he'd been thinking, he would have come back last night with Chester and put something over the hole, instead of counting on the weather report. If he had, the ceiling would have held.

"I'll get a mop and clean the floor."

Surprised, he turned and looked at her again. More light filtered into the room, revealing her calm expression. If she was mad, she had a strange way of showing it.

"When Margaret gets here, I'll have her get started in the kitchen." She faced him, consumed with the confidence he'd been attracted to from the moment they met. "We won't have a normal workday, but that's all right."

Zeke couldn't help but smile. He couldn't say he wouldn't be irritated after being doused with cold rainwater. Yet after the initial shock, she now seemed unfazed. He'd never met anyone like her before.

"Goodness, what happened?"

Zeke turned around to see a blond-haired woman walk through the open door, her steps hesitant. Physically she was Naomi's opposite—light blue eyes, fair skin, and about an inch shorter than he was. But both women seemed to be about the same age, which he guessed to be in their early twenties.

"More problems with the leak," Naomi said. She crossed her arms over her chest.

The other woman's gaze darted to the stream of water coming out of the ceiling. "I can see that. What are you going to do?"

Zeke listened as Naomi gave the woman, who was apparently her assistant, instructions. Not wanting to inter-

rupt, he slipped past them and went outside to the buggy. The rain seemed to have lightened up. If it stopped completely he could get up on the roof and replace the tar paper and missing shingles. But until then, he'd have to make a quick repair job inside using the plastic sheeting he'd gotten from Chester that morning. He slipped on his tool belt, then grabbed his supplies.

When he went back inside, Naomi had disappeared. The blond woman stood by the stove, holding her hands above it.

"Where's Naomi?" he asked.

"Getting a mop. Downstairs. I was just trying to get warm." She looked at her feet for a moment, then met his gaze again. "I'm Margaret," she said, her voice cracking on the last syllable of her name.

"Zeke Lapp." He didn't mean to sound curt, but he wanted to repair the ceiling. "Do you know if Naomi has a stool or an old chair I could stand on?"

"Sure. It's in the kitchen. I'll be right back."

A few moments later he climbed on the small step stool. He glanced at Margaret, who watched. "Could you give me a hand?"

"Sure!" She hurried over to him. "What do you want me to do?"

"Hold this," he said, giving her the plastic sheeting. He grabbed three nails out of one of the pockets of his tool belt, then slipped the hammer from its leather loop on the other side of the belt. "Now hand me the plastic."

He couldn't be sure, but when she gave him the plastic, he thought he heard her giggle. He glanced down at her and stifled a sigh. Being one of the few bachelors in his community had made him a target for single females between the ages of nineteen and thirty. He'd heard that shy

giggle more than once. *Naomi, hurry up!* He had come to Paradise for his cousin's wedding, not to find a wife.

CHAPTER THREE

Naomi clasped her fingers around the handle of the mop, grateful that the roof had collapsed when it did. If it had happened during the winter, the small stove wouldn't do much to keep the house warm, not with cold air and possibly snow coming through the ceiling. As she made her way from the back porch to the front room, she thought about how Zeke's coat had felt around her chilly body. She had breathed in the mix of scents emanating from the sturdy, dark blue fabric. A smoky wood smell, as if the coat had been hung in front of a fire to dry. The underlying aroma of coffee, which made sense when she saw the small brown stain on the lapel as she took the coat off to change. And a scent she couldn't identify, but one that had triggered another shiver through her body. One that had nothing to do with being cold.

A pounding sound came from the front room. Knowing that even in the rain she might have customers soon, she quickened her steps. When she walked into the living room, she saw Margaret beside Zeke. He stood on tiptoe on a footstool, hammering a corner of a plastic tarp over the hole in the ceiling while Margaret held the other end. The rain had ceased, but water still dribbled, making hollow plinking sounds against the plastic.

Naomi started to ask if they needed help. Then she

saw the look on Margaret's face as she gazed up at Zeke. And remembered her promise.

"Can you hand me the other end?" Zeke said to Margaret. She complied, and in a few moments he had the hole secured. He stepped down off the stool.

Naomi watched Margaret follow Zeke to the stove, never taking her eyes off him. Zeke tossed a few more pieces of coal into the stove and shut the door. Margaret moved in close and said something, but Naomi couldn't make out the words. Zeke turned to her, giving her the same polite, charming grin he'd given Naomi when they first met.

For the briefest of moments, something ugly twisted inside her. She ignored it as Zeke walked toward her, again with Margaret in tow.

"That plastic should keep the leak at bay," he said. "Now that the rain has stopped I'll get up on the roof and fix the flashing."

"But the roof's wet," Margaret said, her eyes growing wide with concern. "You could slip and fall."

Naomi had the same thoughts. Yet before she could say anything, Zeke shook his head. "I've been on all kinds of roofs. Wet ones, icy ones. I'll be careful." He kept his hazel eyes on Naomi as he spoke. Then he flashed her a smile and went outside.

As soon as he disappeared, Margaret moved right next to her. "Where did he come from?" Excitement edged her tone. "I've never seen him before."

"He's Chester's cousin. He arrived from Middlefield, Ohio, yesterday." She looked at her friend, noting her dreamy expression. Whatever ugliness had appeared in Naomi's heart, it wasn't there now. Margaret was smitten.

"He's very *schee*. And nice." Margaret's smile dipped.

"I don't know why I'm even talking about him. A *mann* like him would never give me the time of day."

"You don't know that. He could be thinking about you right now." She put her hand on Margaret's forearm, wishing her friend wasn't so down on herself. "I think we should find out if he is."

"But how? It's not like I can just walk up to him and ask him out on a date."

"Leave that to me," Naomi said. She heard the thud of Zeke's footsteps on the roof. She hoped he would keep his promise and not do anything reckless. Somehow she knew he would stay safe.

NORMALLY ZEKE MAINTAINED singular focus when he was working on a roof. Any loss of concentration could result in his slipping and falling off the slanted surface. But despite his attempts at paying attention to tacking down the tar paper, he couldn't get his mind off Naomi.

He put two tacks in his mouth and positioned the tar paper in place. He'd spent the last twelve years of his life praying for God to bring the right woman along. When he was younger his prayers weren't exactly earnest—he was too busy working and didn't mind being single. But in the past couple of years, the loneliness had caught up with him.

Seeing his siblings, his friends, even men he didn't know married and with children triggered a bit of desperation inside him. Yet despite his desire to find a wife, he wouldn't settle for just any woman. Not because he had to have the most beautiful one, or the finest caretaker, or even the best cook—although being able to cook was a plus. He wanted his marriage to be blessed by the Lord, and influenced by Christ in every way. He trusted that

God would let him know who the right woman was. He wasn't sure how, but he had faith. And so far he hadn't felt anything for the women he had met.

Until now.

The hammer came down on his thumb. "Ow!"

Thanks for the reminder, Lord. I'll pay attention to my work from now on.

He managed to shove Naomi out of his mind for a few moments. A buzzing sounded in his ears. He assumed it was a fly. He waved the pest off and started hammering again. Then he felt a sharp pain on the side of his neck. He slapped his hand against his skin, only to feel another stinging sensation on his left leg. Turning, he dropped his hammer. *Hornets!* He leapt up as several more stung him. He skidded down the roof, batting at the hornets. "Ow!"

"Zeke? What's wrong?"

He saw Naomi when he got to the edge of the roof. "Hornets!" he yelled. One stung him on the cheek. His foot slipped on the eave.

"Zeke!"

He regained his balance, then was stung again as he clambered down the ladder, his tool belt slapping against his waist. "Inside," he gasped. "Quick!"

They both ran inside and shut the door. Zeke leaned against it, his breath hitching.

"Are you okay?" Her hand rested on her chest, her soft brown eyes round.

Suddenly he felt every single hornet sting at once. He shook his head, closing his eyes against the pain.

She ran up to him and grasped his arm. "How many times did you get stung? Never mind, we'll find out." When they reached the kitchen she led him to a chair. "I need a bowl, baking soda, and a glass of water."

"What happened?" Margaret asked, retrieving the items.

"Hornet stings." Naomi leaned over and looked at Zeke. "One on your face for sure. Where else?"

"Neck. Arm. Leg."

She nodded, then turned around as Margaret put the bowl on the table. In a few seconds Naomi had mixed the baking soda and water into a paste. She took some in the palm of her hand and dipped her finger in it. She applied it to the sting on his face with a gentle, confident touch.

Despite the pain, he couldn't take his eyes off her as she continued to apply the thick white paste to his neck. She was even prettier up close.

"You've been stung before, *ya*?"

He nodded. "Not like this." He held up his forearm. A bright red dot appeared among the dark hairs.

"Are you feeling okay, other than the pain?" She paused, a thick coating of baking soda paste on her finger. "Dizzy? Nauseous?"

"*Nee*. The stings are enough."

A knock sounded on the front door. "I'll take care of whoever it is," Margaret said.

"I haven't had a chance to put anything out," Naomi told her.

"It's all right. I'll tell the customer what we have." Margaret disappeared from the kitchen.

Naomi turned her attention back to Zeke. "Where else did you get stung?"

He pointed to a spot under his collarbone. Already the pain had started to ease. The paste was doing the trick.

She moved her paste-covered finger toward his shirt, then paused, her cheeks suddenly turning red.

He looked down. His shirt collar was open, making

it easy for her to slip her hand underneath the fabric and apply the paste. Instead he reached for the bowl. "I can get the rest of them, Naomi."

"Ya." She stepped back, then hurried to the sink to wash her hands, not looking at him. He quickly put the paste on the stings on his chest. The one on his thigh would just have to do without. When he set the bowl on the table, she turned off the tap and dried her hands. She walked toward him, handing him the towel. He wiped off his fingers.

"I'm so sorry. I had no idea there was a hornets' nest up there."

"I'm not sure there was." He looked at her, touched by her concern. "They seemed to come out of nowhere." He took off his damp hat and tapped it against his other hand.

"I'm glad you weren't stung more. Do they still hurt?"

"Not too bad. Don't worry, I'm fine." A different kind of warmth traveled through him as he met her relieved gaze. "I'll figure out where that nest is and finish up the roof." He started to stand.

"You don't have to do that now." She put her hand on his arm, then jerked it back. "I mean, I don't want you to get stung again."

"I won't. I'll make sure of that." Zeke rose from the chair and started to leave the kitchen.

"Wait." Naomi opened the cabinets under the sink and withdrew an aerosol can with a yellow lid. "Bug spray. Not sure if it will work on hornets, but it's worth a try."

Two hours later Zeke was finishing the last of the repairs on the roof. He'd located the hornets' nest, which was underneath the extended roof that covered the back porch, and sprayed it down thoroughly. He hadn't been stung since. Even though the stings still smarted a bit,

he wasn't going to let that keep him from finishing the job. By the end of the afternoon he'd repaired the hole in the ceiling as well. He was rolling up the plastic sheeting when Naomi came into the living room. She looked up at his repair and smiled.

"I can't thank you enough for all your help. And on your vacation too. I still feel awful about the hornet stings."

"I survived." He grinned. "And I didn't mind doing the job."

"I want to repay you in some way. Other than the money for the materials, of course." She looked up at him. "I'd like to invite you to supper at my *haus* this Saturday evening. If you're free, that is."

"I just so happen to be free. What time?"

"Around five?"

"I'll be there."

She nodded, her cheeks plumping as her smile widened. "I should get back to the kitchen. Margaret left a little while ago, and I've got a couple of spice cakes in the oven. Oh, I almost forgot." She left the room, returning a moment later with his jacket. "I should have given this to you earlier. Maybe it would have helped against the hornets."

"I doubt it." He took the jacket and slipped it on. "Well, guess I'll see you Saturday."

"*Ya.* See you then."

As he walked outside, he couldn't stop smiling.

SATURDAY EVENING ZEKE removed his hat and smoothed down his hair, then put it back on. He stood in front of Naomi's door, suddenly a bundle of nerves. He glanced around the property, taking it in closely for the first time.

The Kings didn't live too far from his aunt and uncle's house, and like them they had a nice piece of land. Naomi's small white house was situated behind the backyard, with a stone path leading from her front porch to the back of the main house. Two large maple trees had already started shedding their vibrant red, orange, and yellow leaves, but Naomi's porch, which ran the front length of the house, was spotless. Two potted orange mums were on the ground on either side of the door, and a flower box filled with marigolds hung beneath the window to the right.

Flowers. He should have brought some. Obviously Naomi liked them. But he couldn't dash out and find some now.

His palms grew damp as he reached to knock on the door. He'd been thinking about seeing Naomi as he did odd jobs on Chester's house while his cousins and uncle were at work. *Get it together, Lapp!*

Zeke knocked on the door, then quickly ran his palms down his thighs. The door opened right away. As soon as he saw her, his anxiety disappeared.

"Come in, Zeke." Naomi smiled and opened the door wider.

When he crossed the threshold, he inhaled the most delicious aromas, the strongest being a robust, smoky smell. Was that steak? He detected the faint scent of cinnamon and fruit. Apple pie? His mouth watered in concert with his growling belly.

"Let me take your coat."

He handed her his jacket and hat, and she hung them on a peg next to the door.

"What would you like to drink? I have water, iced tea, lemonade, soda, and coffee."

"Iced tea will be fine."

She gestured to the couch in the living room. "Please have a seat, and I'll bring it to you. Supper will be ready shortly." She smiled, then disappeared into a narrow hallway that led to the back of the house.

Zeke frowned slightly. She was acting so formal. Maybe she was a little nervous about tonight, although she seemed more distant than nervous. He wished she'd invited him into the kitchen. He'd rather talk and watch her cook than sit here waiting for her to serve him.

He perched on the sofa, his hands clasped between his knees. Glancing at the ceiling, he could see where he'd repaired the hole. It didn't look too bad, but the spot was a little whiter than the rest of the ceiling. Maybe he should offer to paint the whole thing so it would all match. The interior of the house was as neat as the outside, and simply furnished. He eyed the pale green couch, matching chair, and an end table with a plain gas lamp on top. Next to the chair was a basket filled with what looked like a neat stack of blue and white quilt strips. As he'd noticed the first time he stepped into the house, everything about the room reflected Naomi—tidy and practical.

She was the first woman he'd met who lived on her own. And he had to wonder—did she get lonely like he did? He didn't like the idea of her being here by herself, even though he could tell she was capable of living alone. But he hoped she didn't feel the same hollow loneliness he knew.

She entered the room, and he stood up, noticing her rosy cheeks and the small spot of grease on her apron. He doubted she knew it was there. She handed him the glass of iced tea and said, "Supper is ready. I don't have a formal dining room, so you'll have to eat in the kitchen."

"I don't mind." He breathed in the sweet scent of apples again. He was more than ready to tear into the meal. But even beyond that, he was eager to get to know Naomi better. Smiling, he followed her to the kitchen, more excited about being alone with her than he'd ever been on any of the dates he'd gone on in Middlefield. Then he entered the kitchen, and his smile slipped.

Sitting at the table was Margaret. She gave him a shy smile, then looked down at her plate. And he saw something that made his stomach drop.

Two place settings. *Only* two.

CHAPTER FOUR

NAOMI WIPED HER hands on her apron and glanced at Margaret. A blush bloomed on her friend's cheeks as she looked at Zeke. Naomi understood why. He looked particularly handsome this evening in his light blue shirt, black suspenders, and denim broadfall pants. He combed his fingers through his bangs and sat down across from Margaret.

Another pinch of jealousy ran through Naomi. In a way, she wished she were joining them for supper. But she had planned this meal for Margaret and Zeke. She needed to serve it, then get out of their way. She brought out the freshly grilled steak where it was keeping warm in the oven and put it on the table.

Zeke's eyes rounded as he grinned. "Smells *appeditlich*," he said, staring at the steak. Then he looked at her, his grin widening.

Her pulse quickened and she looked away. Suddenly she'd become as shy as Margaret. She put three more dishes on the table—creamy broccoli and cheese casserole, roasted potato wedges with thyme and rosemary, and homemade knotted rolls. She placed a pitcher of tea near Margaret and said, "If you need anything else, I'll be in the living room. Enjoy your meal." She turned to leave when Zeke's voice stopped her.

"You're not joining us, Naomi?"

Was that hope she saw in his hazel eyes?

"*Nee.* I ate earlier during my cooking class. We always sample the dishes after we prepare them." She gave an encouraging smile to Margaret, who looked a little deflated by the attention Zeke was giving Naomi. "You two enjoy the meal. Just make sure you leave room for the apple pie later."

Before Zeke could say anything else, she went to the living room and plopped down in the recliner.

She closed her eyes, fatigue seeping into her. She'd spent the day teaching her cooking class, then a couple more hours preparing supper for Zeke and Margaret. Plus Margaret had been a mess when she arrived. It had taken Naomi at least ten minutes to calm her down. She wondered if her friend was always this disconcerted around men. No wonder she needed help in the dating department.

Naomi opened her eyes, concerned that if she kept them closed much longer she would fall asleep. She picked up her sewing from the basket on the floor near the chair and laid the four connected quilt strips on her lap. While Naomi felt confident in the kitchen, sewing was another matter. Yet from the time she heard Priscilla say she wanted a wedding ring quilt, Naomi decided to make one for her as a wedding present. She'd started it three weeks ago, but she couldn't get the pattern to match up. As she inspected the curved strips, which she had cut from a template, she could see places where the stitching was uneven. But she couldn't rip it all apart again. She didn't have as much time as she wanted to piece the material, add the batting, and quilt it together. She had to settle for imperfect stitches if she was to have the

quilt completed by their wedding. Hopefully Priscilla wouldn't notice.

Naomi picked up a quilt block from the basket and matched the edges to the pieces she'd already put together and pinned them in place. After threading the needle, she had just started on the first stitch when Margaret burst into the room, nearly in tears.

"Naomi, you have to help me. This is a disaster!"

ZEKE CHOKED DOWN the juicy piece of steak he'd been chewing and looked at the empty spot across the table. The food was delicious, but the company awkward. It wasn't that Margaret wasn't a nice girl. She was kinda pretty too. But Naomi had been gone barely five minutes before conversation between him and Margaret ground to a halt. She'd gaped at him, her eyes as wide as full moons, her face turning bright red. Then as soon as he put the bite of steak in his mouth, she fled the room.

None of this made sense. Why would Naomi invite him over for supper to thank him for helping her and make this wonderful meal, only to leave him alone with Margaret? She had specifically used the word *date*.

Then it became clear—Naomi had no intention of dining with him tonight. It had all been a ruse to set him up on a date with Margaret, not her. To say he was disappointed was an understatement. He'd looked forward to spending the evening with Naomi. Now even the tender steak tasted like rubber in his mouth.

He put down his knife and fork and eyed the back door. The kitchen, like the rest of the house, was tiny, and he looked out the window to the back porch, which led to a small yard. The fleeting thought of sneaking out while the women were occupied entered his mind, but he wasn't

capable of doing something that cowardly. Still, he didn't appreciate being brought here under false pretenses.

He glanced around the kitchen, spying a bud vase with two small sunflowers and three orange carnations on the windowsill. It was October, so Naomi obviously had bought them in a store. Or maybe someone had given them to her. The idea of her getting flowers from some man twisted something in his gut.

After a few more minutes he pushed away from the table, intending to go home. This so-called date was a disaster. He didn't know what he had said or done to offend Margaret, but she should have been back by now. Just as he was about to get up, both Margaret and Naomi came back into the kitchen.

"Sorry." Margaret sat down and put her napkin in her lap. She stared at her plate, her chin dipped so far that he could only see the neat part of her blond hair and the black bobby pins that pinned her *kapp* to her head.

"It's all right." But his attention turned from Margaret to Naomi, who was getting another dish down from the cupboard. Without a word she filled her plate and sat down between him and Margaret at her round kitchen table.

"I decided I was hungry after all." She gave Zeke an awkward smile. She picked up the butter dish and set it beside her plate. "Hope you don't mind if I join you."

"Not at all." He glanced at Margaret, who was shoving pieces of roll into her mouth. She still wouldn't look at him. This was one unusual girl.

"So, Margaret," Naomi said as she cut her steak. "You and Zeke have something in common."

Margaret looked at Naomi with those wide eyes of

hers. Naomi tilted her head to the side, prompting Margaret to look at Zeke as she swallowed.

"Oh. *Ya.* Naomi said you have a lot of *bruders* and *schwesters.*"

"Chester mentioned it," Naomi said at Zeke's questioning look.

"I do." He scooted his chair toward the table. He turned his gaze to Margaret and smiled, hoping to put her at ease. "I suppose you do too, *ya?*"

Margaret opened her mouth to say something, but no sound came out. Instead she glanced at Naomi with a helpless expression on her face.

Naomi's eyes flitted toward Zeke, then back to Margaret. But still Margaret remained silent, so Naomi spoke. "Margaret's the oldest of eleven. All *maed.*"

"Eleven *maed?*" His brow shot up.

"ElisabethRuthCarolMaryRachelRebeccaAmandaHannah LydiaandKatherine."

Zeke's brow shot higher as Margaret spoke. "What?"

"*Mei schwesters.* ElisabethRuthCarolMary—"

"I think Zeke got their names the first time, Margaret." Naomi picked up the basket of rolls and handed it to her. "Would you like some more bread?"

"Oh, *ya.*" Margaret snatched another roll, tore it in half, and stuffed it into her mouth.

Zeke had been on plenty of awkward dates, but this one beat them all. He glanced at Naomi, who reached out and squeezed Margaret's hand for a second, then let it go and put her hands in her lap. Nice to see how much she cared for her friend.

Naomi turned to him while Margaret chowed down on the roll. "Is the *haus* coming along, Zeke? I haven't had much of a chance lately to ask Priscilla about it."

"Coming along well enough. I installed some cabinets in the kitchen yesterday. The *haus* is going to be a *gut* one when it's finished."

"I'm sure it will. Although I hope you're not working too hard. This is your vacation, after all."

"*Ya*, but I don't mind." He took a forkful of broccoli and cheese casserole. "I'd rather be busy then just twiddling my thumbs. I'm hoping to take a drive through Lancaster County sometime before the wedding. I'm sure it's changed a lot. Would be nice to have someone show me around." He looked at Naomi, hoping she might take the hint.

Suddenly Margaret made a choking sound. Zeke's gaze darted to her face, which was turning a reddish-purple. He jumped up from the chair.

NAOMI WATCHED IN horror as Margaret's eyes bulged. But before she could move, Zeke was behind Margaret. He yanked her from the chair as if she were a rag doll and put her in front of him. He placed his arms around her from behind, clasped his hands together under her rib cage, and squeezed. A chunk of bread flew out of Margaret's mouth, landing on the floor. She leaned against him, gasping for breath.

Naomi popped up from her chair. "Are you all right?" Her gaze went to Zeke, who still held on to Margaret.

Margaret finally nodded. "*Ya*," she said, her voice raspy. Then, as if she just realized what had happened, her face turned red again and she moved out of Zeke's grasp. She ran out the back door.

"I'll check on her."

Zeke nodded as Naomi followed after Margaret. She

found her friend standing by her buggy, leaning her forehead against the side.

"I'm an idiot." Margaret didn't look at Naomi. Instead she kept her head pressed against the buggy, her hands down at her sides.

"*Nee*, you're not." Naomi moved to stand beside her. "It was an accident. And now you're all right."

"Thanks to Zeke, I am." She looked at Naomi, her eyes brimming with tears, her face still red.

Naomi couldn't tell if it was embarrassment or from her choking.

"I'm sure he thinks I'm a fool."

"If he does then he's the fool, not you." She put her hand on Margaret's shoulder. "Why don't you come back inside? I'll get you a glass of water."

"I'm not going back in there." Margaret wiped her cheeks with the tips of her fingers. "I've embarrassed myself enough for one day." She sighed, clasping her hands in front of her. "For a lifetime, actually."

"Margaret, you're not the first person ever to choke. And from how quickly he acted, Zeke knew exactly what to do. I'm sure he understands."

"But it's not just the choking. I made a fool of myself way before that. I can't even talk to him like a normal person. I'm always like that around *mann*. It's like my brain goes *seltsam* or something. I can't think straight, I trip over my tongue, and I end up doing something stupid."

More than anything Naomi wanted to give her friend a hug. But she didn't want Margaret to think she pitied her. Which she did, a little. She'd had no idea Margaret, the capable, confident baker, fell completely apart whenever she was around a man.

"I'm going home." Margaret moved to unhitch her horse.

Naomi followed her. "Without telling Zeke good-bye?"

"Can you tell him for me?" She untied the horse and brought the reins to the front of the buggy, then climbed in and turned to Naomi. "I can't face him right now."

"But, Margaret—"

"I'm sorry, Naomi. I appreciate your helping me. I really do. But I think I'm a lost cause." As Naomi opened her mouth to protest, Margaret guided the buggy down the driveway.

Naomi stood there, watching her go. Now she had to explain everything to Zeke. She'd been so sure he and Margaret would hit it off. How could she have been so wrong?

When Margaret disappeared down the road, Naomi went inside. Her brow lifted when she saw Zeke standing at the kitchen sink, washing the dishes.

"Hope you don't mind," he said, up to his elbows in soap bubbles. "I figured we were finished with the meal anyway."

"You didn't have to do that." She went to the sink, then stopped. What was she going to do, pull his hands out of the dishwater?

"I know." He looked at her and smiled. "But I can't sit still. Been a problem for me ever since I was a *kinn*. I always had to be moving. Gave my *mudder* and my teachers fits."

Naomi nodded. "Sarah Mae is like that. My youngest *schwester*." She picked up a dish towel. "If you're washing, then I'm drying."

"Deal." He rinsed off a plate and handed it to her. "I take it Margaret left?"

"*Ya*. She said to tell you *danki* and that she's sorry." Naomi wiped down the dish and set it to the side next to the stove. "I tried to convince her to stay, but she refused."

He frowned. "Hope it wasn't anything I did."

Naomi sighed. She might as well admit the truth. "*Nee*. It's what I did." She looked at him as he handed her two dripping forks. "I should have told you about Margaret."

"*Ya*, you should have. I don't appreciate being set up without knowing about it beforehand."

His tone wasn't overly harsh, but stern enough that her cheeks heated. She rubbed the towel on the forks until it squeaked. "I'm sorry. And you're right, I shouldn't have done that without your permission."

He gave her another dish. "It's all okay," he said, his voice softer this time. "I guess I wouldn't be so touchy about it if it hadn't happened so many times before. Seems everyone thinks I need to be paired off. Even you."

When he put it that way, Naomi felt worse. She just assumed he would want to go out on a date. Maybe he had a girl back home. Maybe he was like she was, and not interested in dating anyone. "I shouldn't have assumed." She put the dried dish on top of the other clean one. "I've really made a mess of things." Without looking she reached for another plate.

Instead she found Zeke's hand.

CHAPTER FIVE

NAOMI KNEW SHE should pull away, but for a moment she didn't want to. His hand, covered with watery bubbles, was a little larger than hers. She could feel the calluses on his palm. A shiver coursed through her body. She hadn't felt this sensation since she last held David's hand. Even then, her reaction hadn't been this intense.

Her ex-boyfriend's intrusion into her thoughts jerked her back to her senses. But before she could move, Zeke cleared his throat and pulled his hand away. He thrust it into the dishwater and washed a tea glass. This time when he gave the glass to her, she made sure their hands didn't touch. They didn't say anything for a moment.

Finally Zeke spoke. "You didn't make a mess of things, Naomi. We misunderstood each other." He paused. "Margaret seems like a nice *maedel*."

His assessment of Margaret gave her a bit of hope that she could salvage the situation. "She is. You should see her in the kitchen. She's an excellent baker and a really *gut* cook. She has some great ideas for special Christmas cookies and she's always interested in trying new recipes and techniques."

He nodded and pulled the stopper out of the sink. The kitchen filled with the sucking sound of the water swirling down the drain. "Sounds like she's very *gut* at her job." He looked at her for a moment.

For the second time that day, a strange fluttery feeling came over Naomi. As her gaze met his, something in his hazel eyes pulled at her.

"Naomi?" he said, his voice low and husky.

"Ya?" The word came out of her mouth in a breathy sound.

"Could I have the towel? To dry my hands?"

She yanked her gaze from his and looked at the damp towel in her hand. "Oh. *Ya.*" Handing it to him, she made sure she didn't look at him. Instead she moved to the oven a few steps away and opened the door. Warmth covered her face, but it wasn't completely from the low heat of the oven. "Would you like some apple pie?" she asked, more to the oven than to Zeke.

"Sure."

She grabbed the pot holder near the stove. She pulled out the pie and set it on top of one of the cold burners. Behind her she heard the scrape of the chair as Zeke sat down. She sliced into the flaky crust, steam curling up from the piping-hot pie filling. She handed him a piece, making sure she didn't look into his eyes again. She seemed to lose her senses every time she did. "Be careful, it's hot. It also might be a little runny. The longer it sits the more the filling sets up."

"I don't mind." He took the pie from her. She dished herself a small wedge and joined him. She cut into her piece and blew on the rising steam. When she heard him groan she looked up.

His eyes were closed as he chewed, seemingly unaffected by the temperature of the pie. Then he shook his head and opened his eyes, looking at her directly. "Hands down the best apple pie I've ever had."

Naomi smiled. "Really?"

"Absolutely. Naomi King, you know how to cook." He dug back into the pie with relish.

Naomi couldn't help herself. She watched him eat, glad he appreciated her cooking. It was different from baking for her business. His reaction was more…personal. And other than her weekly cooking class, she didn't have anyone to really cook for, other than herself. Occasionally she helped her mother cook in the main house, especially when they hosted church or other gatherings. But when she ate alone at her house, she usually didn't go to the trouble to make a complicated meal.

"Does all your *familye* live in Middlefield?" she asked.

"*Nee*. Three of my *bruders* live in Holmes County with their families. One *schwester* lives in Ashtabula with her husband and *kinner*. The other two *schwesters* live in Middlefield."

"So they're not married?"

"Oh, they're married. All my siblings are." He paused. "Between them I've got twenty nieces and nephews."

"Twenty?"

"*Ya*. And they're all terrific *kinner*."

Naomi smiled at the pride in his voice. Although humility was a prized quality among the Amish, it touched her to know how much Zeke loved his family and wasn't afraid to express it. She was more convinced than ever that he was widowed. She couldn't imagine him not ever having had a wife.

"What about you?" he asked. "You seem to know a lot more about me than I know about you."

"Besides Priscilla, I have two other sisters. Hannah is already married and expecting her first *kinn*. Then there's Sarah Mae. But we're not holding a wedding for her anytime soon."

"Why not?"

"She's five." Naomi chuckled. "My parents call her their little surprise."

"So how long have you lived here?" Zeke asked between bites.

"In Paradise? My entire life."

"*Nee.* I mean here." He tapped on the table with his finger. "In this little *haus.*"

She dipped the side of her fork into the warm pie. "About two years. Our grandparents passed away when we were young, and it seemed a shame to leave this house empty. So after my younger sister Hannah married, I moved in."

She ate the bite of pie, savoring the explosion of apples and cinnamon in her mouth. Zeke was right, this was good, one of her best pies yet. Then she frowned, feeling bad that Margaret didn't get the chance to enjoy it.

Zeke paused in his eating. "Something wrong?"

"I wish Margaret hadn't left on such poor terms." Any good feelings Naomi had before disappeared at the thought of how miserable her friend looked when she left. "I'd hoped she would have stayed."

"Me too." Zeke polished off the last bite of pie.

Naomi looked at him for a moment. Could it be that he'd seen past Margaret's awkwardness to the sweet woman beneath? If so, why did the idea suddenly bring on a twist inside her? Wasn't this what she'd wanted— to help Margaret? Maybe they both would be open to a second chance, but she would have to go about it a different way.

"You mentioned you wanted to have a ride around Paradise."

He nodded. "*Ya.* I'd like to take a look at the town, to

see what's changed, visit old places. It's been a long time since I was last here."

"That sounds like a *gut* idea." She put down her fork. "When were you planning to do this?"

"Anytime in the next week or so."

"Would you like a tour guide?"

ZEKE GRINNED. He felt bad that Margaret had to leave, but he wasn't too disappointed. It gave him more time to be alone with Naomi. He thought about how their hands had touched. How she hadn't moved away. But uncertainty had flashed through her eyes, and he didn't want to take advantage of the moment, even though he easily could have.

Everything about this woman felt right. God had to have a hand in this, he was certain of it. He'd prayed for a woman like Naomi. And it had been a long wait, but now she was sitting right in front of him.

Yet he had to be careful. Although unlike Margaret, Naomi didn't seem to scare easily. He tempered his emotions before he spoke. "I'd appreciate some company. I would get pretty bored talking to the horse while I drove around."

When she smiled, his heart did a tiny backflip.

"I know the perfect guide for you." Naomi's smile grew larger.

"Ya? And who might that be?"

"Margaret! She knows Paradise inside and out."

Zeke's smile deflated. "I don't think she'd be interested, Naomi."

"I know she feels bad about this evening. This would be a *gut* way for you two to get back on track. If you're agreeable to that, of course."

She smiled again, but Zeke thought it looked a little forced. Which didn't make much sense. Actually none of this made sense. Why was she so determined to pair him and Margaret together?

"No offense to Margaret, but I was hoping you'd like to *geh* with me."

His comment seemed to take her aback. She stared at him for a moment, her chestnut eyes widening. Then she rose from her chair and picked up his plate. "*Danki* for the invitation, but I can't."

"May I ask why?"

"I'm much too busy." She took his plate to the sink.

He was hoping to have another piece of pie, but apparently that was out of the question. "Oh."

She faced him, her cheeks and forehead flushed. "I don't mean I'm too busy for you. But with the wedding coming up, the bakery, and I have one more cooking class before the wedding, plus I'm working on a quilt for Chester and Priscilla…" The words came out in a rush. "There's just so much to do, Zeke. I'm sorry. That's one reason why I suggested Margaret."

"It's okay." He stood, suppressing a sigh. Maybe he'd been wrong about Naomi. "I guess I should be going, then. There's still some daylight left. I'll head over to Chester's and see if he needs some help." His voice sounded flat to his own ears, but he couldn't help it.

He started to leave the kitchen when Naomi called his name. He turned and looked at her, hope blooming inside him. Had she changed her mind after all?

"Should I ask Margaret about giving you a tour?"

Zeke paused. "Sure," he said, with about as much enthusiasm as a dog being thrown into the tub for a bath.

It didn't matter anyway. After the way Margaret left, she would probably turn Naomi down.

"How about next Thursday?"

"Fine."

"I know she'll be happy to do it." Naomi smiled.

Zeke fought to return it. He just wished she would smile for him.

"I DON'T THINK it's a *gut* idea, Naomi."

Naomi finished sponging off the excess white flour from the table. She dropped the yellow sponge into the sink and turned to Margaret. Her friend was placing brown sugar brownies onto square pieces of white Styrofoam and slipping them into plastic bags. "It's a great idea, Margaret. You'll get a chance to talk to him again, and to show him around Paradise. Also, you'll get to thank him in person for saving your life."

Margaret twisted a red wire tie and fastened the bag in place. She sighed. "I know. I should have thanked him Saturday." She set the package to the side and started on another one. "How am I ever going to face him again?"

"By taking him on a tour of Paradise." Naomi turned on the faucet and squirted some dish detergent on a large baking pan.

Margaret shrugged. "I don't think it matters anyway. He has to *geh* back home eventually. So what's the point?"

Naomi paused, the water trailing over the silver pan. Margaret was right. After the wedding Zeke would go back to Middlefield. Why did that thought disappoint her? She shook the feeling away and scrubbed the crumbs off the pan. She rinsed it off and put it in the dish drainer.

"I'm not asking you to marry him, Margaret. Just *geh* with him on a buggy ride."

Margaret tied up the last package of treats. "I really do appreciate your trying to help me, Naomi." She glanced over her shoulder. "But maybe I'm beyond helping."

"I don't believe that." Naomi turned off the faucet and faced her. "Even if you and Zeke aren't meant to be a couple, that doesn't mean you can't show him around town. Besides, he's such a nice, easygoing *mann*. He might be able to help you get over your, uh, your…"

"Awkwardness?" Margaret displayed a half smile. "I don't know why I can't be myself around men. Maybe it's because I have all sisters and my *daed* is always so busy working. I just get so nervous." She lifted up her hands. "Just thinking about going on that buggy ride gives me the shakes."

"Are you nervous when Ben Hooley picks you up?"

Margaret paused for a moment, then shook her head. "That's probably because he ignores me for the entire buggy ride. He's just trying to get into *Daed*'s *gut* graces. I might as well be a sack of horse feed sitting next to him." She sighed. "But Zeke—and every other *mann* I know—they're different."

This was worse than Naomi thought. "Then you absolutely must *geh* with Zeke. He really does have a way of putting people at ease. And obviously you didn't scare him off."

"That's true."

"Plus, if you can get over your anxiety, then you'll be able to be yourself around everyone." Naomi touched her arm. "He said he'd come by and pick you up on Thursday after work."

Margaret's eyes widened. "I can't—"

"*Ya*, you can. Remember the Scripture we heard on Sunday?"

"God did not give us a spirit of fear and timidity," she said.

"Exactly. I think that applies to this situation as well. Don't be afraid of Zeke."

Margaret shook her head. "Naomi, I'm not afraid of Zeke. I'm afraid of myself." Then she burst into laughter. "That sounded silly, didn't it?"

"A little." She gave Margaret a hug. When she drew back she said, "Just remind yourself of that verse and you'll be okay."

"I will." Margaret drew in a deep breath. "I promise. And I'll show Zeke places in Paradise he's probably never heard of. We'll have a *gut* time." It sounded like she was trying to convince herself.

"I know you will. Now, *geh* on home. I'll finish straightening up here."

"Okay. *Danki*, Naomi."

"For what?"

"For keeping your promise. And for not giving up on me." Margaret grinned as she took her jacket off the peg and left the kitchen.

Naomi smiled. But her mind kept wandering back to the conversation with Zeke. About how he wanted Naomi to go with him on the tour, and his reluctance when he agreed to Margaret showing him around. She was sure he'd asked Naomi to be polite, or possibly out of friendship. She did consider them new friends. But the way he looked at her when he said it…the memory made her warm inside, like drinking smooth hot chocolate on a winter day. She'd given him a list of legitimate reasons why she couldn't spare the time to go with him, but to

her own ears they sounded like excuses. From the look on Zeke's face, she could tell he thought so too.

But what else could she have done? She couldn't have said yes to Zeke, not when she had made a promise to Margaret. And even though chances were slim that he and Margaret would be a love match, she didn't want to be the reason they weren't. But there was another, deeper reason she refused to go with him. Even after her talk with Margaret, even after thinking about the verse in Timothy about God not giving her a spirit of fear, she couldn't deny the truth.

She was afraid. Not of Zeke, but of her feelings for him, feelings she was certain he didn't have. How could he? They barely knew each other. There was no such thing as love at first sight.

And even if there were, she couldn't forget what David had done to her. She couldn't take the same risk with Zeke. She had promised herself long ago that she wouldn't open her heart to anyone unless she was absolutely sure about his feelings. And right now she wasn't sure about anything.

CHAPTER SIX

THURSDAY MORNING DAWNED bright and clear, with only a few cottony wisps of clouds in the blue sky. The temperature was crisp, but refreshing. A perfect day for a buggy ride. Naomi stood on the front porch of the *daadi haus*, ignoring the twist inside her that came every time she thought of Zeke and Margaret alone in the buggy. It was stupid and irrational, and she'd always considered herself practical. Being jealous of an innocent buggy ride was as far from practical as she had ever been.

By the time nine o'clock came, however, her jealous thoughts had turned to worry because Margaret had failed to show up for work. Naomi was mixing up a batch of sweet roll dough when someone knocked on the front door. She wiped her hands on her apron as she walked to the door. She opened it to see Margaret's father standing there.

He tugged on his thick salt-and-pepper beard, which hung a few inches past his chin. "I dropped by on my way to work to tell you Margaret's sick. Got a stomach bug or something."

"Oh *nee*. I'm sorry to hear that. She seemed fine yesterday afternoon."

"Ya." He gave his beard one more tug, then shrugged. "It came on all of the sudden. Just hope none of the other *kinner* get it."

It passed through her mind that maybe Margaret was faking the illness to get out of going with Zeke. Yet now that she thought about it, Margaret had seemed unwell near the end of the day yesterday. Naomi had chalked it up to nerves. Guilt nagged at her for doubting her friend.

"She wanted me to make sure you understood that she was really sick. She threw up in my buggy this morning." He made a face, his lips tugging down. "That's one reason why I'm late for work. Made her *geh* straight to bed after that."

"Please tell her I hope she feels better soon. She can take tomorrow off too. I want her to get completely well."

"I'll let her know. Have a *gut daag*, Naomi."

"You too." Naomi shut the door and returned to the kitchen. The day flew by. By the end she was tired, but satisfied not only with the baking she'd gotten done but with the steady stream of sales throughout the afternoon. Still, she wouldn't want to run the bakery alone every day. Margaret's absence drove home how much Naomi needed her help.

Naomi tidied the kitchen, the rich smell of fresh baked bread still hanging in the air. She kept one ear out for Zeke's approach, and ten minutes later she heard the *clip-clop* of a horse's hooves outside. She slipped on her navy blue sweater and pulled it closer to her body, then went outside. Squinting in the sunlight, she recognized Chester's horse and buggy—she'd seen it enough times at her parents' house in the past couple months. Zeke was tethering the horse to the hitch when she went to him.

"Hello." He grinned, his hazel eyes bright. "Is Margaret ready?"

Naomi breathed in the cool afternoon air. "That's what I came to tell you. She's not here."

"Oh?"

"She's ill with the stomach flu. I'm sorry you had to drive all the way out here. I didn't have a way to let you know."

He frowned. "That's too bad. I hope she feels better."

"Me too." Naomi crossed her arms over her chest. A few clouds hovered in the sky, but they didn't block the sunshine. Colorful leaves skittered across the gravel drive. A couple swirled around Zeke's ankles as the breeze kicked up. "Again, I'm sorry you wasted a trip."

"Maybe the trip's not wasted." He moved closer to her, a twinkle in his eyes.

SINCE HE'D AGREED to let Margaret guide him around Paradise, Zeke had prayed about today. He had nothing against Margaret, but it seemed wrong of him to be spending the afternoon with her when he really wanted to be with Naomi. God would want him to keep his word and pick up Margaret today. But it wasn't fair to her that he would spend the afternoon wishing a different woman sat beside him.

He didn't need wisdom for the drive. He needed help to figure out what to do about Naomi. He couldn't ignore his attraction to her. Now another opportunity had presented itself, and he wasn't about to let her put him off again. Though he could see she was going to try.

"I promise we won't be gone long." He moved to stand in front of her. She was only a few inches shorter than he, and he could easily look into her pretty brown eyes, which right now were darting back and forth as she thought about her answer.

"I need to work on Priscilla's quilt."

"You could bring it with you."

"It's not easy to sew while riding in a buggy."

"Oh," he said. "I suppose not. But we won't be gone long. I promise."

She turned around and looked at the *daadi haus*. "I appreciate your offer, but I have too much work to do."

His shoulders drooped. She was giving him excuses, and they both knew it. Time to be straightforward. "Naomi, please. Take a ride with me."

She looked at him, uncertainty in her eyes. "But what about Margaret?"

"This isn't about Margaret." He took a step closer to her, lest she misunderstand him again. "This is about us. About me getting to know you better." He heard her breath catch, and she stepped away, her eyes filled with indecision.

"Zeke, I don't know what to say."

"Say *ya*. Just for a little while. Half an hour, that's all I ask."

She didn't answer him right away. As the seconds ticked by, he knew he'd missed his chance.

Then she blew out a long breath. "All right."

His brow arched. "What?"

"I said all right. But just for a little while. Let me run inside and get my coat."

He had no idea why she'd changed her mind, but he wasn't about to question it. She returned, slipping her arms into her navy blue coat as she headed toward him. With a sweeping arc of his arm, he gestured toward the buggy. "Your chariot awaits."

She laughed. "That's a funny looking chariot."

"I hear the bishop in these parts frowns on real chariots," he quipped. "A buggy will have to do."

"*Gut* thing you know how to drive one." Her lips curved into a smile, and she climbed into the buggy, then slid to the other side of the seat.

He jumped in, pleased that she was playing along. If he'd made that comment to some of the women back home they would have given him a weird look, or worse, not understood he was joking. For some reason most of the women he'd been fixed up with in the past were all very serious. Naomi had a nice sense of humor.

As he picked up the reins he said, "Where should we *geh* first?"

She steepled her thin fingers under her chin. He stared at her hand for a moment, remembering the soft feel of it. He pulled his gaze away as he yanked back his thoughts. *Tread carefully. Don't scare her off.*

After a moment she spoke. "Are you hungry?"

"Are you cooking?"

"*Nee*, I'm not cooking." She chuckled. "But there's a great restaurant in Paradise. We call it the Pantry. It's been around for a while. You haven't eaten there yet, have you?"

He shook his head. "Nope. Been getting fattened up by all the great cooking my *aenti* feeds me."

"You won't be disappointed with the food here, I promise. It's about twenty minutes away."

"Hmmm." He smirked. "Then we'll be gone at least two hours. Sure you can spare the time?" He wiggled his eyebrows, making sure she knew he was teasing.

She opened her mouth, then shut it. Sheepishly she said, "I decided the quilt could wait."

Zeke smiled. *Danki, Lord.* "I'm glad you did."

WHEN ZEKE AND Naomi entered the Pantry, she saw Rose sitting at the table in the back corner of the restaurant, sipping a cup of tea and talking to her *aenti* Tabby.

"Before we sit down, there's someone I want you to meet."

"Sure."

He followed her as she went to Rose's table. Rose smiled at her and gave Zeke a welcoming nod.

"Rose, this is Zeke. Chester's cousin. From Middlefield, Ohio."

"Nice to meet you," Zeke said.

"Nice to meet you too. Are you enjoying your time in Paradise?"

Zeke looked at Naomi and grinned. "Very much."

Against her will, Naomi's face reddened. Hopefully Rose and her aunt didn't notice.

Zeke glanced over his shoulder at an empty table behind them. "Why don't I find us a seat, Naomi?"

As soon as he was gone, Rose's smile widened. "You're blushing."

"It's a little warm in the restaurant." Naomi pressed her teeth against her bottom lip.

"I don't think it's warm. Do you, *Aenti*?"

Aenti Tabby shook her head. "Not at all."

Rose gestured for Naomi to lean toward her. When she did, Rose said, "I approve."

"It's not what you think. We're just having supper."

"If that's what you want to call it, fine by me." Rose sat back. Her gaze went to Zeke, who had found a table. She nodded. "He's waiting for you."

"Because he's hungry."

"Whatever you say, Naomi." Rose smiled again, then hid it behind her menu.

Naomi shook her head and joined Zeke at the table.

A few seconds later the waitress, a young *Englisch* girl wearing several silver bangles, showed up. She pulled a pencil and pad out of the pocket of her apron. "What can I get for you two today?"

Zeke flipped open the menu. He scanned it, then looked at the waitress. "I have no idea. What do you recommend?"

Naomi hid her frown behind her menu as Zeke flashed the waitress a charming smile. Both she and Margaret had been on the receiving end of that same smile. The man could charm a hungry horse out of its oats. The waitress's shy smile and pink cheeks testified to that. Now Naomi wished she had stood firm and not gone with him. She already felt like she was betraying Margaret.

The waitress leaned over Zeke's shoulder and pointed at the menu with the eraser end of her pencil. "If you're really hungry, I suggest the meat loaf platter. It's a Pantry specialty."

"Then that's what I'll get." He shut the menu and handed it to the young woman. Then he looked at Naomi. "Have you decided?"

"I'll just have a piece of cherry pie. With ice cream." She looked up to see the waitress still looking at Zeke, even though his eyes were trained on Naomi. When she didn't respond, Naomi cleared her throat.

"Oh, sorry." The young woman scribbled on her pad. "Peach pie and whipped cream. Got it."

"No, I said cherry pie and ice cream. Two scoops." Suddenly she was craving something sweet, and a lot of it. She handed the waitress the menu.

"I'll bring your drinks and bread out in a minute," she said, looking at Zeke again.

When the waitress left, Naomi glanced down at her lap, disappointed with herself. After what happened with David, she worked hard to keep jealous thoughts at bay. She'd been thrilled at Hannah's marriage. She'd brought Chester and Priscilla together. But in the course of a few days Zeke Lapp, whom she barely knew, made her practically teem with jealousy. *Lord, forgive me.*

"Naomi? Is something wrong?"

She looked at him, seeing the concern in his eyes. Genuine concern, which broke through her envy like a stone tossed into a still pond. "*Nee*, there's nothing wrong. I'm fine. Just ready for that pie."

"With two scoops." He smiled. "I like pie too, especially homemade. I usually make black raspberry pie in the summer."

"You bake too?"

"*Ya*. Had to learn, living on my own for so long. I'm not a great cook, but what I make is edible. Nothing like your cooking, though. That's in a class by itself."

He knew the right thing to say.

"Why have you never married?"

"What?"

Naomi bit her bottom lip. The question had just flown out of her mouth, and she'd do anything to reel it in. Now she understood how awkward Margaret must have felt the other night. "Never mind. It's none of my business."

"I don't mind answering. I've got nothing to hide." He put his hands on the table, palms up.

"Here you go." The waitress appeared with their sodas and a basket of fresh bread. She looked at Zeke. "Can I get you anything else?"

"*Nee*." After the waitress left, he pushed the basket toward Naomi. She shook her head, and he grabbed a slice.

"Where were we?" he said, spooning a healthy amount of thick peanut butter spread on the soft slice. "Oh *ya*... you wanted to know why I never married."

She waved her hand at him. "I don't need to know—"

"I think you do."

He stared at her with such intensity, she couldn't pull her gaze away.

"The reason I haven't married is simple. I haven't found the right woman. God has a special *frau* in mind for me, and when He's ready, He'll bring us together." He took a bite of the bread, then set the slice on his plate. "You don't seem surprised," he said when he finished chewing.

"Of course I'm not. Isn't that what we're supposed to do? Wait on God and His timing?"

"Not everyone does that. Some people marry for the wrong reasons."

The look on his face told her he was speaking from personal experience. "Did that happen to someone you know?" she asked. She'd already pried once, she might as well pry all the way.

He nodded, looking down at his bread. "My parents. Whatever love they had in their marriage left a long time ago."

"But they're still together."

"*Ya*, because the church says they have to be." When she frowned, he waved his hand. "Don't misunderstand me. I believe that marriage is for life. That's why it's so important the woman I marry be the right one."

"How will you know?"

He looked at her, and his hazel eyes, with their vivid hues of brown, green, and gold, darkened. "I'll feel it in

my heart." Then he smiled. "So what about you? I'm surprised you haven't married yet."

"I guess my reason is the same as yours. I haven't found the right one." But her motivations were different. She hadn't prayed to God for the right *mann* to come along. Instead she kept herself busy, too busy to think—and sometimes even pray—about much of anything. It had worked after David left, and it continued to work for her now.

The waitress showed up with Zeke's meat loaf and her pie. They both bowed their heads and said a silent prayer. Naomi watched as he dug into the food with great enthusiasm, much as he had at her house. After he finished chewing a huge bite of gravy-smothered mashed potatoes she asked, "What do you think of the food?"

"Gut." His gaze met hers. "But not as *gut* as yours."

She blushed, unsure whether he was speaking the truth or being polite. While she preferred homemade food, she thought the meals at the Pantry were delicious. She decided he was being his usual charming self and pressed her fork into the flaky crust of her cherry pie.

As they finished their meal, they fell into easy conversation. She made sure to avoid anything personal, and he seemed fine with that. When he polished off his meat loaf supper, he looked at her half-eaten pie. She'd been talking so much she hadn't paid much attention to it.

"You going to finish that?" he said, a twinkle in his eye.

"Nee." She pushed the plate forward. "You can have the rest if you want. Although I'm surprised you still have room for it. I don't know where you put all that food."

He took the plate from her and started on the pie. "Two stomachs. At least that's what *mei mudder* used to say."

Naomi laughed. "I'm thinking she might be right."

Zeke finished the pie just as the waitress came over. She pulled out her order pad again. "Can I get you anything else?"

He shook his head. "No thanks, but everything was delicious. Give the cook my compliments."

The waitress smiled. Her bangles jingled as she peeled their ticket off the pad and placed it on the table. As she'd done since they arrived, she ignored Naomi and looked at Zeke. This time Naomi couldn't blame her. She was finding him a bit irresistible herself.

"You have a nice evening," the girl said, giving Zeke one last look.

Naomi reached for the ticket, but he snatched it away. "My treat."

"At least let me pay for my dessert."

He shook his head. "Wouldn't hear of it. Consider it part of my thanks for giving me a tour."

"You didn't have much of a tour," she said, sliding out of the booth. "Just from my *haus* to the Pantry."

He stood and took a step toward her. "Maybe we can fix that. Can I pick you up on Monday evening? You can show me around the rest of Paradise."

She bit her bottom lip. Technically she was free. But there was still so much more to do to help with the wedding—

"If you're busy, I understand."

But she could see the disappointment in his eyes. *There's nothing wrong with showing a friend around.* And Margaret probably wouldn't be well enough. Before she could talk herself out if it she said, "All right. I'll be happy to show you around Paradise."

He smiled in response, and her pulse jumped.

The trip back home seemed to take only seconds. When she got out of the vehicle, Zeke met her at the other side and walked her to her door. "What time should I pick you up?"

"About six o'clock?" She questioned herself even while she answered him. She shouldn't be running around Paradise with Zeke. Then she looked at him, taking in his handsome face and mischievous grin. And suddenly she realized—she wouldn't cancel.

She expected him to leave, but instead he glanced down, shuffling his foot against the gravel, his smile dimming. Then he looked at her again, his expression more serious than she'd ever seen it. "Naomi, I need to be honest with you."

"All right." She'd never suspected he'd been dishonest. A sudden, familiar pang of betrayal ran through her. She'd never suspected David would betray her either.

"I like you." He closed the distance between them. "I mean, I really, really like you."

Her breath caught in her throat as his words scrambled her brain, making her forget David, forget everything on her mile-long to-do list. He shouldn't be speaking to her like this. Or looking at her with such genuine care. Yet his words, his tone, reached a part of her that had died three years ago. The strength of the emotion rendered her speechless.

"So when I asked you to take me around Paradise, I was asking you for a date. I just wanted to make that clear." He gazed into her eyes. "If you don't want to do that, then let me know now. I'll walk away and leave you alone."

Her chest tightened. She'd convinced herself they were friends, but she couldn't deny a part of her wanted more.

Yet to have more she'd have to open herself up again, and she wasn't sure she could. "I...I don't know..."

He leaned toward her. His proximity caused her confusion—along with something more. "At least you didn't say *nee* right off the bat. I'll take that as a *gut* sign."

CHAPTER SEVEN

"SURE THAT'S STRAIGHT?"

Zeke looked at Chester, then at the row of kitchen cabinets on the wall in front of him. "The level says it is. I wouldn't eyeball something like that."

"I know. I didn't mean it that way." Chester sighed, then moved to sit on the blue ice chest in the middle of the room.

Zeke turned and looked at his weary cousin. "Tough day at work?"

"*Ya.* That and worrying about getting the *haus* built." He looked up. "Didn't realize getting married would be this stressful."

"Cast your cares upon the Lord, and He will sustain you." Zeke grinned. "You're not casting enough, cousin."

"I'm casting plenty, believe me. But lately those cares have been multiplying faster than I can get rid of them. I just want everything perfect for Priscilla."

"I know you do." Zeke leaned against the counter he'd installed earlier that day while Chester was at work. He'd had to do the job twice, thanks to Naomi ruining his concentration. Again. Not that he minded. But he wasn't telling Chester any of that. He seemed worried enough as it was. "Tell me something. Do you think Pricilla will love you any less if things aren't perfect?"

"Of course not. But I want her to be happy. She's

so excited about getting married. I don't want to disappoint her."

Zeke nodded. "Well, maybe I'm not the best person to give advice about marriage, but seems to me you're gonna disappoint her somewhere down the road. Probably more than once. She'll disappoint you too. It's how you handle the disappointment that will make your marriage, not what happens on your wedding day."

Chester stood. "Sounds like something *mei daed* would say. So how did you get so wise in the ways of marriage? Being a lifetime bachelor and all." His cousin's tone was genuine, not mocking.

"Sometimes you learn a lot from paying attention." He remained silent about the state of his parents' marriage. Zeke was pretty sure his cousin's family didn't have any idea that his parents barely spoke to each other. They always put up a good front for family and friends. Home... well, that was a different story. He picked up one of the cabinet doors and started screwing it on. "I don't plan on being a lifetime bachelor, by the way."

"Oh?" Chester grabbed another door and got to work. It was dark outside, but the gas lamp they'd set up in the middle of the kitchen cast plenty of light. "You've got your eye on someone back home, *ya*?"

"Not exactly." He pushed the door back and forth, making sure the hinges worked and didn't squeak. Satisfied, he put on the opposite door.

"Someone here, then?"

When Zeke didn't answer, Chester asked, "Who? You haven't been here that long. There's only been one *maedel* I know that you've met—" His cousin stopped working. "Naomi?"

Heat suffused Zeke's face. He wasn't used to talking about such things with Chester. Or with anyone.

"It's Naomi." Chester grinned. "You could do a lot worse."

Zeke looked at him. "What do you mean by that?"

Chester held up his hands, gripping the Phillips screwdriver in one of them. "*Nix.* I just meant that Naomi's a nice *maedel.* I can see why you like her."

Zeke hadn't realized he'd been that obvious. Although telling Naomi straight out that he liked her qualified as pretty obvious. He recalled her reaction, a mix of surprise and uncertainty, and, if he wasn't mistaken, a little distrust. That bothered him more than anything. Being up front with her made her suspicious. At least she hadn't rejected his request for a date outright. Somehow he would convince her that she didn't have to be wary of him. "She's smart. Confident. Not to mention pretty."

"And you're gone." Chester chuckled. "You sound like I did when I fell for Priscilla." He checked the door the same way Zeke did and nodded. "So when's the wedding?"

"Hold up. I haven't gotten a date with her yet."

"Then ask her."

"I did." Zeke put down the screwdriver.

Chester looked at him. "She turned you down?"

"She didn't give me an answer either way." A thought occurred to him. "She's not seeing anyone, is she?"

Chester scoffed. "Not that I know of. I can ask Priscilla to make sure. But, Zeke, Naomi's not that kind of *maedel.* If she's with someone, she'd let you know."

"*Ya*, I figured as much." The men went back to work, but a couple of nagging questions remained in Zeke's mind. If she was available, why wouldn't she agree to

go out with him? And if she was so *against* dating him, why didn't she tell him no outright?

When they finished putting the doors on the cabinets, Chester said, "I'm calling it a night."

"Sounds *gut* to me. I'll come back in the morning and start on the floor." There were planks of sanded, stained oak floorboards in the brand-new barn out back.

Chester looked at his cousin. "Thank you, Zeke. I don't know how to repay you."

"By not saying things like that." Zeke clapped him on the shoulder.

"If you and Naomi ever need anything, let me know. I'll be there."

Zeke shook his head. "I shouldn't have said anything. You already have us married off."

"Of course." Chester made a funny face. "We Lapp *mann* are impossible to resist."

Zeke laughed. He hoped Naomi thought so.

"WHY CAN'T I get these stitches straight?" Naomi looked at the curved quilt strips laid out on her kitchen table, frowning at the fabric puckering on one seam. She grabbed her seam ripper, then heard a knock on the front door. When she opened it, she saw her youngest sister standing there.

"Sarah Mae." Naomi tamped down her frustration and opened the door wider for the little girl to come inside. She crouched down to meet Sarah Mae at eye level. "To what do I owe this surprise visit?"

"I made something for you." Sarah Mae held out a plastic pitcher filled halfway with red juice. "Cherry Kool-Aid!"

Naomi wasn't thirsty, but she smiled at Sarah Mae and

took the pitcher. She didn't want to risk Sarah Mae tripping and spilling it. "Why don't we *geh* in the kitchen, and I'll pour both of us a glass?"

"Nee." Sarah Mae patted her stomach, the pleats of her light green dress covering her rounded tummy. "I've already had my share."

Knowing Sarah Mae, and seeing the bright red strip across her upper lip, Naomi suspected her little sister had had more than her share. "Then I'll pour myself a glass and give you the pitcher back."

"That's okay. I made another one for everyone else." She yawned, and Naomi noticed she wasn't wearing her small black *kapp*. Thick locks of her dark hair hung loosely from the bobby pins struggling to keep it in place.

"Does *Mamm* know you're over here? Or did she tell you to *geh* upstairs and get to bed?"

Sarah Mae looked sheepish, and Naomi had her answer. She set the pitcher on the coffee table. "Get back to the *haus*, Sarah Mae." She grasped her little sister's shoulders and gently turned her around. "You don't want *Mamm* mad at you."

Sarah Mae looked over her shoulder. "I wanted you to have some before it was all gone."

"I know. And *danki* for thinking about me. Now, *geh* home." She kissed the top of Sarah Mae's disheveled hair and gave her a gentle nudge out the door. She could only imagine what the rambunctious girl had gotten into tonight. With her mother preoccupied with wedding preparations, Sarah Mae sometimes got lost in the shuffle. Naomi made a mental note to spend some special time with her when the wedding was over.

When her sister had left, she took the pitcher and set it on the kitchen table, then sat down to figure out how

to fix the quilt. She should have volunteered to bake a cake instead. She'd wanted Priscilla and Chester to have something they could enjoy for years, and possibly pass down to their children. But at the rate she was going, she'd finish it by the time they had grandchildren.

Thinking about Chester and her sister drew Zeke back into her thoughts. She had to get control of the situation with him, but she still had no idea how. Pushing him out of her mind, she focused on the quilt. She spent the next hour bent over the kitchen table, removing the stitches and carefully redoing them. She had just flattened out the fabric to inspect her work when she heard another knock on the front door. Glancing at the clock, she frowned. It was past eight thirty. Who would stop by for a visit at this hour?

She got up and answered the door, and her stomach dropped. "Hello, Zeke."

He took off his hat and turned the battered brim in his hands. "I hope I'm not interrupting anything," he said.

In fact, he was interrupting everything—her organized routine, her placid emotions, and for the past twenty-four hours, every facet of her life. But she couldn't just turn him away. She shook her head. "You're not. I was just working on Priscilla and Chester's quilt. Come inside."

As he walked through the doorway behind her, she heard him sniff. "Chocolate?"

"I made some brownies earlier." Although she wasn't emotionally prepared for him to stay, politeness over-ruled. "Would you like one?"

"Sure."

The grin she was used to seeing on his face returned, and he followed her into the kitchen. She put a brownie

square on a plate as he sat down at the table. "Would you like something to drink?"

"This looks interesting." He pointed to the pitcher on the table.

"Oh." Naomi smiled a little. "Sarah Mae's special-recipe Kool-Aid. She usually doesn't put enough sugar in, so I don't recommend drinking it with the brownie."

"Pour me a glass anyway. Never could resist cherry Kool-Aid."

She laughed despite herself. She poured him a small glass and joined him at the table. She started to fold up the quilt fabric when he stopped her.

"This is what you're working on?" He studied it for a moment, and she squirmed under his scrutiny. Did he notice the uneven stitching? The puckered seam? "This is going to be a beautiful quilt, Naomi."

His compliment brought a blush to her face. She ran her hand across the soft fabric. "I don't know about that. I'll probably have to take half of it apart and redo it. Again."

"Why? It looks fine to me."

"Spoken like a *mann*."

He smirked. "Are you saying that I don't know my quilts from my roofing shingles?"

She smiled. "That's exactly what I'm saying."

"You know, living on my own for a while, I learned to do more than cook. I couldn't *geh* running to *mei mamm* every time I ripped a seam in my pants. I learned how to manage a needle just fine. I just don't *geh* around advertising the fact."

She hadn't thought about that before. She looked down at the quilt section again. "You really think it's okay?"

"I do. And even if it's as bad as you think it is, which it's not, Priscilla and Chester won't notice or care."

"I know. I just want it to be perfect for them."

He chuckled. "You sound like Chester. He was saying the same thing an hour ago at the *haus*." He looked at her steadily. "Perfection is impossible to attain." Then his eyes turned dark, almost smoky green in color. "Although I think you're pretty close."

She sucked in a breath, surprised and touched by his compliment and his intense expression.

He pulled back, and his elbow knocked over the glass. Naomi yanked on the quilt and jumped up from her chair, watching helplessly as the white background fabric turned pink.

CHAPTER EIGHT

ZEKE GAPED IN horror at the ruined fabric. He'd come over here to reassure her that he wasn't going to push her into anything, and not only did his mouth get the best of him, but he destroyed something she'd worked so hard on.

"Naomi…I'm sorry."

The words were weak. He expected her to yell at him, or at the very least tell him to leave. But she just rushed to the sink and ran cold water over the fabric, then poured dish detergent over it and started scrubbing. After a few moments, she shut off the water and leaned against the sink, tossing the fabric to the side.

He scrubbed his hand over his face. *Dummkopf.* A dripping sound caught his attention, and he looked down to see the Kool-Aid dribbling over the edge of the table and onto her spotless floor. He spotted the napkins in the holder in the middle of the table, snatched a few, and started mopping up the mess, trying to think of something to say to salvage the situation.

"It's all right." She knelt beside him, paper towels in her hand. "I'll get this." When he protested she put her hand over his, stopping him. "Let me do it."

He let go of the napkins and stood while she finished cleaning up. "At least let me get the table."

When she didn't answer he took that as a yes and wiped up the rest of the mess. He tossed the red-stained

napkins into the trash, glancing at the now-pink quilt segment lying limply in the metal sink. He turned to face her, swallowing hard. "I'll pay for the fabric, Naomi. The thread, anything else you need."

She shook her head. *"Nee."* Her voice sounded thick, as if she were trying to speak through a mouthful of peanut butter. "It was an accident. I should have put the quilt away."

"I should have been paying better attention." The defeat in her eyes tugged at him.

"It's probably for the best," she said, sounding a little clearer now. "I wouldn't have finished it in time for the wedding anyway. I'll have to think of another gift for them." But while her words sounded nonchalant, he saw the strain on her face.

"I can help you with the new one," he said, desperate for anything to cheer her up. "I don't know how to quilt, but I can help you piece it together. I can put all that bragging about my sewing skills to *gut* use."

She gave him a half smile that quickly disappeared. "I think you should *geh*."

"Naomi, I'm really sorry. Give me the chance to make it up to you."

She shook her head. "You don't need to make it up to me. I meant it when I said it was okay. Accidents happen. I could have spilled the whole pitcher on it." She paused, biting her lip. "I just think…we shouldn't be here alone like this."

"That's what I came here to tell you." He longed to move closer to her, but that would only make her more skittish. The last thing he wanted to do was make even more of a mess of things. "I shouldn't have been so straightforward with you after the Pantry. Believe me

when I tell you I don't normally put my feelings out in the open like that."

"Zeke—"

"And I want you to know I wouldn't do anything to pressure you or make you afraid."

She didn't say anything for a long time. Instead she stared at the damp fabric, running her finger over one of the seams. Then she looked at him. "I'm not afraid of you, Zeke." She licked her lips. "I couldn't be."

His pulse went into overdrive. Here he was praying she wouldn't hand him his hat, and now she'd given him more hope than he deserved. "I'm glad you believe that."

"I do." She took a breath. "But I don't think we should see each other anymore."

THE DISASTER OF the quilt was forgotten as Naomi took in the pained look on Zeke's face. The hold he had on her emotions amazed her. Just a moment ago she'd been in near tears over the quilt being ruined, and then just as quickly ready to laugh at his offer to help her start a new one. She couldn't imagine any man being willing to do that, sewing skills or not. And at the same time that she'd told him she didn't think they should see each other, her heart spoke something else. Being here with him felt right.

But it had also felt right with David. Her feelings were unreliable, and she couldn't trust them. She forced a lie off her tongue. "I'm flattered, but I believe that's the way it has to be."

He straightened his shoulders, but she could see doubt creeping into his eyes. "I didn't tell you my feelings to flatter you, Naomi. Or to take advantage of you."

"I know."

"I told you I liked you because I meant it. And I thought…" He sighed, his shoulders rounding. "I thought you might feel the same."

She nodded, not trusting herself to speak.

"And I'll *geh* and not bother you again. But before I do…" His gaze bore into her, challenging her to speak the truth. "I would like to know why you think we shouldn't see each other."

"It's not practical."

He frowned. "Practical?"

"We barely know each other, Zeke."

"I'd like to change that."

She drew in a breath. "You live in Middlefield, Zeke. You have your own business. Your *familye* is there. Are you willing to leave that all behind because of some infatuation?"

He tilted his head. "I'm not infatuated. And I still don't think you're being completely honest with me." His voice lowered. "What are you really afraid of?"

"I'm not afraid of anything." But when he kept his gaze focused on her, she glanced away. "I'm not being unreasonable. You said yourself you don't waste time dating. I'm trying to save you from wasting your time, just to find out that we weren't meant for each other."

He moved toward her. "But you were willing to let me waste my time with Margaret, *ya*?"

"I thought…I thought you two might be *gut* for each other." But she thought about everything that had gone wrong with Margaret and Zeke, while she and Zeke got along from the very beginning, even easier than she had with David. Was God trying to tell them all something? The practical side of her dismissed it. "I still think you should give her a chance."

"Even though you won't give me one?" He sighed. "Naomi, I don't know why you're so determined to hand me off to Margaret, when I can see—*nee*, I can feel—that you like me. But maybe you're right. If you don't trust me enough to tell me the truth, then this won't work."

She was tempted to tell him about David, only to remember all she'd tried to forget over the past three years. David had said the same things Zeke did. He'd cared for her. Thought she was special. That she was the one God had made for him.

Then he left and never came back. There was no guarantee Zeke wouldn't do the same. She couldn't glue her heart together again if he did.

He let out a breath, and the pain in his hazel eyes slashed at her. "I think I've got my answer."

She turned around, unable to speak. With each thud of his boots against the wood floor as he left, she blinked back the tears.

ZEKE CLIMBED INTO the buggy, whipped off his hat, and slammed it against the seat. He leaned forward and let his head drop into his cupped hands. *Was I wrong, Lord? Did I let my feelings cloud my thoughts and Your will?* If he'd asked those questions before seeing Naomi tonight, he would have answered no. But now he wasn't sure.

The sun had already disappeared behind the horizon, bringing on the chill of the night. He couldn't sit in Naomi's driveway trying to figure things out. He picked up the reins and made his way back to Chester's house, trying to calm his rocked feelings. He wasn't an immature kid who didn't know his own heart. He'd felt loneliness before. Even physical attraction, which he'd always made sure not to act on. And now, an attraction that ran deeper

than the physical, deeper than anything he'd known before. But he'd never experienced this kind of rejection before, and it was like someone put his heart in a vise and tightened the screws. A big part of him wished he hadn't taken the risk in the first place.

Risk. He pulled up on the reins, slowing the horse to a near stop. A beam of headlights shone in his face, but he barely noticed. That had to be what she was afraid of. She'd been hurt in the past, he was almost sure of it. Why else would she be so reluctant to trust him? He had to reassure her that he wouldn't hurt her. If he waited much longer she would be too caught up in the wedding preparations to see him. Or she would use that as an excuse. Naomi King had no shortage of those.

A car whizzed by, honking its horn, and he realized he was going slow, even for a buggy. He spurred the horse to a trot, paying more attention to the road. But in the back of his mind he prayed. *How can I reach her, Lord? Please, tell me—*

He stopped midprayer, realizing this wasn't about him. He'd lived his life striving to obey the Lord, to do His will. "Do you want me to reach her, Lord?" he said aloud. "If so, show me how."

CHAPTER NINE

"ZEKE, THERE'S SOMEONE here to see you."

Zeke looked up from the book he was reading in the guest bedroom and looked at his uncle. Who in Paradise would be coming to see him on a Sunday night? Then his heart gave a little flip. *Naomi.* Maybe she'd changed her mind about talking to him. "Tell her I'll be right down."

"I didn't say who it was," *Onkel* Emmanuel said, frowning. "How did you know?"

"Had a feeling." Zeke grinned.

When his uncle shut the door, Zeke turned back to the mirror, smoothed down his hair, and pulled up his suspenders. Then he took a deep breath and rubbed his hand over his clean-shaven chin. He bounded down the stairs two at a time, then skidded to a stop before walking into the living room. *Slow down. No need to pounce on the* maedel. *I'm trying to woo her, not terrify her.*

With measured steps he walked into the living room. But he couldn't help the grin that appeared in anticipation of seeing Naomi again.

"Hello, Zeke."

Zeke halted, disappointment slamming into him. He kept the smile plastered on his face. "Hi, Margaret."

She twisted the end of the *kapp* ribbon between her thumb and forefinger as she stared at the ground. Her face was flushed, but he couldn't tell if it was from shyness or

if she was still ill. He also couldn't figure out what she was doing here. When she didn't say anything for a moment he said, "Would you like to sit down?"

"*Ya.*" She nodded a little too briskly and made her way to the chair. Her foot caught on the wooden stool in front of it, and she pitched forward.

Zeke grabbed her arm to keep her from falling. When she looked at him this time, her cheeks were the color of pickled beets.

"Sorry." Her voice was barely audible. She sat in the chair and smoothed out the gray skirt of her dress.

"It's okay. I've tripped over that thing a couple of times." He sat down on the couch across from her and ran his hands over the tops of his pants. "What brings you by, Margaret?"

She finally met his gaze, and the brightness in her blue eyes took him aback. Had Naomi convinced her to try their date again? He wouldn't put it past her. But Zeke had no intention of leading Margaret on. He opened his mouth to say as much when she suddenly spoke again.

"I came by to apologize." She started twirling the ribbon again, then stopped and glanced away.

"Apologize? What for?"

"For running out on you during supper after I choked. I shouldn't have done that, especially after you saved my life."

Zeke shook his head and shifted on the seat. "It's okay."

She shook her head. "*Nee*, it's not. I didn't even thank you properly." She sighed. "I don't know what's wrong with me. I always turn into a klutz when I'm nervous."

He couldn't help but smile a little. "You're not a klutz, Margaret."

"And you're being nice." She looked at him, her shoulders relaxing a bit.

"Well, maybe you're a little klutzy, but we all are at times."

"I've seen you working on the roof. I have a hard time believing you're klutzy."

"On roofs, *nee*. But I've taken my fair share of spills." He leaned forward. "You don't have anything to apologize for. Or to thank me for. I'm the one who's thankful, that I was there to help."

Margaret stared at him, then sighed. "Why is it all of the *gut* ones are taken?"

He furrowed his brow. "I don't know what you mean. I'm not taken."

"Not yet. But you will be. Soon, I hope." Margaret stood. "When I saw you and Naomi together, I knew there wasn't a chance for me. I saw the way you looked at her. The way she looked at you." She sniffed and brought out a tissue she held in her hand. "You two are meant for each other."

Zeke popped up from the couch and went to her. "I'm sorry. I didn't mean to hurt your feelings. I didn't even know about the supper the other night. I thought I was having dinner with—"

"Naomi. I know." Margaret wiped her nose. Her eyes started watering. "We kind of tricked you, a little." She brushed away the tears with the back of her hand.

He had no idea how to comfort her. "Margaret, I feel really bad about this. Please don't cry."

"Cry?" Margaret looked at him, frowning. "I'm not crying." Then she looked at the tissue in her hand. "Oh, this. I'm still nursing this cold. Can you believe I got one on top of the stomach flu?"

Zeke moved a few inches away from her.

She chuckled. "I don't blame you for not wanting to get sick. Although I feel better today than I have in a while." She smiled. "I'm not upset, and my feelings aren't hurt. Naomi deserves a *gut mann*, Zeke. I think you've proved more than once that you are one."

Zeke cleared his throat, embarrassed by the compliment. He stepped away from Margaret to gather his thoughts. He thought he'd dreamed that he'd seen something special in Naomi's eyes when she looked at him, but now Margaret confirmed it. "I'm glad you think Naomi and I should be together. I happen to agree with you. But she's determined to push me away."

Margaret nodded. "That doesn't surprise me. We've been *freinds* for a few years, and she's headstrong sometimes. I don't think she realizes how stubborn she can be. But don't give up on her."

"I don't plan to. But right now I don't know what to do."

Margaret tapped her finger on her chin. Then her brow lifted. "I think I do."

Zeke listened to Margaret's plan. "Do you think it will work?"

"*Ya.* I think it will. As long as we give her a little bit of time before we do anything. The question is, are you willing to do it?"

He nodded, despite a few doubts. But he couldn't be choosy right now. "I'll do anything to get her to talk to me again."

NAOMI OPENED HER eyes to the sunlight streaming through the window. Sunlight! She sat up in bed and looked at her alarm clock. Nearly seven o'clock. How could she have

overslept? But she knew the reason why—she'd tossed and turned the night before, wondering if sending Zeke away had been a mistake. She hadn't seen him for days. She missed him.

Then she remembered David's abandonment and convinced herself she'd made the right decision. She remembered a quote she'd read long ago. *Better to have loved and lost than never have loved at all*. But she had loved and lost, and she couldn't go through that again. Yet today her soul wasn't any more at peace than it had been last night.

The rest of the day everything seemed off balance. She burned the peach turnovers and miscounted a customer's change. At the end of the day she went to her parents' house, not wanting to be alone with her thoughts. She hadn't seen much of her mother and father this week. She followed the smell of fresh baked bread back to the kitchen.

When she walked inside, Sarah Mae jumped into her arms. "Naomi!"

"*Gut* to see you too, little one." She kissed Sarah Mae's cheek and set her down, her sister's exuberant greeting just what she needed to hear. Sarah Mae ran over to the table where she was helping Priscilla peel apples. Naomi set down her book satchel on the corner of the kitchen counter and joined her sisters.

"You look tired," Priscilla said, quickly winding a paring knife around a ruby red apple.

"I am." She looked at her sister, who seemed pretty calm considering she liked things to be on schedule and under control. Naomi saw Sarah Mae struggle with the apple peeler. She settled the child in her lap, put her arm around her and her hands over the peeler, and guided her

It wasn't long before Sarah Mae got bored. She wiggled out of Naomi's lap and landed on the floor. "I'm going to find *Mamm*," she said and flew out of the kitchen.

Priscilla chuckled. "I'm surprised she stayed here this long. At least she got one apple peeled."

"What are these for?" Naomi picked up the discarded peeler and an apple and started peeling with quick, practiced movements.

"Applesauce. We thought we'd make a couple extra batches beyond what's needed at the wedding."

Naomi frowned. "I didn't know you were all getting together."

Priscilla put down the finished apple. "It was a last-minute thing. Plus you'll be busy with your class tomorrow."

Naomi shook her head and picked up another apple. "I canceled my classes for the next couple of weeks. I thought you knew that."

Priscilla looked at her. "Oh *nee*. I can't believe I forgot to tell you. Margaret called for you last night."

"What did she need?"

"She called about your cooking class, and she asked if you could do her a favor."

"Sure." Naomi moved to get up. "I'll go outside to the call box and give her a call."

Priscilla put her hand on Naomi's arm, keeping her in place. "You don't have to do that. She already gave me the message. She has a special friend who wants to take your class tomorrow."

"But she knows I've canceled my classes until after the wedding."

Priscilla nodded. "That's why she needs the favor. She

said her friend is leaving in a couple of weeks and won't be able to take another lesson."

Naomi frowned. "Is this friend *Englisch*?" She had to be. Naomi couldn't imagine an Amish woman desperately needing a cooking lesson.

"Margaret didn't say." Priscilla leaned back in the chair and crossed her arms over her chest, covering the thin white ribbons of her prayer *kapp*. "What if it is their only trip to Paradise?"

Naomi considered this. Some of her cooking students traveled from as far as the West Coast to Amish Country. She hated the idea of disappointing someone, and Margaret wouldn't have asked her for a favor if she really didn't need one. This friend must be very special. "Maybe I can teach one of my shorter lessons."

"What about strudel?" Priscilla uncrossed her arms and gestured to the white-handled paper bags of apples on the table. "We have plenty of apples. All you would need would be the ingredients for the pastry."

Naomi nodded. She always kept plenty of pantry staples on hand. Then she frowned. "But what about tomorrow? Are you sure you and *Mamm* won't need my help?"

Priscilla shook her head vigorously, her bright expression the exact opposite of what it had been a moment ago. "Hannah will be here. Between the three of us we can handle it." She grinned. "*Danki*, Naomi."

"Why are you thanking me?" Then she paused. "Do you know the student?"

"*Nee*, of course not." Priscilla snatched an apple and began peeling it, keeping her head down. "I just appreciate you not being upset with me for forgetting to tell you Margaret called." She hesitated and looked at Naomi. "It

seems like everything has been going wrong lately. I'm a little worried about the wedding."

"Don't be. Everything will be fine." She smiled. "Just think, if you and Chester can get through this, you can get through everything."

"I hope you're right. About getting through it, that is."

Naomi's smile dimmed, wishing she could say something that would give her sister confidence. There had been a cloud of bad luck surrounding them lately. Besides the accident with the quilt and Abe breaking his wrist, progress on the house was much slower than expected. But despite the catastrophes happening around them, Chester and Priscilla loved each other. That was what really mattered.

Later that night Naomi went home. She'd intended to start over on the quilt this evening, but instead she had to prepare for her unexpected student tomorrow. She hoped the woman would be a quick study and that the lesson wouldn't last too long. But she wouldn't shortchange her. As Naomi prepared the ingredients, Zeke came to mind again. How he'd offered to help her with the quilt. The way she felt when their hands accidentally touched as they washed dishes. The rejection in his eyes when she told him to leave.

She sighed and plopped down on the kitchen chair. Why couldn't she stop thinking about him? At least she didn't have to worry about seeing him again. Until the wedding. But even then she could avoid him by making sure she was busy in the kitchen or serving the wedding guests. Then he would go back to Middlefield, and she would never have to see him again. Or think about him. Which relieved her. Or so she tried to tell herself.

NAOMI SET OUT the mixing bowl on the table and stood back. She had everything ready for her lesson, including an index card with the recipe neatly written on it attached to the gift bag she usually gave her students—a long-handled wooden spoon, a metal eggbeater, a handcrafted pot holder, and a collection of her favorite recipes written on cards and bound with a silver ring. She glanced at the clock on the wall above the table. Nine forty-five. Her classes started promptly at nine thirty. Maybe the student changed her mind. Naomi had to admit she wouldn't mind if that were the case. It wouldn't take her much time to clean up everything and get started on the quilt, which was weighing on her mind.

She heard a knock at the back kitchen door. On Saturdays she put a sign on her front door instructing her students to enter through the kitchen. She smoothed her apron, said a quick silent prayer that the lesson would go well, and answered the door. "Oh. Zeke."

Zeke's brow shot up. "Wow. That's some greeting."

"Sorry. It's just I'm expecting a student to arrive at any time." She started to close the door. "So I can't talk right now, but I'll see you at the wedding."

Zeke put his palm against the door. He didn't push back, but he held the door in place. "Hold on a minute."

She stopped. "What?"

"You're expecting me."

Naomi frowned. "What?"

This time he did push back. Not forcefully, but enough to make her take a step backward. "I said, you're expecting *me*."

"Zeke, I don't have time to figure out riddles. I have

a *cooking* student coming any minute. You really need to *geh*."

He stepped into the kitchen and removed his hat. "Naomi, the cooking student you're expecting...is me."

CHAPTER TEN

NAOMI GAPED AT ZEKE. "*You're* my surprise student?"

Zeke nodded and walked farther into the kitchen. "*Ya.*" He breathed in deeply. "And from the smell of things in here, you're going to teach me how to make something *appeditlich*." He turned and grinned.

She stormed toward him. "This isn't funny, Zeke. My cooking classes aren't a joke."

His smile faded. "I never thought they were. I'm serious. I'm here to take your class." He dug into his pocket and handed her several bills. "Here's the payment for the class and supplies."

She looked at the money in his outstretched hand, but didn't take it. He shrugged and set it on the nearby countertop. He looked completely calm, while inside she was bubbling like a pot of forgotten stew.

"Priscilla told me that Margaret had a friend who wanted a cooking lesson."

"That's true."

Her eyes narrowed. "Since when did you and Margaret become friends? Or did you lie to her to get her to help you?"

All traces of humor in his eyes disappeared. "Just a minute, Naomi. I didn't lie to Margaret. It was actually her idea." He gave her a pointed look. "You're not the only one who can play matchmaker."

Naomi sucked in a breath. "Why would Margaret do this?"

"Because we both knew you wouldn't see me otherwise."

She couldn't deny his words. Her gaze dropped to the money on the counter. Three twenty-dollar bills, neatly folded. She picked up one and handed it back to him. "I only charge forty."

He didn't take the bill. "The twenty is to pay for quilt fabric, since I ruined yours."

She hesitated, then put the twenty back on the counter. By the determined tilt of his chin, she could see he wouldn't budge. All right, if he wanted a lesson, a lesson he would get. She'd deal with Margaret later. And once she and Zeke finished, he would leave her alone. She hoped.

"Fine. Let's get started." She crossed the room and picked an apron off the peg on the wall. She tossed it at him. "First, put this on."

He stared at it as if it were a snake in his hand. She knew he wouldn't put it on. What Amish man would risk someone seeing him in an apron? But he didn't say a word as he wrapped it around his narrow waist and tied it tightly in the back. "Next?"

Naomi glared at him, then turned her attention to the lesson. She let out a deep breath. *Treat him like any other student. Don't bring up anything personal. Keep the lesson succinct and quick.* As she mentally prepared herself, she heard him come up behind her.

"Naomi?"

He stood close to her, his deep voice low in her ear, making goose bumps rise on her forearms.

"I don't want you to be mad at me."

The remorse in his voice made her turn around.

He took a step back. "This isn't going like I thought." He pushed his bangs back.

She barely noticed the birthmark this time.

"I wanted to talk to you one more time. I knew if I just showed up on your doorstep you wouldn't see me. I thought maybe this would work...but I see it's a bad idea." He let out a deep breath and moved to stand beside the stove, putting ample space between them. "I'm not trying to trick you, Naomi."

"It sure seems that way."

He shook his head. "Then I'm sorry. I should have known better. I've had more than a few *maed* back home who've tried to pull the wool over my eyes."

His words took her anger away. She couldn't be mad at him, since she'd been less than innocent in her dealings with him concerning Margaret.

"It's just that..."

For the first time since she'd met him he seemed unsure.

"I wanted...Naomi, I *needed* to see you again."

She gripped the back of the chair, looking away from his intent gaze. Her fear heightened, feeding her drive to send him away. "Zeke, we don't have anything more to say." She fought to keep her voice steady. "I thought I made my feelings clear to you."

"How can you do that when they're not clear to yourself?"

When she looked at him, he nodded.

"I can see the confusion in your eyes, Naomi. Honesty is important to you, right?"

"Of course it is."

"Then be honest with yourself. And while you're at it, be honest with me."

Naomi turned away, her knuckles snow-white against the dark wood of the chair. She stared unseeing at the ingredients and cooking utensils neatly displayed on the table. Zeke Lapp tapped feelings deep inside that she hadn't realized she had. Feelings David hadn't begun to reach. But how could she trust Zeke, a man she'd known only a short time, when a man she'd known all her life had betrayed her?

His hands lightly touched her shoulders, making her flinch. She hadn't heard him approach. Her mind told her to shrug him off, to tell him to leave, but she couldn't form the words. The warmth and comfort of his touch broke the dam in her heart.

"He promised he'd come back." She turned and looked at him.

"Who?" he said softly.

"Do remember my friend Rose? The one we met at the Pantry?"

He nodded.

"Her cousin David. We had been dating for a year. I had just started teaching, and he was trying to find a job. We'd spoken of marriage, but we wanted to be practical. We wanted to save up enough money to build us a *haus*, like Chester is doing for Priscilla."

"That sounds smart to me." He nodded, his rough-ened palms still covering her shoulders. She continued.

"He couldn't find work here, so he went to Florida to help out his cousin, who owned a construction company. He said he'd be back in a few months, and he promised to save every penny, just as I promised to do from my job. By the time he returned, we'd have enough money to get

married. I waited for him." She closed her eyes briefly. "I never doubted him for a moment."

"He didn't come back, did he?"

She opened her eyes. "I wrote him dozens of letters. He wrote me two. Six months after he left, I found out through Rose that he'd married someone he'd met in the settlement there." Even though the pain wasn't as acute as it had been, it still smarted.

"I'm sorry." Gently he rubbed his hands over her shoulders.

"You don't seem surprised."

He shook his head. "I'll admit, I suspected someone hurt you. I figured that was the reason you were pushing me away." He cupped her cheek. "But I want you to listen to me carefully, Naomi. I'm not David. I would never hurt you like he did. And I promise, I'm not going to leave and never come back."

"But you're going to leave."

He dropped his hand from her cheek. "I have to. Middlefield is my home. But—"

"So you see how this won't work?" She pulled away from him, her eyes burning. "I can't *geh* through that again, Zeke. I can't sit around and wait to see if you'll come back, then discover you've met someone else."

"Naomi, that won't happen. I wouldn't hurt you."

"But what if—"

Zeke put his finger to her lips. "Naomi, you can't live your life like that."

"Easy for you to say. You've never had your heart broken."

"You're right," Zeke said. Finally, she'd admitted why she didn't want to see him anymore. But he knew she

wasn't any closer to giving him a chance than she'd been when he first arrived. Still, he wasn't going to give up. Pursuing a woman was new to him—usually he was the one being pursued. "I've never had my heart broken," he had to admit. "But here's something you don't know. You're breaking my heart now."

She brought her fingertips to her mouth. "I don't mean to." She turned away from him again.

Frustrated, he reached out to touch her, wanting her to face him, wishing she could see how much he wanted her to give them a chance. *Lord, what do I say? What do I do?*

Then he realized he'd done everything he could. Said everything that could be said, at least right now. And still she hadn't changed her mind. "Okay," he said, trying to keep defeat from straining his voice. He fought to speak the words he knew were a lie as he let his arms fall to his sides. "I understand."

She spun around, a surprised expression on her face. "You do?"

He nodded, even though his heart was shattering. Now he fully understood how she'd felt when David abandoned her. And through his pain, he could honestly sympathize with hers. Which made the fact she wouldn't let him comfort her even more difficult to take. "I can't make you trust me."

He'd always known God had someone special for him, a woman who would complete him. But the Lord had never promised Zeke things would be easy. Maybe that was part of God's plan after all. The Lord didn't always answer prayers the way people expected Him to. Zeke knew that firsthand when he'd prayed for years that his parents would stop fighting with each other. They finally did, but in exchange they barely spoke to one an-

other. And here was Naomi, the woman he'd prayed for, who seemed to be within his reach, but might as well be on the opposite side of the world. Zeke didn't pretend to understand it or to derive comfort from it, but he had to trust in God above everything else.

He untied the apron and handed it back to her. "I promise you won't see me again until the wedding." When she took the apron from him, he turned to leave.

"Zeke. Wait."

NAOMI CLUTCHED THE apron in her hand as Zeke turned around. His name had flown out of her mouth, and now she didn't know what to say. Her gaze met his gorgeous hazel eyes, eyes that were filled with pain. And she realized he did understand, so much that he was willing to walk away because she asked him to. Now she suddenly didn't want him to.

"Naomi?"

How could she ask him to stay when she'd made it clear she wanted him to leave? She glanced at the money on the counter beside him. "Your lesson," she said, moving toward him. "Don't you want your lesson?"

"I figured it was canceled, considering the circumstances."

"But you already paid for it." She snatched up the money before he could grab it. More confusion entered his eyes, mirroring her own. What was she doing? *Following my heart.* "And, uh, I don't give refunds."

"Okay." He tilted his head, uncertainty edging his tone. When she thrust the apron at him, he hesitated, and she expected him to refuse. Instead he put it back on and walked over to the table. She thought she heard him release a quiet sigh.

"I see flour, sugar, and apples." He picked up the edge of the plastic wrap covering the bowl of apples. "Apple pie?"

"Strudel."

"Oh, even better." But his voice lacked his usual enthusiasm.

She couldn't blame him for that. And now that she had him here, she didn't know what to say. So she focused on the lesson, something she could do in her sleep. He was a model student, asking questions at the right time and following her directions while they made the apple filling. By the time they'd finished rolling out the pastry dough, she realized he'd downplayed his cooking skills. "You could teach your own class," she said.

"Nah. I don't have the patience for it." He looked at her, seeming a little more relaxed. A short while later they put their strudels in the oven, and Zeke helped her clean up. They had the kitchen put back to rights by the time the strudel was finished. As they pulled the desserts out of the oven, Zeke murmured his approval. "They both look perfect."

"I can wrap one up for you to take back to Chester's."

"That would be *gut*. I'm sure my cousin's *familye* would like to have some." He looked at her. "I should get going."

But she still wasn't ready for him to leave. "Unless you want to try a piece?" she said, struggling to sound unaffected. "While it's warm, I mean?"

His smile faded. "Are you asking me to stay, Naomi?"

She licked her lips. "*Ya*. I want you to stay."

He faced her, looking directly into her eyes. "First you want me to *geh*, now you're asking me to stay. I don't understand."

She opened her mouth to speak, fear nearly stopping her words. But she wasn't going to give into it this time. The verse from 2 Timothy came back to mind, and she prayed for strength. "I'm afraid, Zeke."

"I know." He moved toward her, his voice low. "But you don't have to be. Not with me."

"I'm not." She took a deep breath. "I'm afraid of me." Before he could say anything she added, "When David left, I blamed myself. I thought it was my fault he didn't come back."

"It wasn't your fault. He was the one who left you, Naomi."

"Because I asked him to. When David and I started courting, he wanted to marry me right away. I'm the one who wanted to wait. I wanted to make sure we had enough money." Her bottom lip began to tremble. "I'm the one who pushed him to *geh* to Florida. He wanted to stay here, but all I could think about was the money."

Zeke's eyes were filled with compassion. "You were being practical. Nothing wrong with that."

"Maybe there is." She moved away from him. "I'm always practical, Zeke. I'm always planning, always thinking ahead."

"Except when it comes to yourself."

She nodded. "When David didn't come back, I was devastated. I loved him, Zeke. At least I thought I did. But if I'd loved him enough, I wouldn't have put money above our relationship. I wouldn't have pushed him away."

Zeke looked at her. "Or maybe you pushed him away because deep down you knew you weren't right for each other." He took a step toward her. "Maybe this wasn't your decision alone."

Naomi mused on his words for a moment. Could he

be right, that she'd been reluctant to marry not because of money but for some other reason?

"Maybe this was part of God's plan all along. Because if you had married David, I wouldn't be able to do this." He touched her cheek. "Or this." He leaned forward, his lips brushing against hers. He pulled back, his gaze meeting her eyes. "I wouldn't be standing here, enjoying every moment I spend with you."

Tears sprang to her eyes. Something was happening to her heart. The ice encasing it started to melt away. She shivered as he wiped his thumb across her cheek.

He grinned. "So does this mean you'll *geh* on that buggy ride with me?"

She started to nod, then paused. "But what about the future? What happens to us when you *geh* back to Middlefield?"

"Naomi," he said, his voice low. "Whatever God's plan is for us, I promise...I won't hurt you."

She wanted to believe him. And for the most part, she did. But even though she tried, she couldn't completely erase the doubt.

CHAPTER ELEVEN

"So HOW ARE things between you and Zeke?" Margaret pushed the white thread through a thin silver needle, then knotted the ends.

Naomi looked at her friend across the table, then back at the quilt laid out in front of them. Because of time constraints she wouldn't be able to make the quilt the size of a bedspread like she wanted to, but it would make a decent lap quilt. She had also abandoned the wedding ring pattern for simple white and blue blocks. With Margaret's help over the past couple days, she'd made good progress. At least she would have a wedding gift to give to Chester and Priscilla. She was pleased with the result.

She adjusted the thimble on her right middle finger and began making small quilting stitches through the two layers of fabric and the batting. "Things are going...well."

"Hmmph." Margaret stuck the needle into the underside of the fabric. "That didn't sound too confident, Naomi."

Naomi pressed her lips together. While she had seen Zeke several times this week, including the buggy ride they'd taken last Saturday afternoon, she still couldn't dispel the doubt that their relationship was too good too last. Knowing he would be returning to Middlefield two weeks after the wedding didn't help. They had avoided

talking about that, and she tried not to think about it. But she couldn't help it.

"We're fine, Margaret. We enjoy each other's company. There isn't more to tell than that."

"Okay, I won't pry." She paused, looking at Naomi. "I'm glad you're not angry with me about the cooking lesson."

"*Nee.* How could I be? You were just giving me a taste of my own medicine."

"I was trying to help you. And Zeke."

"I know." She grinned. "And it worked."

Margaret nodded, her eyes filled with satisfaction. Then she bent her head down and started stitching in earnest. Suddenly she chuckled.

Naomi looked up. "What's so funny?"

Margaret's cheeks flushed. "Oh, *nix.* Just thinking about something Ben said the other day."

"Ben? Are you talking about Ben Hooley?"

With a nod, Margaret looked up. *"Ya,"* she said softly.

"I noticed he picked you up a couple times last week." Naomi tried to hide a smirk, but failed. "I suppose he's still trying to appease your *daed.*"

"Maybe." Then Margaret put down the needle and leaned forward, the ribbons of her prayer *kapp* brushing against the quilt. "Oh, Naomi. I think Ben might be the one."

"What?" Naomi raised her eyebrow. "Four weeks ago you couldn't stand him."

"I know, but things have changed."

"What happened?"

"He started to talk." She held her hands up and shrugged. "When he picked me up on Monday he asked me about my day. Then before long he was telling me

all kinds of things. Like what a troublemaker he was in school."

Naomi couldn't imagine a man as polite as Ben being a troublemaker. It gave her hope for Sarah Mae. "So that's it? He started talking, and you fell in love with him?"

"I'm not saying I'm in love." Margaret looked away, but her smile widened. "I'm just saying that I think I... might be." She looked back at Naomi. "I feel ridiculous even saying it out loud, but he's so different from anyone else I know. I can be myself around him. I don't even get tongue-tied, and I haven't tripped over my feet once."

"Does he feel the same way?"

Margaret nodded. "Last night he admitted that he'd had a crush on me for months, but he thought I didn't like him, so he kept it a secret. All this time I thought he was being quiet because he didn't like me. Turns out he did all along."

"Do you know what made him admit that to you?"

"He'd heard about me having supper with Zeke. Fortunately he didn't know how the evening ended." She cringed. "But he realized he couldn't sit by and let me slip away." She sighed, leaning her elbow on the table and cupping her chin in her hand. "Isn't that the most romantic thing you've ever heard?"

Naomi's heart soared. "I'm really happy for you, Margaret."

"I'm happy for both of us." She reached over and took Naomi's hand. "To think, we both might be getting married next year!"

"I wouldn't plan any weddings yet." Naomi pulled her hand away. "At least not for me."

Margaret's smile disappeared. "Why not? You and Zeke are a perfect match."

Naomi couldn't help but smile. She thought the same thing herself.

A knock sounded at the back door. Naomi answered it, pleased to see Zeke standing there. But her pleasure turned to worry when she saw the stricken look on his face. "Zeke. Is something wrong?"

"I need to talk to you." He looked over her shoulder at Margaret, giving her a curt nod in greeting. "Alone."

Margaret stood. "I'll see if your *mamm* needs any help, Naomi." Her gaze flashed from Zeke to Naomi before she hurried out of the room.

Naomi stepped to the side. Zeke strode to the table and took off his hat, but didn't remove his coat. He slid his fingers through his bangs and pushed them away from his brow, revealing his birthmark.

She moved toward him. "You're worrying me, Zeke."

"I don't mean to." He put his hat on top of the table, covering one corner of the lap quilt. "I just got a call from one of my *schwesters*. *Mei daed* had an accident today."

She put her hand on his shoulder. "Oh *nee*. What happened?"

"He was chopping wood with his ax." Zeke swallowed. "He's getting too old to do that, and his eyesight isn't real good. I had split plenty of wood for my parents before I left, but I should have known he would try to cut more." He glanced at the ground, then looked at Naomi again. "He missed the wood and the blade landed in his shin."

Her hand covered her mouth. "Is he all right?"

"*Ya*. He will be. Lots of stitches, and he's on crutches. *Mei schwester* Barbara said he's home now. But he and *mei mudder* need my help." He pressed his lips into a grim line. "Naomi, I have to *geh* home. I have a taxi waiting outside to take me to the bus station."

Her stomach twisted into a double knot. He was leaving. She knew this day would come, but she didn't think it would be so soon. "I understand." She fought to keep her voice steady. "You have to be there for your *familye*."

He nodded. "I don't know how long I'll be gone."

Naomi's head started to spin. She took a step back. David had said almost those exact same words before he left for Florida.

"But I'll be back. I promise."

It was happening all over again. The doubt she'd tried to suppress for the past week came rising to the surface.

"Naomi?" His brow furrowed, and when he walked toward her she moved away, until her back was against the counter.

He tilted his head to the side and let out a breath. "Naomi, I'm not going to go back on my word. I told you I wouldn't hurt you like David did."

"I know." She could barely get the words out.

"You say that, but I don't think you believe it." This time when he took a step forward, she had nowhere to go. "I didn't want to do it this way. I thought I'd have more time." He threaded his fingers through his hair again. "I even planned to stay in Paradise after the wedding, so we could keep seeing each other."

"You did?"

"*Ya.* But now that's changed." He looked up at the ceiling and groaned. "I didn't want to rush this, but I have no choice." His gaze met hers again. "Remember our conversation at the Pantry?"

She nodded.

"You asked me how I would know if I found the woman God set apart for me. Do you remember my answer?"

Her throat thickened with tears. *"Ya,"* she said thickly. "You said you'd feel it in your heart."

He took her hand and pressed it against his chest. Even through the thick wool of his navy blue coat she could feel his pounding heartbeat. "I love you, Naomi. And I probably sound *ab im kopp*, because we've only known each other for a short time, but I know what I feel. I know my heart." He ran his work-roughened thumb over the back of her hand. "I'm coming back to Paradise, Naomi. You have to believe that. I'm coming back because I love you. I want to marry you."

His declaration not only swept away her breath but robbed her of speech. She opened her mouth, only to close it when he shook his head.

"I don't expect an answer right now. I didn't say those things to pressure or scare you. I said them because I want you to trust me. Most of all, I want you to trust God." He let go of her hand, then brushed her cheek with the back of his hand. "I'll be praying for you while I'm gone, Naomi. I'll be praying for *us*." He retrieved his hat from the table and walked out the door.

Naomi turned and stared at the open door. Cold air rushed over her. Yet that wasn't what chilled her heart. She heard the crunch of car tires on her parents' gravel driveway, the sound of a car engine as Zeke sped away. Back to Middlefield. Away from her.

Slowly she closed the door, then leaned against it, closing her eyes. She couldn't do this again. All those days and weeks and months without hearing from David, checking the mail every day for a letter, her heart cracking every time she didn't receive one. Then finding out he'd found someone else. She couldn't live through that pain. Not again. And it would be worse this time, because

she loved Zeke, more deeply than she'd ever loved David. But Zeke hadn't even given her the chance to tell him. He disappeared, just as David had.

Her fists clenched as she fought for control of her thoughts. She wasn't being fair to him. She was the one who had urged David to leave. Zeke was leaving because of his family; she couldn't fault him for that. But she couldn't deny the sense of betrayal growing in her heart.

Zeke's words echoed in her mind. Not his words of love. Or even his proposal.

"Most of all, I want you to trust God."

Zeke trusted God in everything. She thought she did too. But somehow this man had seen deeper into her heart than she had ever dared to look. Did she truly trust God? If she did, why did she allow her doubt over Zeke's promise to overshadow everything? Why did she think she would fall to pieces if he didn't return?

She had to surrender this. Everything—her past with David, her future with Zeke. *Lord, show me how.*

THE NIGHT BEFORE the wedding, Naomi folded up the finished lap quilt and placed it in its box. She'd used every minute of spare time to complete the quilt. As she fitted the lid over it, a sense of peace settled through her spirit. She had fretted over this quilt, and in the end she had finished it. Although it wasn't the size she had intended it to be, it was still beautiful. Her worry about Priscilla's gift had been for nothing.

She sat down in her living room and closed her eyes, tired but content. The soft hiss of the gas lamp filtered through the room. She hadn't heard from Zeke. At first it had been a struggle to keep the doubts at bay, to not worry that she'd never see or hear from him again. But

through prayer she was able to see thin beams of hope. Instead of expecting Zeke not to return, she chose to trust that he would come back. She opened her eyes and smiled. It might not be in her timing, which would be right now if she had her way. But in God's time. And she was content to wait on that.

She yawned and got up to turn off the lamp. Earlier that day she had finished up Priscilla's cake, but she planned to get up early and add a few finishing touches to the frosting. She had started for her bedroom when she heard a knock on the front door. Probably Sarah Mae sneaking over to the house again. She'd become more of a handful than usual as Priscilla's wedding approached. Naomi turned the light back on low and answered the door. "Sarah Mae, it's too late for you to be out—" The words froze in her mouth when she saw Zeke.

He looked himself up and down. "Last time I checked, I wasn't Sarah Mae."

"Zeke!" She started to throw her arms around him, then stopped. "Wait, what are you doing here? How's your *daed*?"

"Can I at least come in? It's a little cold out here."

"Of course. Sorry." When he crossed the threshold, she clasped her hands behind her back, forcing herself to stay calm. He'd come back much sooner than she'd anticipated. "I can't believe you're here."

He shook his head, frowning.

"*Nee*, that's not what I mean. I knew you'd come back." She smiled. "Just not so soon."

"To answer your earlier question, *mei daed* is doing great. Seems *mei schwester* exaggerated a little bit about the injury. He's still on crutches, but he's going to be fine."

"I'm so relieved." She brought her hands to the front and held them together. "I've prayed for him."

"That means a lot to me." He looked at her intently. "Did you pray about anything else?"

She gave him a teasing glance. "Was I supposed to?"

He grinned and took off his hat. "Very funny." Then he grew serious. "I meant what I said before I left, Naomi. I love you."

"I know."

"And I want to marry you."

"I know." She moved to close the space between them. "I love you too, Zeke Lapp. And I want you to know, I would have waited for you to come back. One week, one month, or even a year, I would have waited. Although if you'd stayed away that long I would have come to Middlefield a few times."

He touched her chin with the tip of his finger. "I know."

"Then you know the answer to your question. I'll marry you, Zeke."

He grinned, cupping her face with his hand. His lips touched hers in a brief, featherlike kiss that made her knees wobble. "I can't tell you how long I've waited for you to say those words to me," he whispered, drawing her into his arms.

She laughed. "A whole month?"

His expression sobered. "*Nee*, Naomi, not a month. I've been waiting my entire life."

* * * * *

ACKNOWLEDGMENTS

Thanks to my wonderful editors, Natalie Hanemann and L.B. Norton. Again, you've worked your magic on another story! To Beth and Kelly, for being such great partners in this writing journey. To Tamela Hancock Murray, for her friendship and support. Thanks to Jill Eileen Smith for reading the story and giving me wonderful advice. You're a treasured friend. And thank you to everyone who reads our stories, visits with us on Facebook, Amish Living, and Amish Hearts, takes the time to write us letters and e-mails, and all the other wonderful things you do. You're the best!

ABOUT THE AUTHOR

Kathleen Fuller is the author of several best-selling novels, including *A Man of His Word* and *Treasuring Emma*, as well as a middle-grade Amish series, The Mysteries of Middlefield. Visit her on the web at kathleenfuller.com, look for her on Facebook, www.Facebook.com/pages/Kathleen-Fuller/625583260853477, or follow her on Twitter: @TheKatJam.

A PERFECT SECRET

KELLY LONG

For my girl, Gracie

In Hebrew, perfect *means "whole or complete." It is God's desire for our lives that we become perfect or whole in Him. He is slowly revealing His perfect secret for each of our lives.*

PROLOGUE

"THAT'S IT? THAT'S my wedding proposal?" Nineteen-year-old Rose Bender stared at her best friend in the waning light of the cool summer evening.

Luke Lantz's dark blue eyes held steady as always. "*Ya*, what more do you expect?"

Rose half bounced in the buggy seat, trying not to let Luke's typical calmness rile her into a temper that would match the unruly black curls tucked beneath her *kapp*. What more did she expect? It was a fair question.

She'd known Luke for all of her young life, and he was right—a marriage was something that would please both of their families and have the strong foundation of their friendship at its base. It would also unite two lands, the rich soil that ran parallel in property. And, perhaps most importantly, it would bring a woman's touch to the motherless Lantz household. But it might have helped if Luke could have conjured up a few romantic words to add to the moment. Yet, at twenty-three, he was what he was: Placid. Faithful. Secure. And when Rose was with him, it was rather like skating on a pond that had been deep-frozen for months—no chance for a crack in the ice. Perfectly safe. Not that she should desire anything more.

"I accept," she said with determination and not a little defiance. She wanted to silence the doubts that echoed inside—that suggested she knew him too well to have a

romantic marriage. And the realistic fears that she could never live up to the legacy of domesticity and kindness his mother had left behind just two short years ago. She told herself that it had to be more than enough to fulfill the expectations of Luke's father and her parents and to find a strong base in a wealth of memories—school days, sledding and ice-skating together, long walks and throwing horse chestnuts into the pond, and serious conversations about life—though not necessarily about love.

"*Gut.* I thank you, Rose. I believe, with *Derr Herr*'s blessing, that it will be a successful match."

She nodded, then slid closer to his lean form, reaching to trail her fingers in the brown hair at the nape of his neck. She felt him tense, but she ignored it.

"Luke," she whispered, "now that we're engaged, maybe we could kiss a bit more?"

His strong jaw tightened, and he turned to peck neatly at her lips, moving away before she could even close her eyes. He disentangled her hand from his hair and gave it a cool squeeze, then picked up the reins. "We'd best move on," he said. "It's getting late."

And that's that, she thought ruefully, comforting herself with the knowledge that he would be too dutiful to maintain such distance once the marriage ceremony was over. She stifled a sigh at the unusually irreverent thought and focused on the dim road ahead.

CHAPTER ONE

Two months later...

THE SUNLIGHT OF early autumn filtered through the clear windowpanes and made passing shadows on the wide fir floor of the Bender farmhouse. The family was gathered for a hearty meal, and the *gut* smells of cooking mingled with robust conversation.

"I tell you that it's downright odd, that's what." Rose's father gestured with his fork to the lunch table at large. "Two of our hens—our best layers, mind you—a goat from the Lamberts', and the sheets from old Esther Mast's clothesline. All of it missing, and dozens of other things from the community over the past few months. I say there's a thief hereabouts, and that's the truth."

Rose's mother calmly passed the platter of sauerkraut and kielbasa to Rose's two older brothers to take seconds. Then she offered the fresh platter of airy biscuits to *Aenti* Tabitha, Father's sister, and nodded her head as her husband sputtered himself out.

"Maybe it's a Robin Hood type of thief," *Aenti* Tabitha ventured, her brown eyes shining. At fifty, she often seemed as young as a girl to Rose with all of her romantic ideas and flights of fancy. Yet her suggestion stilled Rose's hand for a moment over the saltshaker.

What would it be like to meet such a romantic figure of a man? Dark and mysterious in nature…

Abram Bender shook his head at *Aenti* Tabitha. "Tabby, you always have had a heart of gold—looking for the best in others. But Rob in the Hood, like the *Englisch* folktale? Taking from the rich to give to the poor? Who's poor in our community? Don't we all see to each other? *Nee*, this is just a thief, plain and simple. And I don't like it one bit."

"The weather'll change over the next month or so," Ben remarked over a forkful of boiled potatoes. "Any thief is likely to drop off in his ways once there's snow on the ground to track him."

"Or her," Rose said, for some reason wanting to provoke.

"What?" her father asked.

"I said *her*. Your thief could be a female, *Daed*." She didn't really think the thief was female, yet she had a strange urge to enter the suggestion into her father's mind.

Her *daed* gave a shout of laughter, then resumed eating. Ben turned to her with a smile while her other brother, James, just rolled his eyes.

"Rose, no woman in her right mind is going to go thieving about," *Daed* said. "It's a *gut* thing you're marrying Luke come December. Maybe he'll settle down some of your wild ideas."

"Perhaps." She smiled, her green eyes flashing heat for a brief second.

"Well," Ben interjected, "Rose's *narrisch* thoughts aside—there's a storm due tonight, supposed to be a doozy."

"*Ya*, I heard." Father rose from the table and hitched up

his suspenders. "Come on, boys. We'd best tighten down a few things." He bent to pat *Mamm*'s shoulder. "*Danki* for lunch." Then he pinched Rose's cheek fondly. "And no more foolish thoughts from you, my miss. Remember, you're to be a married woman soon."

Rose didn't respond. She toyed with her fork instead, making a mash of the potato as an idea began to take shape in her head.

As Rose cleared the lunch table mechanically, she avoided her *aenti*'s eagle eyes. Ever since she'd been little, she'd felt as though *Aenti* Tabby could see the subdued thoughts churning inside her head, and just for a moment she wanted to debate the merits of her plan undisturbed. Still, she knew the intent look on her aunt's face and had to admit that the older woman's intuition had fended off trouble for her many a time. But today—something was different. Today Rose *wanted* trouble. She drew a sharp breath at the hazardous thought, but the idea fit with her nature of late. It seemed as though her spirit had grown more restless, less satisfied with life, ever since she'd accepted Luke's proposal. She'd tried to pray about it, stretching her feelings out before the Lord for guidance, but nothing had come to her.

Aenti Tabby caught her eye in an unguarded moment as they washed and wiped the dishes. "I'd like to see you in my room, Rose, after we clean up a bit. If you don't mind?"

"Um…sure, *Aenti* Tabby, but I have to hurry. I'm going to bake some pies this afternoon."

"Bake? Pies?" Her aunt and *mamm* uttered the questions in unison, and Rose concentrated on dabbing at a nonexistent spot on a dish. The whole family knew that

she was a hard worker, to be sure, but baking was not a skill that she possessed or an activity she particularly enjoyed.

"Ya." She nodded vigorously, forcing a soft curl to spring loose from the back of her *kapp.* "I need to practice, you know? Luke likes a *gut* apple pie, or perhaps blueberry." She stretched to put the plate away in the cupboard. "But I'll be glad to come and talk with you before I start."

AUNT TABBY, WHO had never married, lived with the Benders and was a cherished part of the home and family. Rose and her brothers often sought the sanctuary of their aunt's room for advice, comfort, or a smuggled sweet long after supper. But Rose knew that she had been distinctly absent lately from any visits with her beloved *aenti* and mentally prepared to face what might be some pointed, but truth-provoking, questions about herself and Luke.

Aunt Tabby sank down onto the comfortable maple bed with its patchwork quilt and patted a space next to her. *"Kumme* and sit, Rosie."

Rose blew out a breath, then came forward to relax into the age-old comfort of the well-turned mattress. She half smiled at her *aenti*, remembering times she'd jumped on the same bed and had once taken a header that nearly landed her in the windowsill. But that was childhood past—long past, or so it seemed to her heart.

"I'll not keep you long, Rose, but I want to ask—why did you agree to marry Luke?"

"What?"

The question was even more probing than she'd braced for, and a thousand answers swirled in her mind.

"Luke. Why did you accept his proposal?"

"Well…because he's…we're…we've always been best friends."

Aunt Tabby frowned. "I've never married, child, but I do wonder if that is reason enough to build a life together."

Rose said, "It's made both of the families happy."

"That's true, but what about you? Are you happy?"

There was a long, disconsolate silence that wrung Rose's heart as her aunt touched her shoulder.

"I'm supposed to be happy," Rose said, thinking hard.

"*Ya*, that's true."

"I just—I expect too much, I guess. Like wanting some kind of—I don't know."

"Like wanting someone mysterious and romantic?"

Rose gazed in surprise at her *aenti*, who laughed out loud.

"I was young once too, and I think it's perfectly normal to want more from a relationship than just friendship. But maybe—maybe there's more to Luke Lantz than meets the eye. Have you thought of that?"

Rose shrugged as her aunt cleared her throat. "Luke's father—well, we courted some. He was always shy, but then…well. He had it in him to do some fine kissing now and then."

Rose stared at her *aenti*'s flushed face. "You and Matthew Lantz? *Aenti* Tabby—I never knew you dated him. Why didn't you marry him?"

"It wasn't what the Lord wanted for me."

Rose marveled at the simple statement. She knew her people lived by the will of *Derr Herr*, but to give up a relationship because of faith was difficult for her to comprehend. She knew she had spiritual miles to go before she would make a decision like that.

"Haven't you ever regretted it? Not even when—well, when Laura Lantz died of the influenza? You're still young, *Aenti* Tabby. Maybe you and Mr. Lantz could—"

"Nee," the older woman gently contradicted. "I've never regretted it, not even when Laura died. In truth, I believe I would have regretted more if I had not obeyed what I felt was the Lord's leading. And just think—had I married Matthew, there would be no Luke for you."

Rose frowned. "*Ya*, you're right."

"So, you will try, Rosie? To see all there is of him?" Her aunt gave her a hug.

"*Ya, Aenti* Tabby—all that there is."

CHAPTER TWO

A HAWK GAVE a keening cry as it began its twilight hunt while the evening shadows stretched across the grass to wend through the windows of the Lantz woodworking shop. Luke closed the heavy ledger and glanced at his watch. Six o'clock. He was done tussling with another day's accounts for his family's furniture-making business, and his head ached from the numbers and the customers. But his father wouldn't trust an outsider with the books, and although Luke was as skilled as any of his brothers in woodworking, he was the only one "with a head for business," as his *daed* liked to say. So he sat in the stuffy office and dutifully did his job, though he would much rather let his hands run down the fine smoothness of a wood grain than the tally of a day's earnings.

He leaned back in the chair, letting himself drift for a moment until the familiar pleasure of imagining Rose came to mind. In truth, he couldn't believe she'd accepted his proposal so readily. He wasn't always the most persuasive of persons, and Rose could be headstrong.

He didn't jump when his father clapped him on the back.

"Dreaming of your bride, *sohn*?"

Luke smiled, looking over his shoulder. "She's worth the dreaming, *Daed*."

"To be sure. But now's the time to see what Joshua's managed for supper. *Kumme*."

He followed his father into the old farmhouse and stifled the urge to look about for his mother as he came through the door. It was difficult for him to believe that she was gone, even after two years. She'd been what the Bible called a "gentle and quiet spirit," but she'd been a vigorous light to each of them as well. He knew that part of what he loved about Rose was her own light and sweetness, and that her spirit was a balm to his grieving soul. He knew she'd bring that comfort to the whole house once they married, and he mentally charged himself once again with making sure that she wasn't overtaxed physically or emotionally with the inherent burden of taking on a household of men.

His brother Joshua looked up rather sheepishly from the stove when *Daed* asked what was for supper. "Fried potatoes and bacon."

Luke stifled a groan. He longed for variety—vegetables, pie, anything. Even when kindly members of the community brought them hot meals, it wasn't the same as having someone cook for them with love. And there had been no one to maintain a kitchen garden since *Mamm* passed, so they were restricted to more plain fare. Still, he knew it was food in his belly, and he was grateful for it. And so he told the Lord when *Daed* bowed for silent grace.

ROSE SQUELCHED A sudden cry as the blueberry juice from the bubbling pie dripped over onto her hand. She hastily deposited the pie onto a rack and ran to soak the burn in the bowl of cool milk and vinegar she'd used in making the crusts. She glanced at the kitchen clock as she blew

a loose tendril of hair away from her damp forehead and was glad to see that it was only just past seven. Her family was relaxing in the adjoining room after supper, and she'd volunteered to clean up alone so that she could finish her pies in peace. Now, if she could just keep Ben and James from wanting a taste...

She lifted her hand from the milk and gazed ruefully at the half-inch-long red mark on the back of her hand. But it gave her an idea. Taking a scrap of dough, she opened the woodstove and threw the pastry piece inside. Within seconds, the smell of burning piecrust filled the air. She smiled and scooped up the pies, this time carefully holding a dish towel around each pan as she bumped open the back screen door with her hip.

She ignored the groans of her brothers as the burning smell hung in the early evening air, then set the pies on the porch rail. Now, if only no animal would take a nibble before she caught her real prey...

"Rose!" Her *mamm*'s voice echoed, and Rose flew back inside, closing the door carefully behind her. The unpleasant smell had wafted throughout the house.

"Mercy, child! What are you doing? Where are your pies?"

Rose sighed. "Outside."

"Burned that badly?" her mother asked as she fooled with the damper on the stove and waved a damp dish towel through the air.

Rose said a quick prayer for forgiveness as she delayed her response. She wasn't used to withholding the truth.

"Well, open the window then, so we can get some more fresh air in," *Mamm* urged.

"*Ya, Mamm*—open the window!" Ben bawled from the other room.

"And teach Rosie to bake before she kills poor Luke and the whole Lantz clan!" James's voice joined in the banter.

But Rose simply smiled as she wrestled with the heavy window; she had put her plan into action.

CHAPTER THREE

IN THE CROWDED confines of the well-concealed tent, oil lamps held the encroaching night at a cheerful distance. A hodgepodge of gathered furniture, dishes, quilts, and other small items filled the contours of the vinyl walls, while a thick, hand-braided rug covered the bulk of the pine-needled floor.

"It's too much, really. You have to stop." The *Englisch* woman's tone was torn between gratitude and remorse as she balanced a blueberry pie in her outstretched hand and a fussy toddler on her lean hip.

Her benefactor shrugged as another child, slightly older, clung to his leg in a familiar game.

"Mommy! His shirt's all dirty. Wash it!"

He laughed and brushed at the blueberry juice stain on the front of his sweatshirt.

"Never mind, Ally." He glanced around the tent, then back to the woman. "There's a storm coming tonight. Supposed to be bad. I don't like the idea of leaving you here."

She smiled. "The Lord will protect us. You staked the tent so well, and I doubt anything can shake this stand of pines."

"Have you had any word—I mean—do you know when?" He stared with intent into her eyes.

"No—nothing."

He nodded. "All right. I'd better go." He set the other pie down on the washstand near the quilt-covered cot and noted that he'd need to bring more blankets soon. He disengaged the little girl from his leg, then bent to receive her sweet kiss. "Good-bye," he whispered.

She clung to his neck. "Thank you for the pies. Tell the lady thank you too."

"The lady?"

"Who made the pies."

He smiled. "Maybe I will."

ROSE WAITED UNTIL the house had been asleep for more than half an hour before she crept from her room, avoiding the third step from the bottom of the back staircase and its telltale squeak. She almost giggled to herself as she maneuvered, remembering a time she'd sneaked out to see Luke when they were young. They thought they could catch the biggest bullfrog from the local pond, the one with the baritone that soothed the locals to sleep on summer nights, if they could only get there late at night. They'd ended up with no frog, muddy clothes, and stiff reprimands from frustrated mothers the next morning. It had been fun, but that was a long time ago.

Rose told herself that she wasn't a child anymore, looking for grandfather frogs on moonlit nights. No—she was a woman who wanted to hunt for something, someone—whose very nature seemed to call to her. Rob in the Hood, as some of her people called him from the old German rendition of the tale. She tiptoed across the kitchen floor and then gained the back porch. She switched on a flashlight and caught her breath, then smiled; both pies were gone without a trace. Of course, she told herself, as she stole into the wind-whipped air, a possum could have

gotten them, but an animal would have left an overturned plate, a trail, a mess. A thief more likely would not...

She glanced without concern to the moon and dark gathering clouds overhead; the incoming storm suited her mood. She passed the kitchen garden, still sprawled with the bulging shadows of pumpkins yet to be harvested, then broke into a light run toward the forest that encircled the back of the farmhouse. She knew nearly every inch of the woods between her family's home and the Lantzes'—though she had to admit she hadn't been walking there in the months since her engagement. It seemed that courting, as well as the usual influx of work of the farm during harvest, had kept her too busy. But now she trod the pine-needled ground with secret delight. She could tell from the air that the rain would hold off for a while, and she pressed more deeply into the trees, certain that the best place for a would-be thief to hide would be the woods.

After an hour of actually navigating the rocks and root systems of the dark forest, she began to question if she truly had her wits about her. What had she expected? That the thief would just pop out and introduce himself? Suppose he really was dangerous and much more than a thief? She thought of the comfort and safety of her narrow bed and shivered, deciding she'd go hunting for the mystery man some other time. Then she stifled a scream as the beam of her light gave out, and a voice spoke to her from the dark path ahead.

"You're an Amish girl, aren't you? Why are you out in these woods so late and in this kind of weather?"

The voice was a strained whisper. Rose peered into the darkness, trying to see the speaker, when a helpful flash of lightning gave her a brief glimpse.

He was taller than she, clothed in blue jeans and a gray sweatshirt, its hood shrouding his face. Another white streak of light, and the breadth of his shoulders and a dark stain on the front of his shirt were emblazoned in her mind.

"You're the thief," she stated.

"What?"

"The thief who's been taking from hereabouts the past weeks. I put those two blueberry pies out on the back porch. I see the blueberry stain on your front."

He laughed, and she almost gasped in disbelief as the realization hit her with full force. *It was Luke!* Even as a confusion of thoughts rushed past her like the waters of a swollen creek, one instinctual idea took control of her brain—she would not let him know that she recognized him.

"Very smart," he said. "My compliments. But you'd better get home to your husband. These woods are no place for a lady."

CHAPTER FOUR

"I'VE RUN ABOUT this land since I was a child," she announced, trying for normalcy in her tone. "And why do you assume I'm married?"

Was in der welt was he doing—dressed as an *Englischer* and stealing pies from her porch? He didn't seem to recognize her in the dark...but then why was he out talking about marriage with a strange girl in the woods?

"Aren't most Amish girls married young?" he asked in the same husky whisper that seemed to tickle at her shoulder bones in a way that his normal voice didn't do.

"*Ya*... Yes, I mean—some are. I'm just engaged." She almost clapped her hand over her mouth at the word *just*.

"Just?"

She wet her lips in the dark and tried to infuse her voice with warmth. "I'm going to marry my best friend in a few months."

"And does your...er...best friend realize how enthused you are about the whole affair?"

He does now, she thought, trying to keep a rein on her emotions. "I *am* happy," she asserted finally, then swallowed, finding herself voicing to the supposed stranger the concern that had haunted her for weeks. "It's just that—he—my betrothed—doesn't notice anything—not about me anyway. He's very—practical and smart."

She felt a palpable silence between them, then sensed

him step toward her. She lifted her chin, wondering what he would do next.

"Smart or not, he's a fool—not to notice you," he muttered.

"How can you say that? You can't even see me properly," she said.

"You saw me, at least enough to know my—secret. And I saw you, like meeting destiny in a strike of lightning. White sparks and moonlight—they suit your beauty, Amish girl."

In the cascading roll of thunder that followed, she heard the deafening sound of her own heartbeat as his words penetrated. They were so unlike him. And proof that he did see her in the waxing light. Beguiled and bewildered, Rose held her breath, waiting.

Then he reached out one hand to stroke her cheek in a slow caress. She wanted to lean into the mysterious yet familiar hand, its strong warmth coupled with a heavy tenderness that transmitted to every delicate nerve ending the flush that she felt burning her skin.

"You don't even know me," she said, trying to keep her voice level. "Maybe I'm too wild, or a petty shrew, or just plain…boring." She found herself citing all of the things she thought she might seem to him at times.

He laughed again, then backed away. "Go home," he said roughly.

She knew she should do as he said to keep up the charade, but there was a mystery here…a mystery man whom she had thought she knew so well. And for the first time in weeks she'd unburdened herself to someone, and it exhilarated her.

"I'll go when I'm ready."

"Suit yourself. Oh, and by the way, thank you for the pies."

She heard him step through a layer of dried leaves. "Wait!" she called.

"What?"

"I—do you—do you need some more?" She could have bitten her tongue at the desperation in the inane question, but he replied with seriousness.

"Apple. Anytime."

Of course, apple...his favorite.

"All right. Do you..." She broke off when she sensed that she was alone, and only the sound of the wind through the trees touched her. She shivered in the dark before turning back toward home, wondering who in the world this man was that she was to marry.

CHAPTER FIVE

THE RAIN PELTED in earnest against the barn roof as Luke stripped off the *Englisch* clothes. He stuffed them into the back of his buggy before changing in the chill air of the barn to his usual Amish wear. All the while, the beauty of Rose's pale face, the warmth of her skin, pulsed through his mind as he recalled the heart-stopping moments in the woods. He was sure that she would have recognized him, but she hadn't.

He was two steps outside when the thought stopped him. He stood stock-still, heedless of the rain soaking him. She'd gone *looking* for the thief…she had thought to find something out there, in the woods, with a perfect stranger, more compelling than she found in her own betrothed. The idea shook him to his core, but then he remembered why he was doing what he was and decided that *Derr Herr* might have plans beyond what he could see himself. He sloshed on through the mud and gained the back porch. He wiped his work boots against the ragged rug with the habit of his *mamm*'s long training and entered the empty kitchen.

THE STORM LEFT the area, leaving behind an almost luminous clarity to the following day. Squirrels hurried to replenish nut supplies across leaf-strewn grass as the

neighborhood cows greeted their fodder with tail flicks and echoing bellows.

"What are you thinking of, Rose?" Luke asked the question in what she considered an idle fashion as they were out driving to survey the damage the storm had wrought. He navigated the buggy down one of myriad country roads, sending the horse around a fallen tree branch with a light touch of the reins.

"Same as usual." Her shrug was noncommittal, but in truth she hadn't been able to stop thinking of him all night—him and his secrets.

"Which is?" He grinned, and she frowned.

Tired and confused, she wondered if she should just admit the truth to him, but something restrained her. She'd rationalized her way through a hundred possible reasons why Luke would resort to disguising himself and thieving from his own people. But after a lot of prayer, she'd decided that she had to trust him until he trusted her enough to tell her his secret.

"Shouldn't you know what your betrothed is thinking, Luke Lantz?"

"What you're thinking? *Nee*—who can ever know what's in a woman's mind?"

Well, after last night...you should know, she thought in irritation. "Take me home."

"What? I just picked you up fifteen minutes ago."

"I don't care." And she didn't. She did not care one bit for Luke's sensibilities, not when she knew that he could be someone like the stranger in the woods who'd noticed her even in the dark. The Luke Lantz in the buggy today hardly seemed the same man. It wasn't just his Amish dress and calm tone; it was also his detached demeanor.

But then, to her surprise, Luke drew the buggy to

a halt. She saw that they were in Glorious Grove—the childish name she'd given to the copse of maples that towered over the dirt road. She was pleased to see that nothing but a stray branch here and there seemed to have been hurt by the storm.

"What are you doing? I told you to take me home." She crossed her arms over her chest and glared at him, unused to his not doing as she asked.

He laughed low, and the sound caught in her mind. She blinked. She was definitely thinking too much about the thief...the thief in the night who'd stolen her dreams. Luke ran a hand down her shoulder to the bend in her elbow, and she snapped back to the moment.

"I'll take you home, Rose, but I've been thinking about what you said—about kissing more."

She opened her mouth in shock. "Now? Now you want to kiss more?"

"Maybe. What do you mean by *now*? Aren't we nearer still to our wedding day?"

She shook her head, confused, and he leaned closer. Against her will, she was intrigued. Luke had rarely been the initiator of kisses in the past.

"Unclasp your arms," he murmured, sliding his hat off.

She lifted her nose in the air. "*Nee*—why?"

He smiled. "So you're not all tense."

"I'm not tense."

"What happened here?" He touched the pinkish burn on the back of her hand with care, and she had to look away from him.

"I made blueberry pies last night."

"Really?"

She'd never have guessed that he knew more than

enough about her pie baking. And she didn't like his teasing tone, even if it was feigned. Sometimes there was no fun in having someone know you well enough to understand even your baking weaknesses.

"*Ya*, really," she snapped.

"I would have liked a taste," he whispered, and she turned to look at him in surprise. Was there some undercurrent of meaning in his words? She searched his familiar face; his blue eyes were as innocent as always. She almost sighed. She was definitely confused by the encounter in the woods.

Then he let his fingers play up along her shoulder to the nape of her neck and slid a curl free from beneath her *kapp*. He moved to press his lips against her hair and gave a soft exhalation of pleasure.

She drew a sharp breath. "Luke!"

"What?" He bent his head, her hair still in his fingers, and tilted forward so that his mouth hovered a bare inch from her own. "What, Rose?" He trailed the tendril across her lips and waited.

Her breath caught, and she felt a near dizzying sense of his closeness. She wanted him to move—to start, to finish the kiss. But he held back, as if he were searching for something in the depths of her eyes. She felt his weight rock against her for a moment, and he placed a very soft, almost brotherly kiss on her forehead, dropping the strand of hair. She blew out a breath of frustration when he picked up the reins with an enigmatic smile.

"We've made a start," he observed as he turned the horse.

Rose wasn't sure why she felt such a loss at his idea of a beginning.

CHAPTER SIX

It was a week later when Rose sank down at the Kings' kitchen table to visit with her friend Priscilla. There was a palpable excitement and energy in the air, and Rose wondered if her own home would feel this way when her wedding was only a short few weeks away.

"So, Rose—you've been *baking*?" Priscilla smiled and nodded toward the pie sitting on the table. "I thought you'd rather add up a page of sums than make a pie!"

"As a matter of fact, I would," Rose said flatly. "Just take it and enjoy. It's actually not half bad."

"Okaaay."

Rose took a sip of the tea Priscilla had offered her and tried not to dismiss the past few days from her mind. But a blur of brown sugar, cinnamon, flour, and apple peels swirled in her head until she thought she'd never want to taste another pie again as long as she lived. "How are the wedding plans coming along?" she asked, hoping to dislodge her sugary vision.

Priscilla was engaged to marry in just a few weeks, and Rose was to be one of the attendants. It was a great honor, considering that Priscilla's sister should have served in the position, but Hannah was due to deliver on the day of the ceremony.

Unlike Rose, Priscilla usually glowed with satisfaction over her impending wedding, but now she shook her

head. "We've had a few—incidents, little glitches in our plans, but I'm sure everything will be perfect from here on out. I do think, though, that you and Luke have the right idea in marrying later in the season. It seems I can barely plan, with all of the weddings we have to attend on the weekends."

"I suppose you're right," Rose murmured, breaking a piece of crust from the pie before her and crumbling it between her fingers.

"Rose, what's wrong?"

Rose swallowed. Priscilla was her best friend, and keeping things from her was even more difficult than evading *Aenti* Tabby, but she just couldn't bring herself to tell her Luke's secret. More than that, she knew that her friend would never have gone looking for someone in the night, because she'd found the love of her life—it radiated in her face and convicted Rose's heart.

"Nothing's wrong."

"Rose—I've wanted to ask…does it—well, scare you a little to take on a household of four men? Is that what's bothering you?"

Rose sighed. *If only it were that easy...* It wasn't the responsibility of caring for a ready-made family she feared, but her own treacherous thoughts, and her mixed-up attraction to the man she thought she knew so well.

"Sometimes I'm afraid. But it's just work. I'll delegate. They're managing fine without me now, so one extra pair of hands has got to be a help. Luke would never just let them dump all the housework on me."

Priscilla nodded. "No, he cherishes you far too much for that."

Rose stood up abruptly. "Priscilla, I'd best be going. I just wanted—to give you the pie. Besides, I promised

Luke I'd stop by the office and see him for a few minutes. I suppose I should do it."

"*Bensel*…you sound like you don't really want to!"

Rose summoned a smile. "That's silly—of course I do."

THE *ENGLISCH* SEEMED to have an ever-growing fascination with all things Amish, and Luke considered wryly that he'd much prefer to be wrestling with accounts than doing the other part of his job—dealing with customers.

He blinked from the throbbing in his temples and refocused on the woman across the desk from him. She was young and blond and had bright, carefully made-up blue eyes. She was also spoiled rotten by her husband, as far as he could tell. Mrs. Matthews had very distinct ideas about what she wanted for her own birthday gift, and apparently had even more particular thoughts about men in general falling under the spell of her obvious beauty. Luke had spent a mind-numbing half hour trying to verbally sidestep her, finally deciding that humoring her was the best possible recourse.

"So, let's go over this again, Mrs. Matthews." He leaned forward conspiratorially. "A carved headboard."

ROSE SIGHED AS she looped the reins of the horse over the post outside the woodworking shop and glanced at the car parked there. The vehicle shone with discreet elegance in the filtered sunlight of the row of brightly colored oak trees that lined the Lantzes' lane. She hesitated, thinking maybe a wealthy client might be occupying Luke's time, but she had promised to stop.

She entered the side door, breathing in the pungent smells of many woods—butternut, sassafras, black wal-

nut. The accompanying sounds of hammers and shavers echoed with familiar comfort as she turned to the office. The door to the small room was half closed, and she lifted her hand to knock when a burst of pleased feminine laughter made her jump.

"Oh, Mr. Lantz—tell me another, please. You've got a wonderful sense of humor."

"Call me Luke."

Call him Luke? Rose felt an unfamiliar pang in her chest as she stared at the wooden door.

"Go on in, Rosie," Joshua bellowed as he crossed behind her carrying a brace of two-by-fours. "He's been in there forever."

Forever? Rose frowned and eased the door open.

A blond-haired woman in faded blue jeans, fancy boots, and a becoming pink sweater sat on the edge of Luke's desk. Her betrothed had his hat off and leaned back in his chair. The deep smile on his face revealed a dimple in his cheek that Rose had forgotten even existed.

He turned easily in the chair while the woman looked up. "Rose, *hiya*. I forgot you were coming. I don't know where the time's gone."

He made to rise, and Rose waved him back down with a quick swipe of her hand. Feelings of irritation and jealousy mingled in her mind like the dust motes in the shaft of sunlight from the small window.

"Um… I'll just see you later since you're busy."

But the other woman slid down from the desk, a pile of neatly organized receipts falling after her. "Oh, I'm so silly!"

The woman bent her slender form to pick at the papers, and somehow Luke bent forward at the same time so that they knocked heads, his brown hair touching the

blond strands—and causing a red haze to temporarily mar Rose's vision.

"Do you need some help?" she heard herself ask sweetly. But something in her tone must have conveyed itself to Luke, because he made haste to get up.

"Uh, Rose—don't go. Mrs. Matthews and I…"

"Barbara," the woman interjected with a purr. "Don't forget."

"Right. Barbara and I are finished, really. I was just tallying her bill and telling her some of the odd things people want carved in wood sometimes. Uh… Barbara, this is my betrothed, Rose Bender."

Rose forced herself to shake the hand the other woman extended and resisted the urge to squeeze like she was working a hard milking cow. She was amazed at her own temper. Luke had done nothing but laugh, and after all, he had to be polite to the customers. She felt herself begin to calm down and silently prayed for forgiveness for the way she was feeling.

She cast her eyes quickly over the receipt Luke held and calculated the total with an easy computation in her head. She murmured the figure to him.

"How'd you do that so fast?" Luke smiled his thanks, but Mrs. Matthews was giggling.

"Oh, a wedding. I love weddings. You've got to let me congratulate you both!" She stretched to brush the air near Rose's cheek with a kiss, then wound her slender arms up around Luke's neck.

Not as long as I have breath in my body, Rose thought as she took a step forward and gave a soft cry. She let herself fall with dead weight against the other woman, knocking her clean from Luke to land sideways on the desk, with Rose grimly atop her. Silently asking forgive-

ness for the second time in as many minutes, she took her time letting Luke help her up and couldn't resist a well-placed elbow in the design of the pink sweater.

"I'm so sorry," she murmured, hauling Mrs. Matthews upright. "I must have tripped. You are all right, *ya*?"

The *Englisch* woman looked faintly bewildered, as though she'd been sidelined by some strange forest creature. She grabbed up her purse and nodded to both of them.

"I'll call you when we have your order complete, Barbara," Luke said.

Rose thought she detected the slightest hint of humor in his voice—but she couldn't be sure. In truth, she was appalled at her reaction and hoped that it wouldn't cost the Lantz family a customer. But Barbara nodded vaguely and headed out the door. When she'd gone, Rose raised guilty eyes to Luke, but he just looked at her with a calm gaze.

"Got to get that board fixed," he commented.

"Board?"

"The one you tripped over. Might be bad for future customers."

Speechless, Rose could only nod in agreement.

CHAPTER SEVEN

ROSE HADN'T SEEN the "thief" again since their encounter the night of the storm, but for the third night in a row she set a trap for him. She snuggled beneath the quilt she'd dragged out onto a chair on the back porch and listened to the forlorn sound of occasional raindrops hitting the tightly sealed tinfoil on two apple pies on the rail.

She was a fool to long after another meeting with Luke in disguise.

She thought back again to the image of him laughing with the woman in the office that afternoon and tried to sort out her feelings. She'd watched Luke at singings and youth outings all through the years, and never had she thought to be jealous of his interactions with other girls. Not that he wasn't attractive and well-spoken; he was simply too faithful a friend and follower to ever be doubted. But now...now, he was something else, something more. She was too curious by nature to resist another taste of his disguise. And she had to admit that as the thief he had stirred her senses in a new way. She sighed and wondered what kind of person she was to be attracted to the unknown in someone.

She distracted herself by thinking about the apple pies she'd made. She was becoming adept at the task and yielding a deft hand to the formation of the latticework top crusts. She'd kept her brothers from asking for their

fair share by baking while they were in the fields and had apparently satisfied her *mamm*'s curiosity with her explanation that she was trying to be a better cook. She didn't like the deception, but she rationalized that her doings were certainly harmless enough. She was going to marry Luke, after all, so she might as well give him another opportunity to tell her the truth.

She was half asleep, somewhere between dreaming and wakefulness, when she heard the sound of foil rattling. She popped open her eyes and clicked on her flashlight. The pies were gone, and someone was moving across the yard.

"Hey!" she hissed, arcing the light into the yard. The beam caught against a pair of blue-jean-clad legs, and she dropped the quilt and stood. "Wait!" she called. "Please."

"Put down the light and I'll wait."

She heard the hoarse yet familiar voice, and her hands grew damp with perspiration as she snapped off the light and put it where she had been sitting. She crept to the porch rail and then down into the yard.

"They're apple—the pies, I mean." She toyed with her fingers.

"They'll be appreciated."

"*Ach*…do you…take for your family? Because we have plenty to give… I mean…"

"What do you want?" His question was harsh but penetrating.

"I don't—know what you mean." Rose's heart began to pound, wondering if he'd figured out that she recognized him.

"Yes, you do. A good Amish girl chasing after an *Englisch* thief. Why? What do you want?"

The rain seemed to be melting her sensibilities, her

defenses, the very excuses she'd sustained herself on the past months when she thought of a lifetime with Luke. Suddenly he'd become the center of something she desired with all her heart.

"I want you," she said baldly.

There was a long moment of silence, broken only by the falling of the rain.

"Me?" He laughed. "What do you know about me?"

"I want your way of being, your freedom.…" *Who you are right now…*

"If it's your engagement that you want out of, why not tell your—best friend?"

"I don't want out of it," she cried, amazed at his perception. But then, he'd known her forever…

"Tell him. Tell him you're so hungry to be free that you'd stand in the dark and the rain and long for a stranger's touch—his kiss."

She almost spun away from the deep voice, the mockery, and the powerful allure. *His kiss.*

She heard the shift of the foil, the damp footsteps, and then he swooped so close that she could feel his breath against her cheek, the press of the pie pans against her stomach. He smelled of the forest and something else that was tantalizingly familiar. But then his mouth was on hers, once, twice, two angry kisses, and then a yielding, a softening, and she was kissing him back with all of the withheld passion in her young soul. He broke away with a rasp in his breath, and Rose stood shivering, gasping for breath as the rain increased in tenor.

"Go inside," he ordered, moving away.

She couldn't obey, couldn't think, as she raised a shaking hand to her lips.

"Don't leave," she gasped.

She heard him inhale. "I must."

And then he was gone, running, the rain making an uneven and fading tattoo on the foil as she listened to some part of her dreams move far and away.

CHAPTER EIGHT

LUKE STARED OUT at the gray morning through the kitchen window and wondered if the sun would break through. Rose had promised to come and help with the cider making. He took a deep swallow of the bitter coffee his brother had brewed and tried to suppress his mixed feelings about kissing Rose the night before. To be sure, he could still imagine his mouth stinging with the contact, but he'd been furious too. He'd risked a second encounter with her partially because he'd wondered how far her interest extended to some strange *Englischer*. He also wanted to see her again as he had the night of the storm, so striking in her beauty and so much as one with the wild darkness. He wondered idly whether she'd understand if he tried to explain...

Joshua entered through the back kitchen door. "Saw Abram Bender out this morning."

Luke blinked as he sipped his coffee and turned to his *bruder*. "Mending fence?"

Joshua laughed. *"Ya."*

It was a gentle joke among the Lantz and Bender families how much time Abram spent mending fence. It was almost as if the man could sense a weakening in the stone or wire even before the cows could.

Luke moved from the sink basin to give his brother room to wash.

"Nervous about becoming a married man, Luke?" There was enough curiosity in Josh's voice for Luke to know he wasn't just joking.

"Maybe," he admitted, thinking of Rose kissing a supposed stranger.

"Wish *Mamm* could be here to see it?"

Luke tightened his grip on his cup. "Surely."

Joshua toweled his arms, whistling through his teeth for a moment. "Well, you still going to that *Englisch* homeless shelter to help out like *Mamm* did?"

"*Nee*… I haven't had the time of late."

Joshua nodded. "Just as well. You've enough of your own to care for without chasing after the *Englisch*, no matter how fitting the cause."

"Wouldn't *Mamm* say that helping another is always worth the doing?" Luke's voice was level.

Joshua clapped him on the shoulder. "*Ya*, she would. But not everybody's like she was."

"And that's the truth to be heard," Luke muttered.

"What?"

"Nothing. Nothing at all."

THE DAY WAS one to stir the senses; blue skies and cotton fluffed clouds. Geese flying in south V-patterns, and the mingled scents of nature in its hurried pursuit and preparation for sleep, all joined in a rapturous serenade.

But Rose was uneasy. For once she couldn't discern Luke's mood, and it made her nervous. Of course there was the guilty worry that, from his perspective, she'd been kissing a stranger in the rain. That had to make him angry, and she thought once more of telling him what she knew. But the moment passed and she focused on toss-

ing the quartered apples into the Lantzes' cider press as Luke turned the crank handle.

The smell of ripe apples and the crispness of the fall day seemed to burgeon with life and abundance, and part of her wanted to dance with the red and yellow leaves that swirled in graceful arcs to land on the ground. But Luke was uncommonly silent, moving mechanically, almost as if she wasn't there.

"Are you all right?" she asked at last.

He glanced at her—calm blue eyes and a solemn expression. "*Ya*. And you?"

She frowned. She didn't want to talk about how she felt. "Fine," she mumbled.

He straightened and came toward where she sat on a low stool. His work boots brushed the rounded fall of her dress as it spread upon the ground, and she squinted up at him in the sunshine.

"*Ya*, you are fine, Rose," he said, reaching down to brush the curve of her cheek.

She sat still, mesmerized by his warm fingers and that mysterious side of him that teased at her consciousness.

He dropped his hand and cleared his throat. "I've been thinking of late...our engagement...perhaps we set the wedding too soon. Maybe you'd prefer another year in which to plan?"

"What?" she squeaked in dismay. *Is this why he's so quiet? Does he want to break our engagement?* Surprisingly, the thought made her sick at heart, even as she considered how she might feel if she thought he'd been kissing someone else in the dark.

He turned his back to her and ran a hand over the damp board of the press, shrugging his broad shoulders. "You're much younger than I, Rose."

"I've always been younger than you—it's never mattered before."

"*Nee*, but now...with all of the responsibilities of the house...perhaps you desire still a continued bit of freedom."

Her eyes widened in a rush of feverish thought. What had she said to him last night about freedom? Did he suspect that she knew?

She rose and touched his arm, and he turned to face her. "I want to marry, Luke. I do."

He nodded, but she felt him search her face, and she lifted her chin.

"All right, Rose."

She longed for him to touch her, but he was back to the apple press. The moment was gone, and the day seemed to lose some of its color as she shifted on her feet and tried to sort through her emotions.

When Rose stood behind him, Luke tried to concentrate on the gush of juice from the press and put aside the thought of touching his future bride—kissing her as the "thief" had last night. But he'd meant what he said—perhaps she needed a bit more time. Maybe that's why she spoke of freedom in the dark and yielded to—*nee*, returned a heated kiss with such passion. Yet he didn't want to complicate matters by bringing more physicality into the moment...

He looked up in relief at the diversion when his brother Mark emerged from the woodworking shop nearby. Mark was two years older than Luke, still single, and was the family's tease. But today he appeared frustrated.

Mark dropped onto the stool Rose had abandoned and

sank a dipper into the bucket of cloudy cider. He slurped loudly as Luke ran the last of the apples through.

"What's wrong?" Luke asked.

"What's wrong with you two?"

Luke started to take the apple press apart to prepare it for drying and ignored his brother's question.

"You leaving already, Rose?" Mark prodded. "Seems like Luke could do something to persuade you to stick around more often."

"She has her own chores to be about," Luke observed in a warning tone.

"I'd imagine that a girl would want to spend every second possible with her betrothed."

"Ya." Luke smiled then. "You'd have to imagine it— since it seems no one's standing in line to be your bride."

Rose giggled.

"Watch your mouth, baby *bruder.* Or I may have to watch it for you."

Luke laid the crank down with care. "All right. You are in a fine temper and in front of my future bride. Why is that?"

Mark sighed. *"Ach,* I messed up the piece of burled elm *Daed* had me redoing for that piano front. You know how rare that wood grain is."

Luke turned from the press. "How bad is it?"

Mark shrugged. "I don't know. I was off somehow in the scrolling design, and now the whole thing's lopsided. *Daed*'s gonna have a fit when he and Josh get back from their delivery."

"Let me take a look."

Mark shrugged. "Go ahead. It's on the second workbench."

CHAPTER NINE

ROSE FOLLOWED LUKE'S purposeful strides into the shop. A generator powered several overhead bulbs and cast light onto the worktable that was laden with tools, wood curls, and a beautiful piece of wood. But the design clearly had a flaw. She watched as Luke picked up the foot-long panel and ran his large hands down the unusual sheen of the wood.

His eyes were intent as he scanned the workbench and chose a slender tool from among the gougers and scrapers. There was an air of suppressed energy in his movements, almost a sensuality in the way he turned the wood in his hands.

"Luke?"

"Hmmm?"

He was making small additions to the scrollwork, bending to cast an eye over the wood, then straightening to start again.

"Why don't you tell your *daed* the truth?"

He stilled and stared at her. "What do you mean?"

She gestured to the wood. "You love this; you always have. Tell your father so you can get out of that office." *And away from women like Barbara…*

He bent over the wood again with a shrug. "It doesn't matter."

She was silent, watching him work, liking the way

the dust motes he stirred up played in the fall of light and landed in his brown hair. She'd rarely seen him so enthused, and her throat ached when she thought of the hours he gave without complaint to the work his father expected of him. Perhaps that was why he sought some sort of diversion—dressing like an *Englischer*, playing at being a thief. But still, it didn't quite make sense...

After a few minutes he looked up with satisfaction. "There." He blew the wood off and tilted it toward her as the sound of a wagon and horse echoed from outside. Luke put the wood down, stepped away from the workbench, and caught her hand. He pulled her toward the door as Mark entered, looking hunted.

"*Daed*'s back."

Luke gave him a swift cuff on the shoulder and looked out to see their father coming toward the door.

"*Daed.*" Luke greeted him calmly. "I was about to see Rose to her buggy, if you'll excuse us."

"*Ya*, surely. I wanted to see how Mark did on the—"

Rose watched as he broke off and drifted past them to the workbench. The older man lifted the wooden piece with near reverent hands. "*Ach*, Mark. What is this?"

Mark stepped forward as if to speak when Luke caught his arm.

"It's wondrous craftsmanship, my son. And I'll risk the vanity to tell you so. I've never seen the like of such an intricate design."

Rose watched Mark open his mouth again, and Luke turned abruptly. She felt the jolt through their entwined hands when his elbow connected with Mark's ribs, knocking the breath from him. Then Luke pulled her out the door and into the sunlight.

"WHAT IS WRONG with you?" Rose hissed. She snatched her hand away from him as he moved to help her up into the wagon.

He swung up beside her. "What?"

"Why would you let your *daed* think that Mark fixed that design?"

Luke lifted the reins and tilted his hat back a bit, exposing his handsome profile. He answered slowly. "It would trouble my father—make him feel torn if he knew I could work wood like that. It's less worry for him if I do the books. And he doesn't need any worry—not since *Mamm*...well..."

"You miss her so much, don't you?"

She watched him reach to rub at his neck as if to soothe an ever-present ache. "*Ya*, of course I do."

"I never asked you before...did she know? I mean, how much you love the woodworking?"

"Maybe. I don't know. I planned on telling her once, and then there was the flu. It all happened so fast. And *Daed*, well...it nearly broke him."

Rose took a deep breath and a shot in the dark. "You're afraid. It's not your *daed*, Luke—it's you. You're afraid to be who you really are."

He turned to face her, blinking solemnly. "*Ya*. You're right, Rose. And you'd know, because your secret is that you're afraid yourself. So don't tell me about being who you really are."

"I know who I am," she cried, wanting it to be true. Wanting to banish the meetings with him as the *Englischer* in the woods from her mind. Suddenly, the planned footing of her future seemed treacherously slippery.

CHAPTER TEN

ROSE TOSSED BENEATH the nine-patch quilt of her girlhood bed; she hadn't seen much of Luke the past week and felt distant from him. She sighed aloud and forced herself to focus on her prayers.

"*Ach*, Lord, help me. Help my relationship with Luke to be true. Search my heart, *Derr Herr*, and find those shadows, those secrets that I would hide even from myself, and bring them to light. Forgive me for spending time chasing after Luke as the man in the woods, and help him just the same. Free him from this stealing. Free me from wanting something like the wind, and not the steadiness of the moment. Thank You for Luke. Thank You, *Derr Herr*, for my life and my ability to make choices. Give me wisdom, Lord...please...give me wisdom."

Utterly drained, she pulled the covers up to her chin and dreamed fitfully. Tangled blue threads, the color of the wedding dress she was sewing on a bit each day, seemed to stretch from her mind to wrap around her arms and wrists. The thread was thin but confining, and she struggled against the bonds. Then a dark-hooded stranger stood before her and raised a pair of silver shears high. She felt her breath catch in her throat at the slash of silver against the white of her skin, but then the threads were gone and she was free. She called to him because he was running from her, and he turned. The hood fell

away, and Luke stood before her. Then he caught her up in a swinging embrace and she laughed, free and clear…

Rose jerked awake and sat straight up in bed. Her heart was pounding and she stared out the window, glad to see the first streaks of the morning sun falling across the hardwood floor of her room. She decided that a walk in the woods before breakfast would clear her tangled thoughts, and she hurried to dress. She wanted to slip away before anyone would notice she was gone. She needed some time to herself to consider her dream.

But when she crept downstairs, it was to find everyone wide-awake and already halfway through breakfast at the kitchen table. *"Mamm,"* she cried in dismay. "Why didn't you call me to help with the meal?"

Ben laughed. "We all called you, but you slept like the dead! Don't you remember that today's the first day of the fair?"

Rose bit her lip as she accepted a bowl of steaming oatmeal from her mother and sat down at the table. "I guess I forgot," she mumbled.

The first fall fair in the area was something her family always attended together, but after her poor night's sleep, the outing held little appeal. She kept seeing the moment in her dream when the stranger's hood fell backward to reveal Luke's face.

"As is right," her father remarked, scraping the last of his plate. "Probably dreaming of your wedding coming, like any girl would."

Rose concentrated on the wet lumps of her oatmeal and didn't lift her head. She had no desire to talk about dreaming—wedding or otherwise.

"Are you feeling well, Rosie?" *Aenti* Tabby asked softly.

A sudden inspiration struck Rose. "Well, actually... if you all wouldn't mind—I wonder if I might stay home today to do some sewing on my wedding dress. I've barely pieced the pattern yet, and I feel like time is running away from me."

She saw her mother glance down the table to her father's warm eyes.

"*Ya*, Rose." *Mamm* smiled. "Just for today. Some time alone may be *gut* for you."

Rose nodded. *"Danki."*

James held his plate out for more sausage. "*Ya*, Rose, but just don't go entertaining any Rob in the Hood while we're gone. Luke Lantz might take offense."

She frowned as both of her brothers laughed, and told herself that she'd had enough of fairy tales for a while.

ONCE SHE'D HELPED clean up breakfast, then waved the family off, she decided that a walk in the brisk sunshine would do her good before beginning hours of sewing. Of their own accord, her feet seemed to lead to the forest behind her home. She spent a peaceful half hour praying as she walked, collecting the reddest leaves, and daydreaming. On one level, she continued her prayers for Luke from the evening before, asking the Lord if Luke might one day escape the task of bookkeeping and use instead the ready skill he had with woodworking.

But then she became aware of a rhythmic pounding from somewhere in the distance. She stopped and listened. She couldn't imagine who'd be building on anything out this far. Her steps quickened as a childish memory of an old tumbledown shack on the Lantzes' property surfaced in her consciousness. She crept through

the trees to the sunny clearing and stopped, pressing hard against an old oak.

Clad in blue jeans, work boots, and a loose white shirt, Luke was atop the low roof of the old shack. His back was to her, his head bent, as he concentrated on securing a new white pine board to the roof. The sun caught on the muscles of his arms as he lifted the hammer, and she made an inadvertent sound of pleasure at the sight. He half turned in her direction, then seemed to tense and put a foot back onto the gray wood. There was a brief cracking sound and a muffled cry. Rose gasped as the weathered part of the roof gave way beneath his weight and Luke disappeared in a rain of old wood and an ominous cloud of dust.

CHAPTER ELEVEN

ROSE RAN TO the door of the shack, coughing as she breathed in the dust. She flung open the door and saw Luke lying facedown and still beneath a splintered pile of boards. She began snatching at the boards, heedless of their weight or the scratches from the wood on her arms.

"Luke! Are you all right?"

He gave a faint groan, then sneezed from the mess she was kicking up. "Rose—you know it's me?"

"*Ya*, of course…since that first time in the woods."

Luke sighed, a gusty exhalation, rolled over onto his back, and stared up at her through the dust and shards of wood. "I should have known," he muttered. He closed his eyes and slid one arm up and over his face, revealing an ugly gash on the underside of his wrist.

She dropped to her knees beside him and began to tear a strip from her apron and dab at the blood.

He lowered his arm slowly. "Don't. It needs to be washed first. And I think there's a splinter there."

Even his voice seemed different now—husky, inviting. And his dark blue eyes gleamed up at her with a knowing confidence. She let her eyes trail down his torn shirt to the low-slung blue jeans and shook her head, wondering if she was losing her mind. Was this really her Luke? The irony of her sense of proprietorship struck when she

realized that no woman would take for granted the hold-ing of the man before her.

"I—should have told you that I knew who you were," she said. "But I wanted you to trust me, to tell me what you were doing. You didn't." Her eyes met his, and he caught her hand, pulling her dirty fingertips to his lips.

"Nee," he murmured against her skin. "I was wrong."

He kissed her fingers with lingering passion, as she watched, mesmerized; then he let her go. She snatched her hand back as if she'd touched hot coals, feeling her face grow warm, whether from anger or excitement, she wasn't sure. Her thoughts felt thick, like the oatmeal she'd choked down at breakfast.

"Well, then—what? Why did you go on pretending with me that you were the thief?"

He smiled at her, a flash of white teeth and some-thing fast and wolfish that made her catch her breath. "I am the thief."

"You—you touched me and kissed me, and I thought I was betraying Lu—you! Or that you were betraying me..." She broke off in confusion.

"Let your hair down, Rose, will you?" His eyes were intent, compelling, and she wondered if he'd taken a knock on the head when he'd fallen.

"Wh-what?"

"Please. I want to see you—revealed, like you're see-ing me."

"Revealed?" she repeated slowly. "I don't even know who you are anymore."

"I'm the same person I've always been, Rose. Maybe you just haven't noticed."

She shook her head, inadvertently letting several

strands escape the confines of her *kapp* and brush against his chest.

He smiled, a lazy, sultry smile that made her think of honey dripping from a comb, and she had to blink to keep her thoughts straight.

"We're nearly married," he observed, reaching to catch a stray curl and run it between his fingertips. The sunlight slanted down through the hole in the roof at that moment and fell across the tableau of her hair in his hand.

"Luke!" she snapped, breaking his reverie and yanking her hair from his hand. She ignored the sharp pain at her scalp. She was having difficulty breathing and thought that the dust couldn't be good for either one of them. "We need to get out of here."

"Probably," he murmured. "But I think my left ankle's sprained, so it may present a problem." His eyes drifted closed.

"Hey!"

"Don't worry; I'm here. Just get me up, if you can. We'll go to Dr. Knepp's."

"Fine. But you've got to tell me what you're doing with this shack—in the middle of nowhere." Her fingers pressed down his leg to test the extent of the sprain, and she wondered desperately how she'd ever move his weight.

He laughed, then groaned when she touched his ankle. "That's another story. And don't forget my wallet and pants when we go."

"Is that all you're hiding?" she muttered, reaching to grasp at his shoulders.

"Maybe." He grinned lopsidedly. "But there might be a few more things I should confess to the bishop before we marry."

She stared at him in exasperation and wondered exactly what else her all-too-familiar and at the same time utterly alien betrothed would have to confess before she became his wife.

CHAPTER TWELVE

SHE BREATHED A sigh of relief when he told her that he'd hidden a horse and wagon in a copse of trees behind the shack. She led the horse round to the front of the dilapidated place, then half walked, half dragged Luke outside, trying to ignore the scent of sun and sweat that clung to his dusty skin.

"Your shirt's ruined," she pointed out. "And where are your suspenders?"

He grinned at her and gestured with his chin. "Over on that stump with my other stuff."

She went to gather his wallet and hat. Then she picked up his dark pants with the attached suspenders and turned to him with a frown. He was leaning against the horse for support, and for all of his seeming cheerfulness she couldn't help but see the tense lines of pain around his handsome mouth.

"Do you—do you want to put this on?" she questioned gruffly, extending the hat to him.

Luke nodded. "*Ya*, if you'll help a bit." His eyes danced as he swayed.

"Fine." She laid the items in her hands on the wagon seat, then came closer to where he stood, perching his hat on his head.

"Let's leave the hat, Rose. Just take a back road to the Knepps'. I feel like I'm going to be sick. Sorry."

Rose made a clucking sound of comfort and stood waiting, watching a pallor wash over him and a bead of sweat trail down his cheek. She pulled his hat back off, and he drew a deep breath.

"Do you want to sit down?" she asked anxiously.

"*Nee*, I'm all right now. Glad I wasn't sick in front of you."

"I saw you throw up from gorging yourself on watermelon when you were twelve, remember?"

He smiled faintly. "No secrets with a best friend."

"No secrets," she repeated soberly.

He exhaled. "Let's just go. I'll lie in the back of the wagon."

Somehow she managed to get him there; to half recline, clutching the side of the wagon. She used his dark pants to wrap about his ankle, then set about easing the wagon down back roads to get to the physician's home. And all the while her mind whirled with questions and emotions that she didn't care to examine too closely, choosing instead to focus on Luke's injuries and his need for care.

"A BAD SPRAIN can be as problematic as a break."

Dr. Knepp was a popular *Englisch* physician who'd long been accepted by the local Amish community. And if he thought it strange that Rose brought her betrothed in half dressed in *Englisch* clothes, he didn't remark on it. Instead, he hauled Luke onto an exam table and cut the pant leg of his jeans.

"Got to get that boot off, son," the doctor ordered.

"Right." Luke grimaced.

Dr. Knepp glanced at Rose. "I think you might go have

a cup of tea with my wife, my dear. I'll wrap the ankle and get that chunk of wood out of his wrist."

She was about to protest when something stern in Luke's face made her leave the room. Probably he didn't want her to see him in pain. She wandered down the short hallway that separated the doctor's office from his home, entering the bright and cheery *Englisch* kitchen. Mrs. Knepp looked up from a pile of ironing.

"Rose. Come in and have something warm to drink. Was that Luke I saw you drive up with in the back of the wagon?" She set the iron aside.

"Ya..." She floundered for a moment, not knowing how to explain his injuries and not wanting to lie. "He... uh...we..."

Mrs. Knepp waved a casual hand. "Spare me the details, dear. That's all confidential doctor's information, right? Come have some hot cider and tell me how your wedding plans are coming along."

Rose sat down and accepted the delicate rose-painted china cup. She took a sip of the warm cider. Mrs. Knepp joined her, stirring her own cup with a stick of cinnamon.

"I hear you're to be bridesmaid...er...attendant for Priscilla King's upcoming wedding. A pity her sister's due that day, but a nice honor for you, hmm?"

"Ach, ya. I've known Priscilla nearly as long as I've known Luke." Rose stared into her cider, wondering exactly how long she had known Luke—at least, the Luke who touched her hair and enticed her with his eyes.

A muffled groan from the doctor's wing made Rose stand up. Mrs. Knepp waved her back down. "He'll be fine, Rose. Just relax."

Rose sank back into her chair and toyed with the cup handle.

"Luke will do his own fair share of waiting over the coming years, I'll bet."

Rose looked at her hostess in confusion. "What do you mean?"

"Babies." Mrs. Knepp smiled. "He'll be waiting for you then, though if he's half the man he seems, he'll be right beside you, helping you along."

Rose flushed. The thought of having Luke's children sent her heart racing. Yet, up until a few days ago, she thought she'd known everything there was to him, and not much of that had caused her heart to thrill. But here she was, anxious for his pain, worried about his stealing, and in love with a part of him that she didn't even know. She took a strong swallow of cider, scalding the tip of her tongue and hastily depositing the cup back on the table.

Mrs. Knepp smiled once more. "Engagements are always hard."

Rose had to agree. "What's an *Englisch* engagement like?"

Mrs. Knepp laughed. "Oh, not so much ceremony as your own people's, I suppose, but there's still the fun... and the uncertainty."

"Uncertainty?"

The older woman gave her a sympathetic look. "Has no one told you, dear, that uncertainty is part of an engagement?"

Rose shook her head.

"Well, it is. How exactly are two young people supposed to look down a road where they can't see so far as the nearest prayer in the church?"

"I don't know. I guess I've struggled some with it myself."

"So you're normal. But I saw your face just now when

you thought Luke was in pain…that's love, Rose—the worrying, the hoping."

"And…the future?"

"Belongs to God." Mrs. Knepp smiled and patted her hand. "And with that, we all must be content."

CHAPTER THIRTEEN

"I TAKE IT you'll not be explaining how this all came to be?" the doctor asked, a faint, telling glimmer in his eyes as he wrapped the swollen ankle with gentle hands.

"*Nee*, if you don't mind."

"Not a bit. Just a quick tetanus jab and we should be through here. Keep that ankle elevated a few hours a day, and make sure the bandages on the wrist stay clean and dry. Do you want some help changing your clothes back? I think your jeans are shot."

"*Danki*, Doc. What do I owe you?"

Dr. Knepp chuckled. "The truth—when you care to tell it. Only because I'm curious."

Luke offered his hand and had it shaken with goodwill. "Consider it a future payment then. I've got to get past *Daed* first."

"And your future bride?"

"Don't remind me." Luke sighed as he eased off the examining table.

HALF AN HOUR later Luke's head was throbbing nearly as much as his ankle with Rose's ceaseless round of questions as she drove him home. And the rattling of the wooden crutches in the back of the wagon didn't help matters. Sitting on the bench seat beside her, his leg extended, Luke had the sudden and pressing desire to sim-

ply kiss her quiet, but decided it probably wouldn't be quite as fair as an explanation. Still...he glanced at her berry red lips as she framed her next query.

He moved quickly, dipping his head and slanting his chin so that he met her mouth half open. He kissed her hard, then pulled back a fraction to smile with satisfaction at the surprised *O* her pretty mouth had formed.

She stared at him suspiciously. "Did Dr. Knepp give you something weird for pain?"

"Nee," he whispered. "Am I being...weird?"

"Maybe. For the Luke I thought I knew...yes. For the other..." She slapped the reins across the horse's rump and tilted her head aside. "I don't know if I can say."

He laughed and withdrew. "Oh, I think you can say, Rose."

She flushed visibly at his intimate tone, and he tore his gaze away to glance at the passing landscape.

"What will you tell your family about how you got hurt?" she asked. "I certainly don't know what to say."

He tilted his hat forward and leaned back, closing his eyes. "Don't worry so much. I'll take care of everything."

WHEN SHE BROUGHT the wagon to a standstill at the Lantz home, Rose found that Luke's idea of taking care of things had little to do with explanation and more to do with exhausted dozing. And she couldn't very well give him the elbow jab he so deserved when she was confronted by Mr. Lantz's look of consternation.

"Ach, Rose. What is this?" Mr. Lantz whispered anxiously, peering up into the wagon seat where Luke drowsed.

"Uh, Luke and I..." Her voice rose several octaves.

"We were, um…" She broke off abruptly when Luke half turned to nuzzle against her shoulder.

"Luke!" She rapped his name out frantically, and he woke with a start, blinking his blue eyes warmly at her. "Luke. Your *daed*—we're home." She pleaded with him with her eyes while he got track of his bearings.

"Ach, Daed."

"Is it broken?" Mr. Lantz asked anxiously, reaching up to touch his son's leg above the bandage.

"Just a bad sprain," Luke assured him.

"You are both all right then? Rose?"

Rose could only nod, having no desire to lie to her future father-in-law. Not that she could tell him the truth anyway. She didn't know it.

"I'm sorry," she said, apropos of nothing, and was surprised to feel her lip tremble.

Mr. Lantz misinterpreted her look. *"Ach*, Rosie…never mind. He'll be right as rain for the wedding. I'm sure of it."

The wedding! Rose felt her heart skip a beat as she saw Luke shoot her a warm sidelong glance. Somehow she was supposed to marry a man who had become more than she could ever desire. It was enough to both exhilarate and make her feel like throwing up at the same time.

"Danki," she whispered.

Mr. Lantz came round the wagon and reached up to pat her hands on the reins. "Mark, Joshua!" The old man's voice carried into the workshop, and Luke's brothers appeared in the doorway. "Come—your brother's sprained his ankle. Let's move him inside the house, and then one of you can see Rose home."

"Uh, I'll walk," Rose interjected, slipping down from the wagon seat. "Really. Please—just take care of Luke."

She was two steps away from the wagon when Luke's voice stopped her.

"Rose? Come and visit later?" His tone was pleading.

His *daed* nodded his approval, and she could hardly decline. But first she needed some time alone to think through this strange turn of events.

CHAPTER FOURTEEN

"*Daed*—I'm fine. Really."

Luke noticed that his father's work-worn hands shook a bit as they smoothed the mounded quilt under the injured ankle, and his heart squeezed in his chest. He'd never given much thought to the fact that his father was getting older. Somehow he'd believed that *Daed* would always be healthy and strong.

"*Ya*, surely you are," his father murmured, straightening.

Luke swallowed. "*Daed*... I know none of us has been sick or hurt since *Mamm*, but this is nothing to worry over."

"*Ya*, so they said about your mother." The older man dropped into a nearby rocker and covered his face with his hand for a moment. "Perhaps I grow old in my concern."

Remorse swelled in Luke's throat when he thought of how his selfish behavior could bring more pain to his father. It had never been his desire to assume the role he had—that of a common thief—and what's more, he knew that he'd enjoyed it. But no weight of purpose could outbalance what he'd done. He sighed softly and flexed his wrist in its white bandages.

"*Daed*, we're all a bunch of fool men in this house, who've done little to really talk about *Mamm* not being

here. Rose—well, she likes to talk. I've come to learn through her that talking helps things. It's when we don't say—what we should, maybe—that things are worse."

He waited, and after a moment his father drew a hoarse breath.

"Well, I miss your *mamm*, to be sure. I thought that if I—spoke too much of it, that it would hurt you boys… add to your grieving. I guess I've kept the secret of my hurt inside for too long, and you're right—it's not *gut*." He took out a white hankie and blew his nose prodigiously. "*Ya*, especially with a new bride coming to bring life to these walls again. Your Rosie's got your *mamm*'s spirit, her gentleness and love of life. You're a lucky man, *sohn*—she's perfect for you."

Luke licked at a tear that slipped past his mouth and nodded. "*Ya, Daed*. Perfect."

THE MORE SHE walked, the more confused Rose got. Luke had her coming and going, and she had him in nearly the same position—except for the fact that he seemed so… steamy in his behavior, despite his injuries. Yet she still could explain little to nothing about why he'd done what he had the last months. And he'd kept on as though nothing had happened—except for the day he'd suggested she'd like more freedom…

She stopped so abruptly on the dirt road that she nearly stumbled. He'd offered her freedom, and had she taken it, he'd been willing to let her go, without any guilt or condemnation. Remorse flooded her consciousness, and she felt tears sting the backs of her eyes. What she'd taken for granted—his love—was real. It was giving and patient and all of those other things she knew from church but couldn't recall from her flustered mind.

Aenti Tabby's words teased at her consciousness with sudden importance. *What if there were more to Luke? More. More. More.*

She sighed and resumed walking, swiping at her eyes with the backs of her hands. Luke still had a lot of explaining to do...but then, maybe she did too.

She arrived home slightly breathless with emotion to find that the family had returned from the fair. *Aenti* Tabby was in the backyard making unrefined sugar from the bumper crop of sugar beets they'd had that year.

"*Ach*, some stronger hands than mine for the press," the older woman said with a welcoming smile.

Rose ducked her head so that her aunt wouldn't see the emotion in her face and plunged her hands into a nearby bucket of soapy water. She dried her hands on a clean towel and then took over at the apple press, which currently ran with the bright red and purple of sugar beets. Later the juice would be boiled until nearly all the liquid had evaporated, leaving rough granules of sugar for cooking. The hard part was pressing the liquid from the beets.

Aenti Tabby moved to continue cutting off the rough green tops. "So, have you seen your friend Priscilla lately? I've heard the Kings are having quite a time getting ready for her wedding."

Rose realized she had been too involved in her own issues to be of much comfort to her friend. She'd have to pay her another visit soon. To think that Priscilla and Chester's wedding was only three weeks away. The thought made her heart speed up at the seamless passage of time, and thoughts of her own December wedding to Luke flooded her mind again.

"How is your dress coming?"

"*Gut*. I've got it pieced, and I sew on it a bit whenever I can."

Rose was waiting for it—more pressing questions about Luke from her *aenti*—and decided to forestall the process by talking a blue streak. But as she opened her mouth to speak, her *aenti* gave a shocked cry.

"What?" Rose asked in alarm.

"Your hands, child! You didn't put on gloves."

Rose stared down at her hands and wrists, now stained as purple as the beet juice that gushed through the press.

"*Ach!* I wasn't thinking…"

"Or perhaps you were thinking too much," Aenti Tabby suggested.

Rose laughed aloud ruefully. "I suppose I can try kerosene to get it off."

"Or maybe your Luke would prefer a purple hand to hold until he's feeling better."

Rose opened her mouth in shock. "What?" How did her *aenti* know about Luke's injuries?

Aenti Tabby laughed at her expression. "Dr. Knepp stopped by before you got here to make sure that you were feeling well. Will you tell me what happened?"

Rose stared down at her purple fingers, perplexed, and thought hard about strangling Luke as she struggled for an answer.

CHAPTER FIFTEEN

"Go on up, Rose." Mr. Lantz smiled with what seemed like extra exuberance. "He's just resting that ankle a bit."

Rose returned the smile to her kindly future father-in-law and decided Luke must have handled things all right. She crossed the beautifully pegged oak floors of the Lantz farmhouse with a familiar appreciation. Luke had suggested that they might move into the small house adjacent to the farm soon after they married, but Rose wouldn't think of it. She'd loved the woman who would have been her mother-in-law, and part of her longed to bring back the feminine touches that were missing from the home—the watering can of red geraniums on the kitchen windowsill; the sheen and patina of the beautifully carved furniture, which in recent months seemed always to need a dusting; and just the general feel of a woman about the place to cook and clean, heal and listen. She was no fool though, and knew that unless she drew upon *Derr Herr*'s spirit, drinking from the Living Water to nourish herself first, she would have nothing to bring to her new family.

This thought filled her mind as she moved to the bottom of the staircase and glanced upward. Over the years Rose had climbed the staircase to Luke's room more times than she could count, having always been treated like a daughter by the Lantzes. But today something was

different as she gripped the smoothness of the simple balustrade with one hand and swiped at a stray piece of lint on her dress with the other. Today she was nervous, uncertain, and she hesitated at the closed wooden door at the top left of the steps. It wasn't just her friend who lay within, but her betrothed—and the thief of her heart.

She knocked softly, half hoping he slept, but his voice rang true through the wood.

"*Kumme* in."

She took a deep breath, plastered a pleasant expression on her face, and opened the door. Luke gazed at her with that same rich smile he seemed to have grown out of nowhere, and she felt herself flushing for no reason.

"Rose, *kumme*. Close the door and sit down." He patted the edge of the bed near his hip, and she swallowed.

"*Ya*, but maybe I should leave the door open—your *daed*…"

"My *daed* knows you've been up here a hundred times with that door shut, but suit yourself." He stretched his long arms behind his head so that his suspenders strained across his white shirt, and shifted so that his ankle was better positioned on the heap of pillows. "Will you sit down then?" he asked.

Rose forced herself away from the idea of the chair near the window and went to perch on his bedside, trying to keep away from the length of his black-clad leg.

"How's the ankle?"

"Not too bad as long as I stay off it a bit here and there."

Rose nodded and cast about for something else to say.

"So, it's my fault, I'm guessing," he observed.

"What's your fault?"

"You meeting strangers in the woods." He smiled up at her, but his eyes were searching, compelling.

She hadn't been sure how to bring up the subject of his disguise and her enticement with him, but since he'd provided an opening...

"*Ya*, it is your fault. Both for being the stranger and for being—well, a stranger to me—your supposedly best friend." Her voice wavered a bit. "But I could have told you I recognized you."

"You told that stranger you wanted freedom," he said seriously. "Why did you agree to marry me, Rose?"

She caught her breath. She couldn't tell him the things she'd told *Aenti* Tabby when she'd asked the same question, so she sat silent and miserable, staring at the quilt top.

He reached to toy with her fingers and took a deep breath. "It's not too late for anything, Rose. Engagements can be broken. Friendships can remain."

Her gaze flew to his handsome face, and her heart hammered in her chest. "Is that what you want?"

He gave her a rueful smile. "No fair, Rose. Tell me what you want."

You, her mind screamed with sudden certainty, but she wet her lips cautiously. He'd betrayed her trust, and she did want things from him—the truth, for a start. Yet she hadn't been truthful either. She decided on plowing ahead in the discussion and getting to her own accounting later.

"You have no idea how it's been for me," she declared. "I've known you forever but haven't really known you at all—at least, that's how it seems."

"So you feel like I've taken advantage of you in a way?" he asked quietly.

She blew out a frustrated breath. "No...*ya*... I don't

know. And you've never seemed to well—desire me—when you were—are—really you—"

"Why are your fingers purple?" he interrupted.

"Beet juice sugaring."

"Ach," he sighed, squeezing her fingertips. "Well, I have taken advantage of you, I guess. I didn't mean to. And as far as desiring you, Rose—do you have any idea what it's been like holding back for all these months—these years even?"

"Then why did you?"

"Because I felt like the same kid who chased bullfrogs with you and brought home stray dogs. I felt like you'd grown into something beautiful while I was still this awkward person. And then…when *Mamm* died, I guess I just sort of distanced myself, unintentionally, but the feelings were there, Rose."

"Well, I thought you couldn't stand the thought of touching me, and I wanted—well…" She thrilled at the thought that he'd fought back his feelings for her.

His hand drifted to stroke her arm. "What did you want?"

She shook her head stubbornly in reply, and he shifted his weight fully onto his back. "Rose, listen… I'm sorry. I'll prove it to you. Come here." His eyes burned like dark blue flame as he reached out for her.

Rose leaned forward and reached one purple fingertip to trace the contour of his mouth. She brushed her lips against his, following the trail of her finger. His arms drew her closer and he deepened the kiss, and she felt his chest rise and fall in uneven rhythm.

Rose pulled away. There *was* more she wanted from him…answers, for a start.

"Luke, tell me about the thefts," she whispered. "And

the *Englisch* ways of dress and doings. You were baptized last year."

"I know."

"And?" She trailed her lips to the line of his throat, finding a spot behind his ear and tasting the salty sweetness of his skin.

"And I can't go hobbling out there in the dark anymore…at least, not until this ankle heals up."

She broke away from him at his words, forcing herself to focus on the matter at hand.

"What were you doing in the first place? Why would you steal from your own people when they'd gladly give you anything you asked for?"

He opened his eyes with visible reluctance. "Would they?"

"*Ya*, you know that."

He shook his dark head slowly. "They'd give for me, but maybe not for someone else."

"Someone else?" Her heart began to pound in dismay. "Who else?"

"I can't say, Rose. I'm sorry."

"You can't say?"

"*Nee*, but I do need your help."

Rose was rapidly losing patience. "You need my help—but you can't say why? Are you wanting me to pick up where you left off—rebuilding tumbledown shacks, thieving from the neighbors, and pretending I'm *Englisch*?"

"Actually, something like that."

Rose bounced upward so fast that the bedsprings twanged.

Luke grimaced with pain as the pillows under his foot shifted. "Just sit down and listen."

"*Nee*. Not until you start telling me your secrets."

"It's not my secret to tell," he said finally.

She bristled at his words. "Then whose secret is it?"

"Another woman's." He looked grim. "An *Englisch* woman."

LUKE'S CALLS TO Rose went unheeded, and eventually he sank back against his pillow and covered his face with his bandaged hand. He looked up in surprise when the door creaked back open.

"What's all the fuss?" Mark asked, almost apologetically. "I was next door fixing that windowsill for *Daed*."

Luke lowered his hand, feeling like his mouth still burned from Rose's attention, and glanced at his *bruder*. "What?" he asked finally.

"She sure gets riled," Mark offered.

Luke smiled. "I like that."

"It's no wonder—you like thunderstorms too."

"Did you hear much?" Luke's brow furrowed.

Mark shook his head sheepishly. "Told you I was fixing that sill. I wasn't trying to listen."

"All right. And?"

"Josh and I have been talking. We know you don't like being cooped up in that office all day. And—well—now that you're about to marry, you might find the place even more confining. Women can be a passel of trouble sometimes…"

"And you know this how?"

"Shut up. I'm trying to help you. Josh and I want you to tell *Daed* how you really feel."

"How I really feel?"

"*Ya*, you know, about fooling with the books and the

customers. Tell him you want to do woodworking—even if it's just part of the time. It'll be *gut* for you."

Luke smiled, but rolled his eyes. It felt good to be cared for and thought of with such kindness, even though his brothers could drive him *narrisch*. But he didn't want to listen to another lecture on doing what was true to himself. He had enough trouble just being true, or so it seemed.

"I'm fine, Mark. Really. Somebody's got to do it, but *danki* for caring."

His brother snorted. "You're not going to brush me off that easily. After I got over *Daed*'s praise—which rightly belonged to you—I found something of yours in the workshop."

Luke shrugged. "What?"

"This." Mark pulled a folded piece of paper from his pants pocket and strode across the room to hand it to Luke.

Luke opened the drawing, already guessing what it was. "I wondered where this got to. I must have left it one night." He stared down at the intricate design for a mantel shelf that he had hoped to carve for Rose as a wedding gift.

Mark cleared his throat. "That's a fine vision of work, Luke. Better than anything me or Josh could design. You owe it to yourself to work a talent like that. Maybe you owe it to *Derr Herr* too."

Luke exhaled slowly at his brother's unusually serious tone and leveled his own voice in response. "I said I'm fine as I am. That's all."

Mark gave a wry shake of his head. "All right. I tried. Suit yourself." He cuffed Luke lightly on the shoulder as he turned from the bed.

Luke smiled at the veiled affection. Then he carefully folded the drawing and slid it into his pants pocket.

"Hey." Mark paused. "Do you want me to drive you over there tomorrow to talk to her? It's no fair runnin' away on a one-legged man."

"Would you?"

"*Ya*, but maybe she needs a while to cool down."

Luke smiled. "Told you. I like it when she's riled. Keeps me on my toes."

CHAPTER SIXTEEN

ROSE KNEW HE couldn't chase after her when she slammed the door on his pleas. She jogged down the steps, feeling a bit guilty, and slowed briefly to say good-bye to Mr. Lantz.

"Is everything all right, Rose? I heard the door…" He made a helpless gesture with his hands. "I know the engagement time can be stressful."

Rose gave him a wan smile. "It's nothing. Luke is just tired, and I should leave. Please forgive me for hurrying so."

"All right, child. But if there's anything you'd like to talk about—I'm always here."

Rose nodded her thanks and slipped outdoors. She knew exactly where she was going…

CARRYING A FLASHLIGHT, Rose retraced her way through the woods. The light faded fast in the fall evenings, and the dense trees made it appear even darker. She huddled more deeply in the folds of her cloak as she approached the tumbledown shack. She felt nervous for some reason—not afraid of the twilight or the crack and rustle of small creatures among the forest branches, but rather of what she might find at the shack. It was pure instinct that drove her, searching for something, anything—a

clue to the *Englisch* woman Luke spoke of and her place in his life.

Rose shone the flashlight over the open threshold of the door and shuddered a bit when she saw the pile of rubble from the caved-in roof. Luke could have been hurt a lot worse. The small circle of light played against the walls with their peeling dry wood and then back to the floor again. She almost turned away, feeling foolish, when a piece of paper poking out from under a board caught her attention. She tiptoed across the creaking floor and scooped the paper up, then rushed back outside. She had no desire for another board to come tumbling down while she was out alone.

A safe distance from the shack, she balanced her light in one hand and unfolded the lightweight paper with care. It was the page of a coloring book. Amish parents would sometimes allow coloring books and wax colors to occupy very young children during the long Sunday church service, but the pictures were of simple objects like a wagon or an apple. This was an outline of a beautiful rainbow and clouds, obviously colored with diligence and signed by its artist in uneven block letters—TO DADDY LUV ALLY.

Rose bit her lip to stem the sudden welling up of tears that threatened to pour from her eyes.

CHAPTER SEVENTEEN

LUKE KNEW HE was dreaming, but he was too caught, too enmeshed in the images playing inside his mind to force himself to wake. He was losing Rose in a thousand different ways; fast-forwarded images—Rose in a boat on storm-tossed waves drifting away from him, the eerie lights of a carnival's Ferris wheel and Rose spinning high to the top in a swinging singsong motion, Rose standing on the edge of a cavernous drop while he tried desperately to reach her. Everything that was human in him recognized the fear, the distance, and he knew he had to tell her the whole truth. It was the only way he was going to be able to stay close to her, but when he opened his mouth to speak, he awoke shivering and knew that dawn couldn't come fast enough.

"SURE YOU'RE NOT getting sick, Rosie?" her father asked with genuine concern when she appeared wan and sleepy at the breakfast table.

"Nee, Daed." Though she wondered if she actually was sick, as awful as she felt inside. She had spent the night clutching the child's drawing, examining it by the light of a kerosene lamp from every angle, and was no nearer the truth than she had been standing outside the shack the night before.

She tried to think logically. Ally was not a traditional

Amish name, yet she had no doubt the drawing had been a gift of some kind to Luke. It must have slipped from his jeans pocket when he fell. She noticed that the child had drawn faces on the clouds, so that their raindrops looked like tears. What would clouds weep for? And for so young a life's imagination?

And then that single word: *Daddy*. The letters had rung through Rose's mind with all the cadence of a loud and clanging bell, merciless in intensity and reverberating possibility. Luke was twenty-three… The child had to be at least four or five, judging from her letter formation… That would make Luke eighteen if he were… She couldn't finish the thought, not once the whole night through nor now as she tried to concentrate on her scrambled eggs.

But like a bad canker sore that attracts the tongue, her mind kept running over the possibilities with drawing pain. She and Luke had both had a *rumschpringe*, but it had been nothing like some she knew. At least for her it hadn't been… She'd ridden in a car once, gone to two *Englisch* baseball games, and stayed out all night singing round a campfire with some of her Amish friends. She racked her brain for what Luke had been doing and realized she couldn't fill in all the blanks of time. He'd been to her then what he always was…devoted. But friendship or not, she didn't see him all the time. Could he have met an *Englisch* girl? Could he have had a relationship that she didn't know about?

She poked at her eggs and wished now that she would have stayed and listened to his odd request for help instead of running away like a child. She began to pray for guidance as she determinedly ate her food under the watchful eyes of her father and thought that life could be

as difficult as navigating in the dark sometimes. Then she recalled the Bible verse that said "all the dark was as light" to the Lord; it gave her something to cling to as she ate her eggs.

LUKE KNEW THAT he was probably catching Rose's family right at breakfast, but he hadn't been able to go back to sleep. Consequently, he'd poked Mark out of bed with one of his crutches just after dawn, and they now rode through the chill morning air in the buggy.

"I don't mind takin' you." Mark's teeth chattered as he spoke. "But isn't this kind of early for working out your differences?"

Luke waved a vague hand at his brother. "Never too early to make things right."

"Well, I hope breakfast is still on the table. I'd love to have a stack of pancakes made by a woman's hand."

Mark soon had his wish. Mrs. Bender hustled them in out of the cold, and Mr. Bender filled their coffee cups before they could get their coats off. Luke glanced at Rose and found, to his dismay, that she looked worn and weary. He had to get her alone to talk, but the Bender men appeared to love company at any hour.

And in truth, though he was worried for Rose, there was something infinitely soothing about the stack of pancakes that was placed before him, steaming with goodness and light as air. He toyed with his fork, wondering whether to take a bite or just ask to see Rose alone for a moment first.

"Eat up, *sohn*," his future father-in-law urged him. "And tell us how you're feeling with that wrist and ankle. Rosie wasn't quite straight on how it all happened."

Luke caught the daggered look Rose threw him across

the table and decided she was still mad enough. He al.
had no clear idea how to answer her father. He took
careful bite of pancakes and smiled at Mrs. Bende
"Wonderful."

"Ach, ya," Mark agreed with him.

Mrs. Bender gave a quick nod at their appreciatio
"Danki. Eat hearty—there's plenty more," she said, mo
ing back to the stove.

Luke cleared his throat and looked back to Mr. Bend
as Rose arched a delicate dark brow in expectation of h
response. He knew that look; it was a blatant challeng
He'd seen it enough when she'd dared him to climb high
in the old oak or to ford a rushing stream. He gave h
an enigmatic smile.

"I'm feeling much better today, sir. And, of course,
really wasn't Rose's fault." He took a sip of his coffee .
he let his words sink in and watched Rose turn to hi
across the table with a surprised glare.

Ben looked up from his cup. "Not Rosie's fault, yo
say? What exactly did happen?"

Luke shook his head. *"Ach,* I'm not one for telling tal
on my future bride."

James laughed. *"Ya,* but she's still our sister and *na
risch* in her ways. Go ahead and tell."

"Ya, Luke," Rose murmured through tight lips. "L
tell, but don't leave out the bit about your behavior.
mean, just because we're to be married doesn't mean th
we should…well…" She broke off helplessly, and Lul
almost choked on a laugh as the attention of the who
table now turned with quiet interest in his direction. H
Rose could give as *gut* as she got.

Mr. Bender fixed him with a wary eye. "Perhaps w
should have the whole story then."

"*Ach*, by all means," Luke returned easily. "But I'll let Rose begin."

The attention of the table swung back like a pendulum to Rose as she gave Luke a saccharine-sweet smile. "Certainly, *Daed*. We were in the woods together, Luke and I, near the old shack. You remember that tumbledown place about a half mile back on the Lantz property? Well, the sun was shining and the day was young, and Luke thought that the place might actually be a nice place to..." She paused. "Won't you go on, Luke?"

"*Ya*, go on," Mr. Bender suggested, tapping his empty *kaffee* cup against the wood of the table.

Luke shrugged and took another bite of his pancakes. "I thought it might be a fair spot to build a house for Rose and me—you know, far enough away from everyone for a newly married couple, kind of a pretty spot. I suppose it was foolishness, but I wanted to surprise her with it."

"But I thought you were going to live with—" Mark broke off quickly when Luke gave him a quelling glare.

Then he smiled at the table at large. "You'll no doubt think it was too forward of me to want to lead Rose into the place, to imagine the fire in the old fireplace, the placing of furniture, and where best to carve her windows for light."

Mr. Bender cleared his throat and gave a gusty laugh. "I think that's just fine, *sohn*. Just fine."

Aenti Tabby smiled, her eyes misting, and Rose's brothers were momentarily silent. Then James harrumphed in disappointment at the tale. "Well, what wasn't Rose's fault then?"

Luke shook his head with regret. "*Ach*, she wanted me to test the roof."

The men groaned as one and turned to stare at Rose

with accusation. "The roof, Rosie?" her father asked in disbelief. "How could you do that to a man?"

Luke watched Rose open and close her mouth like a beautiful, gasping fish; then she flung her napkin down on the table and ran from the room and out the back kitchen door.

"She left her cloak," Luke observed, rising to wrangle with his crutches. "I'll take it to her."

He swung himself from the room, listening to the murmured comments behind praising his romanticism and foresight, and grimaced. He had the distinct feeling that he'd won the battle but was about to lose the proverbial war.

CHAPTER EIGHTEEN

ROSE TOLD HERSELF that it was foolishness to cry so, simply because Luke had bested her in an argument. Then she admitted to herself that she was really crying over the drawing in her pocket and the terrible lie he'd told when he'd really been fixing that cabin for another woman.

She nestled more deeply between the hay bales of the barn, her sobs dissolving into hiccups, as she tried to warm herself.

"This might help." Luke's voice echoed from above her, and her cloak fell about her shoulders.

She scrambled into the garment and rose, not wanting to feel trapped by the hay and Luke's presence. "Go away. You've had your bit of fun."

He sighed. "Rose. I'm sorry."

"*Ach*, yes you are, Luke Lantz—as sorry a man as I've ever seen." She pushed past him, almost knocking him off balance as she angrily swung a milk bucket down from a hook on the wall. The barn cats begin to entwine about her as she plunked down on a milking stool near Bubbles, the *milch* cow.

"Look, I should have been more honest with you yesterday, and I shouldn't have let you take the worst of that in there. Please forgive me, and listen." His voice was the husky, cajoling voice of the stranger, and she shook

her head furiously as she concentrated on the rhythm of milking, trying to ease away her hurt.

"Rose, come on, please." He bent near her.

She took deep breaths as she filled the cats' pans, then turned to look up at him from the stool. "Fine. Say whatever you like, but I already know the truth. Or...at least one person of it."

He straightened. "What do you mean?"

"Who's Ally?" she asked, staring him straight in the eye.

She watched him blink in surprise. "How do you—"

"Just answer me, Luke. Who is she?"

"A little girl."

"Is she—yours?"

He shook his head in obvious disbelief. "You'd think that?"

Rose lifted her chin stubbornly. "I went back to the shack last night. I found this." She reached into the pocket of her apron and withdrew the coloring sheet. She handed it up to him without a word.

She watched him balance on his crutches to open the page; then he lifted his head to stare at her, anguish and anger lighting his blue eyes.

"I was wrong," he said slowly. "I thought I was the one wearing the mask, but it's you. You, who would marry me, think that I'd leave a child unclaimed, hidden, who was my own? How little you must truly believe in me."

"Well, what am I supposed to believe, Luke?" she cried. "How does all of this look? You just told me yesterday that you couldn't tell the secret, that it belonged to another woman—an *Englisch* woman! Do you know how much that hurt?" Rose could feel the blood pounding in her ears and knew that she was raising her voice

He drew a deep breath. "All right. You're right. I can see how this must look to you."

She rose and came to stand in front of him, her eyes brimming with unshed tears, her words softer now. "Can you, Luke? Can you understand? I don't think badly of you. I just wanted to know for sure. I—I didn't know if I could accept it, if you'd hidden her from me all this time."

"I didn't hide her from you," he whispered low. "Not intentionally."

Rose reached out to touch the coloring page. "Why is she so sad...this Ally? Her clouds are crying."

He stared down at the paper. "That's the part that's not mine, Rose. It's not mine to tell, but I need you to trust me. To help me, even. To help Ally and her family."

"Her family? They're *Englisch*?"

Luke nodded and met her eyes. *"Ya."*

"And they're important to you?" Rose reached her purple fingertips to stroke his hand where it held the paper.

"They were...important to my *mamm*."

"Your *mamm*?"

He nodded, his mouth set in a grim line.

She could have pressed him further, fought him for answers, but thoughts of what the Lord expected as far as honor and fairness in an individual swirled through her mind. She understood valor, as part of her people, to be that part of self that yields instead of fights.

Rose swallowed. "Then they'll become important to me too. I'll help you." She stretched on tiptoe and sealed her words with a kiss.

CHAPTER NINETEEN

THE WEATHER CONTINUED to track in with the mercurial moods of Pennsylvania autumn. Cold to frost one day, blazing sun the next. The trees were beginning to lose their foliage now, and the leaves underfoot were a sure sign that Rose had let too many days slip past before visiting Priscilla. She knew it for sure as she looked across the table into her friend's drawn face.

"Has it been that bad?" Rose asked, wishing she'd visited sooner.

Priscilla nodded. "I just don't understand what all of this means. I've tried to reason it out, and it almost seems like—well, like maybe all of these things going wrong are a sign that I'm not on the right path."

Rose caught her friend's hand in her own. "Priscilla, you know you love Chester."

But Priscilla was staring down in horror. "Your hand is purple."

"I know. Beet juice. Just think, though, if it doesn't wear off soon, it'll look really nice with the blue dress for your wedding."

"That's not funny."

"Sorry." Rose swallowed her smile.

"Well, tell me about you and Luke. How are your plans?"

Rose stifled a sigh. She'd promised to carry out her

and Luke's "plans" later on that evening, but they weren't exactly wedding related. Or maybe that wasn't completely true, she considered. She certainly was being a helpmate to Luke even if no blessing of the bishop had yet been said between them. But even so, she couldn't reveal any of this to Priscilla, who was looking at her expectantly.

"Fine," Rose murmured at last. "Plans are coming along just fine."

In truth, she knew that her *mamm* and *aenti* were the ones who were beginning to prepare for her December wedding, while she seemed to be off in a world of her own with Luke. She really needed to work on her dress...

"Well, your attendant's dress is nearly finished," Priscilla said with relief in her voice. "If you could come over before the wedding to try it on, that would be *gut*."

"I'll be here," Rose promised. She got up from the Kings' kitchen table, then bent to hug her friend. "Don't worry so much. Everything will work out perfectly. You'll see."

Priscilla nodded. "*Danki*, Rose."

Rose left the Kings' house feeling glad to escape the tension that radiated from her friend. She hoped her own wedding wouldn't be as complicated...then laughed aloud at the irony of her thought.

"I STILL FEEL nervous letting you go alone," Luke commented, frowning as he watched Rose put things into her basket in the Lantzes' barn.

"It'll be light for another two hours," she pointed out as she looked toward the horizon.

Luke rubbed his chin. "Maybe I should tell Mark... let him go with you."

"Mark?" Rose looked up with a smile. "Mark can't be

still with a joke in church, let alone keep a secret. Not that I know all of the truth myself, really…"

Luke ignored her comment. He'd said all he could say. Now he tried to test his weight on his ankle and was forced to catch hold of a support beam to stop from falling. She calmly handed him his dropped crutch.

"Luke, I can be up to that stand of pine trees and back before anyone will ever know I'm gone. Besides—" She grinned at him, her eyes sparkling. "I like being the Rob in the Hood."

"That may be true enough, I've no doubt…but you're not 'in the hood.' Won't you reconsider dressing in *Englisch* clothes, or at least like a boy?"

"Nee," she answered, and he sighed in defeat.

They'd gone over this a dozen times. She wouldn't pretend to be something she wasn't when she went to see the *Englisch* woman and her children. And what could he say? He hadn't told her any more than simply that—an *Englisch* woman and her children. But she was willing to help blindly, without knowing, just trusting him. He couldn't ask for anything more.

"Well"—he balanced to reach one hand and place a thumb against her fair cheek—"no one would take you for a boy, no matter your disguise."

"Really?" She blinked coy lashes up at him, and he had to smile.

"Really."

"And why is that?" She leaned against his chest lightly and looped her basket over her arm so that she could encircle his neck with gentle arms.

He couldn't help the catch in his breath at her touch and bent his mouth close to hers. *"Ach,* perhaps it could be the tip of your nose, or the shell of your ears…or the

taste of your lips." He kissed her lingeringly until she pulled away.

"*Ach*, but I've learned my lesson, Luke Lantz. No more kissing strangers in the woods."

"*Nee.*" He swallowed, trying to regulate his breathing. "None of that."

"All right. Then I'll be going." She patted him jauntily on the arm.

He turned to watch her go. "Don't forget," he called, unable to still a last bit of anxiety. "I'll be waiting out back of your house, and if you're not there in two hours I'll…"

She cracked open the barn door and gave him a sidelong glance. "You'll what?"

"Just be there."

He watched her smile and slip out into the light while he stood fretting in the dimness of the barn.

CHAPTER TWENTY

ROSE CLIMBED THROUGH the woods, excited at the prospect of an adventure, even one as simple as bringing some food and supplies to a woman in need. Of course, she wondered why the *Englisch* woman had not gone to her own people or family, but Rose hadn't been able to press any more information out of Luke and had decided that it didn't matter. It was part of *Derr Herr*'s will that she help those who were less fortunate and in want. And surely a woman living in a tent in the middle of the forest with children was in want.

Time slipped by quickly till she came to the stand of pines. The tent was cleverly disguised from view by branches and bracken, and she might have overlooked it had she not been told it was there. She approached the blue liner of the shelter cautiously, calling out to make her presence known.

"Hello! Heelloo! I'm a friend of Luke's!" she called out, stepping closer. She noticed a goat tethered nearby and a pen of chickens.

Then she heard rustling and the high-pitched squeal of a child, and a beautiful dark-haired woman came out of the tent. She balanced a red-faced toddler on her hip and stared at Rose with worry in her dark eyes.

Rose smiled. "Please...it's all right. Luke sent me."

"Is something wrong with him?" The woman's tone was anxious.

Rose had to bite down on a sudden flare of jealousy; it was more than a fair question when he'd been such a help to the family. "He had a small accident. Just a sprained ankle. But he can't make it up here on crutches, so he asked me to come instead. May I come in?"

"Yes…please. I—I'm Sylvia. This is Bobby, my boy. My little girl, Ally, is taking a nap. There's not a whole lot for her to do when her brother's fussy." The woman held open the tent flap.

Rose entered to find a veritable storehouse of items that had gone missing from the community over the past few months. She had to marvel at the larger items, wondering how Luke had hefted them through the woods alone. Then her gaze fell on the little girl curled up beneath a nine-patch quilt. Her long, black curls cascaded over the fabric squares, and Rose felt a tightness in her chest at the kinship of the skin and hair coloring she shared with the child.

"I suppose Luke's told you everything about us… I mean, for one of your people to come up here." Sylvia tried to put Bobby down, but he began to sniffle, and she scooped him back up with a sigh.

"One of my people?" Rose asked. "You mean Amish."

"Yes, sorry. Does Luke have good friendships with the Amish?"

Rose placed her basket on a small chest of drawers. "Luke *is* Amish," she said.

The woman laughed low, revealing a devastating smile. "Luke? Amish? Are you sure we know the same person?"

Rose began to unpack her basket, not knowing what

to say. Part of her wanted to retort and part of her wanted more of the truth. To this woman and her children, Luke had been *Englisch*. He'd explained to her that the disguise made it easier to move about without attracting curiosity, both in town and in the woods, but she still couldn't help wondering if that was the full reason.

"Hey, I'm sorry if I said something wrong. Maybe Luke just seems different to us." Sylvia's tone was genuine, but her words pricked at Rose's heart.

"It's no matter. Look, I'll probably come again soon. Is there anything else you need?" *And can you tell me why you're here...in the middle of nowhere, with my betrothed as your provider?*

"The Lord has blessed us already with Luke's providing, and now yours. We're grateful for whatever you bring. Hopefully, it won't be much longer until Jim... well, you know."

Rose wanted to say that she had no idea what *until* meant or who Jim was, but she was glad that the woman's tone had lingered longingly over the man's name. She also felt chagrined that the woman mentioned the Lord with such genuineness while she was hardly having Christian feelings herself. Still, Luke could have told her more, since Sylvia didn't seem to have a problem with her knowing.

She'd just placed the final jar of preserves on a stand when a small, cherubic voice spoke up from the little bed.

"Mommy...who's that?" The little girl scooted up to grab at her mother's jeans.

"A friend of Luke's," Sylvia responded, stroking her daughter's hair.

"I'm Rose."

The child's eyes grew wide with interest. "Your hair's

like mine. Does Luke think it's pretty too? Why are you dressed up all funny? Did you see my pet goat? Is it Halloween yet? Mommy, when can I have a costume?"

"Shhh," Sylvia admonished.

"It's all right." Rose smiled. "But I need to be going before it gets dark."

"Wait!" Ally cried. "I always make a picture for Luke to take when he visits my daddy. Shall I give it to you?"

"Certainly," Rose said. She accepted the coloring sheet the child tore painstakingly from the book and made a mental note to bring more toys and things to occupy the little girl the next time she came. *"Danki,"* she said. "That means thank you." She chuckled as Ally tried to get her tongue around the strange syllables.

"Thank you again," Sylvia said as she lifted the tent flap. "And be careful."

"I will. Don't worry." Rose waved good-bye and set out down through the maze of trees, so deep in thought that she didn't notice when she took a wrong turn.

CHAPTER TWENTY-ONE

LUKE HAD DRIVEN the buggy round the back way of the Benders' property at the expense of his ankle and now swung along between his crutches, anxious and in pain. It was already over two hours since Rose had left. *I never should have let her go*, he berated himself.

He kept searching the distant tree line when a voice behind him nearly made him jump out of his skin.

"Is that you, Luke?" *Aenti* Tabby asked with curiosity.

"*Ya*, ma'am... I was just, uh, waiting for Rose."

"Behind the barn? And with your ankle? Wouldn't you be more comfortable inside?"

The older woman walked up to him with a smile, but her eyes were keen. Luke sighed inwardly. It was next to impossible to keep a secret from *Aenti* Tabby.

"Rose went up to the woods to gather...um...late berries or something, and I said I'd wait here until she—"

Tabby crossed her arms over her ample bosom and harrumphed loudly. "Luke Lantz! Has Rose run off because you two were arguing? Is she out alone this time of the evening?"

"Uh...that sounds reasonable, doesn't it?"

"I'll get the boys to go and find her then," Tabby said.

"That would be *wunderbaar*," Luke agreed, relieved that someone could search for her.

"Who needs finding, *Aenti* Tabby?" Rose asked breezily as she came soft-footed from the dark field.

Luke blew out a sigh of relief, but he wanted to holler at her too, for looking so casual and pretty when he'd been worried sick.

"There you are, child!" *Aenti* Tabby exclaimed. "And a *gut* thing too. It's never wise to run off when you're having a bit of a spat. It's better to stay and work things out."

Luke threw Rose a pleading glance as she slowed her steps and brought her swinging basket to an abrupt halt.

"Uh, *Aenti* Tabby, it was my fault, in truth," Luke supplied.

"As usual," Rose murmured, and he had to suppress a smile.

"Well, it's too cold out here. Come inside and warm up, the both of you." *Aenti* Tabby turned to go.

"We'll be along shortly," Rose called.

Luke watched her approach warily, wondering how the time at the tent had gone. Then he caught the heat in her green eyes and thought they wouldn't be going into the house anytime soon.

ROSE WATCHED HIM standing in the twilight and thought how handsome he was, then frowned at the thought. Why her mind would drift to how he looked when she had a thousand questions to ask was beyond her understanding.

"How were they?" he asked.

"Beautiful," she said shortly, speaking the first word that came to mind.

He smiled. "Ally's like you, I think."

She shrugged, flicking her flashlight on and off for a moment. "Sylvia didn't know you were Amish... You are Amish, right?"

He laughed. "*Ya*, Rose."

"It's not funny. Besides the excuse of moving about, why else did you pretend to be something else... *Englisch*?"

He sobered suddenly. "You seemed to like it well enough at times."

She didn't appreciate the reminder and bit back an angry retort, remembering what the Bible said about a soft answer turning away wrath. "That is true. But I hope that it was the real you, no matter your dress, who touched and kissed me those times."

"It was. I'm sorry."

"So, will you finally tell me about Sylvia?"

He sighed. "Her husband's name is Jim—she probably mentioned that."

Rose nodded.

"Well, Jim knew me as *Englisch*, or at least I thought he did..."

He stopped, and Rose sighed and slapped her hands against her sides. "Luke, I know you say this isn't your secret to tell, but I'm involved now. I've seen that woman and her children. They shouldn't be living alone—it's dangerous."

"Do you think I don't know that? Don't think about it a hundred times a day?"

"Then tell me why they are there." She waited.

"All right. All right." He took a deep breath and turned away from her to face the dark fields. "Before I joined the church, and after *Mamm* died, I sort of lost things in my head. One part of me did all the right things—saw you, went to church, worked; but one part of me was wild with pain and anger. But I had to keep that part of myself secret. I couldn't hurt *Daed*...or you."

"Maybe I would have understood," she said softly.

"No, not when I didn't understand myself. So I just kept up two parts of me, two lives… I started going into town and running around with this gang of *Englischers*. They had no idea I was Amish, but this wasn't like *rumschpringe*. They were a dangerous lot…drugs, drinking, crime. When I began to see how they really lived, I backed away. Most of them were homeless, so when I would head back to my warm bed at the house, they were sleeping under bridges, trying to avoid the shelters because they thought they didn't need the help." He pivoted on his crutches to face her. "My *mamm* volunteered at one of the homeless shelters in town. Did you know that?"

"*Nee*…an *Englisch* shelter?"

He gave a bitter laugh. "*Ya*. How many homeless Amish do you know?" He exhaled. "I'm sorry, Rose. I didn't mean to snap."

"And I didn't mean to question… I just…your *mamm* was so busy about her own house."

"She was, but she found time to give to others too… even if it was unusual to find an Amish woman volunteering alone at a place like that."

"Did your *daed* know?"

"We all did…we kind of teased her about it too— 'going looking for trouble,' I said once." He looked grim. "When she got sick, she had me take some jellies and things down there. At first I didn't want to go. I thought it was a dirty place, foul smelling…full of *Englischers* who supposedly wouldn't work. But later I discovered the truth…the secret that nobody *chooses* to be homeless, at least not at first. *Ach*, there were the boys I ran with, to be sure, but there were families too…children."

"Ally?" Rose asked softly, trying to piece the story together.

"*Ya*...the shelter is okay, but it's no place for kids, and every family only has so much time that they can stay. When Sylvia's time ran out, I just thought... I don't know what I thought—that I could honor my mother by helping Sylvia have some type of home... Jim got into trouble with the law a couple months back. He's in the local jail waiting for trial—I go see him when I can. Take him Ally's pictures."

Rose frowned. "But surely there are other *Englisch* means of help—housing, medical insurance..."

"Jim was afraid they'd lose the kids—if the police knew Sylvia was in the area and could question her, he was afraid they might charge her too."

"Charge her with what?"

"Robbery. A series of home robberies. He said he was innocent, and I believe him."

"But then you robbed from your own people to help them. Why didn't you just go to the bishop and tell the truth?" Rose asked.

"The bishop...who'd want no part of *Englisch* law. Who'd not hide a woman and children—"

"You don't know that," Rose cried. "You've not only taken on the role of thief but also judge—of your own people, your own community. You've tried to do this all alone, and it's not going to work anymore, Luke. Cold weather's going to set in, and then what?"

"I don't know," he said. "But I ask you to keep the secret, Rose. Just a little longer. The trial's bound to be soon."

"And if Jim is found guilty? What will you do then?" she asked, closing her eyes against the thought.

"Please, Rose. Just keep the secret. Let me worry about the rest."

"I don't know what to do," she said miserably.

He moved closer to her, and she could feel the heat from his body through his heavy black coat. "I shouldn't have involved you, but this will work out. I promise."

She looked him in the eyes and said the only thing she could think of. "I'll pray."

CHAPTER TWENTY-TWO

LUKE CONCENTRATED ON a particularly complicated gouge in the wood he was working for Rose's mantelpiece wedding gift. It didn't help that he had to do it by candlelight and so late at night, but he couldn't risk starting the generator up and waking his father.

He hadn't seen Rose for a few days...not since the conversation behind the barn. And he wasn't sure what she might be feeling about him at this point. She'd raised a lot of issues that made him think, but the thing that struck home the most was her idea that he was judging his own people.

He wasn't sure when or how it had happened, but some way or another he'd come to a place in his head where he believed that the community would fail him. He sighed as he moved the lantern closer and bent over the wood.

"It was you, my *sohn*," said a voice behind him.

Luke turned to blink at his father. "*Daed*? Why are you up?"

"I might ask you the same thing. But I can see by that workmanship that it was you and not Mark who did that burled elm piano front. It's the truth, *nee*?"

Luke laid the tools carefully on the workbench and braced his hands on his crutches, shifting his weight from where he'd been leaning against the table. "It's just a hobby, *Daed*."

His father stepped closer and lifted the lantern high over the table with a work-worn hand. "A hobby? Such gifts from *Derr Herr* should never be wasted on a hobby. Wasn't it you who told me something about speaking the truth and releasing pain? I'm afraid you've hidden much pain from me, Luke. And I've been too blind and selfish to notice."

Luke met his father's eyes in the light of the lamp. "I never wanted you to know, *Daed*. I am content to do the books. I know it's a help to you."

"Content? Perhaps, but not joyful, my *sohn*. Not working with joy and purpose as the Lord would desire."

Luke hung his head. "*Nee*, sir."

He heard his father put the lamp back on the table, then looked up as he was caught in the older man's loving embrace. "Forgive me," his father whispered.

"There's nothing to forgive. Please don't worry, *Daed*. We can go on as before."

His father stepped away and clapped him on the shoulders. "Not one minute longer. We'll find someone else to do the books. And you will take your place as a carpenter...as The Carpenter would have you do."

Luke's eyes welled with tears. He felt undone inside, like his secrets were slowly being revealed by *Derr Herr*'s hand, one by one.

"*Danki, Daed. Danki.*"

AFTER EVERYONE HAD gone to bed, Rose began to work on her wedding dress in earnest. She'd been to see Sylvia and the children only once since she and Luke had last talked. And she wasn't sure how he was feeling, since she'd had no word from him. She sighed as she fingered the cloth of her wedding dress, wondering what the future

held for them. Shadowy images of dark-haired children danced through her mind. Then she looked up from the kitchen table in surprise as Luke maneuvered himself inside the kitchen door with his crutches. She blinked, feeling her heart begin to pound, and wondered if she simply imagined his presence.

"Hiya!" He smiled brightly.

She glanced with dismay from her wedding dress pieces back to his handsome face and blurted out the first thing that came to mind. "Nobody's up. And I'm working on my wedding dress."

"Well, that's nice, isn't it?" He slipped his hat off.

"Ya… I mean, no… I can't ask you in. I told you— I'm working on my wedding dress. I thought it would be a surprise."

He glanced at the fabric and pattern pieces spread about the table and turned his head a bit. "Suppose I don't look? It's blue, right?"

"You know every wedding dress is blue."

He balanced on his crutches and swung his injured ankle absently. "True. But there're all kinds of blue— the sky on a summer's afternoon, the smoky blue of a kitten's fur, the creek when the light dances off it until it stings your eyes with its beauty…" His voice dropped an octave. "Your eyes, when they're a sleepy blue-green after you've been kissed."

Rose's mouth went dry as she tried to shake off the spell of his words. Since when did he know how to speak so…like he was touching her, though he stood across the room? She cleared her throat and clutched the pair of shears in her hand closer to her chest.

He smiled. "Nervous, Rose?"

"*Nee...* I just...need to get this work done," she whispered.

"Speaking of work—I took your advice and told my father the truth. I've got a new job."

"What?"

"He's going to hire someone else to do figures for him. I want to work the wood. My hands ache for it."

She couldn't help glancing down at his strong hands as he spoke and thought about the moment in the old shack when he'd wound her hair about his hand. "I'm so proud of you," she said and meant it.

"Are you? That's *gut*." He swung himself around to her side of the table and placed a finger against her lips when she tried to protest. "Shhh. I'm not looking."

She fell silent under his touch and barely noticed when he reached with unerring fingers to lift a spool of blue thread from the table. He balanced on his crutches and started to unravel the thread.

"Luke...what are you doing?"

She watched him trail the end of the thread across her bare wrist, which was still the lightest purple from her sugar beets encounter. Then he feathered the blue line up across her arm and shoulder and used it to tickle the tip of her nose. She felt curious, like she was watching herself outside of her own body and could only follow in sensory delight wherever he led the thread. When he traced her lips, she closed her eyes, and soon his mouth followed where the blue had been. She lost herself in the deep silence of the kiss.

When he broke away, his breathing was ragged. "Guess I'm helping you thread your wedding dress."

She bit her lip as an impulse shook her and she picked up the piece of thread where it trailed against her shoul-

der. "Are you? Then maybe you should do a little more work."

She twirled the thread between her thumb and forefinger, then let it drift up across the high bones of his cheeks. She smiled up at his surprised grin and ran the thread behind his ear. Stretching on tiptoe, she let her lips follow the blue tendril down his neck, and he made a rough sound in his throat.

"Any work you like," he whispered.

But the moment was broken by a frantic knocking on the back kitchen door.

Rose dropped the shears and brushed past him, pulling off the thread. Who could it be at this time of night?

She opened the door to reveal a bedraggled and panicked Sylvia. The woman held Ally in her arms and Bobby was asleep in a backpack on her back. "Please," she gasped. "I just took a chance that this might be Luke's house. Please do something. Ally's having a bad asthma attack. She can't breathe!"

CHAPTER TWENTY-THREE

ROSE TOOK THE little girl into her arms, alarmed at the bluish tinge and the rasping intake of the tiny lips.

"Dr. Knepp's," Luke ordered. "I've got the buggy outside."

"*Nee*, it's too far." Something compelled Rose's heart. "We'll go to Bishop Ebersol's. His wife is an excellent healer."

"All right," Luke agreed reluctantly.

"Please, hurry," Sylvia urged.

Luke made short work of the drive despite his ankle, and Rose flew from the buggy with Ally in her arms. She climbed the familiar steps of the Ebersol farmhouse and kicked at the solid front door.

A lamp soon cast eerie shadows on the porch and the shimmering fall of the child's hair as Mrs. Ebersol stared out at them.

"Please," Rose gasped. "She can't breathe."

Mrs. Ebersol was nothing if not practical; she urged them all inside at once. "Is it asthma like our John? Or the bronchitis?"

"Asthma," Sylvia half sobbed.

Luke had taken Bobby from her back and stood with his weight on his ankle holding the sleeping child.

"The child needs steam to breathe in and some menthol. Our John used to have bad attacks. Bring her in here

to the kitchen… I'll wake the bishop when we're through, though he's probably already up."

"Right here." Bishop Ebersol moved quickly, bringing more lamps.

Mrs. Ebersol flew about the kitchen bringing various salves and herbs to where Rose sat holding the child at the table.

"Teakettle's always on the boil when you're a bishop's wife. Now let's make a little tent with this cloth and get her face as near to the steam and herbs as possible. The menthol and peppermint oil act like bronchodilators. Fancy word for opening the airways. That's it. Breathe it in, little one."

The kitchen was quiet as the child's breathing slowly eased. Within minutes, Ally opened eyes and then coughed heartily, trying to pull back from the steam.

"No," Rose crooned, gently holding back the small hands. "Just be still, Ally. It will help you breathe."

In another ten minutes the asthma attack was under control. Everyone sat drained and silent for a moment when Mrs. Ebersol eased the teakettle away.

"What you folks need is some hot chocolate," the bishop's wife announced, tightening the belt of her voluminous housecoat. She rose from Ally's side and laid a reassuring hand on Sylvia's shoulder. "It's all right now."

She and the bishop moved about the kitchen with the accord of those long married, and soon steaming mugs of cocoa were placed on the table. Rose gave Ally back to Sylvia to hold when the child fussed for a drink.

"Let her have a sip," Mrs. Ebersol suggested. "Is your car somewhere about? You're welcome to stay here for the night. Perhaps Luke and the bishop might bring in your things."

Sylvia raised a worried gaze to Luke and Rose. "I—I don't have a car."

Luke rose to his feet. "Bishop Ebersol," he said clearly. "Might we talk for a few minutes in private?"

"*Ya*, certainly. Come this way."

The bishop lifted a lamp, and Rose met Luke's shuttered gaze as she began to pray for him and the words he might feel convicted to say.

CHAPTER TWENTY-FOUR

THE NEXT DAY was church service, and beyond driving her home and telling her that he would speak at the end of the service, Luke didn't go into what he and the bishop had discussed. Rose felt it within her spirit that it was not a time to question, so she went quietly to bed.

"What was all the ruckus last night?" her *mamm* asked when Rose entered the kitchen the next morning. "I thought you and Luke might have been having an argument."

Rose sighed. She'd decided last night that the next time she was asked a direct question about what had been going on lately that she would give a direct answer. She found herself telling her *mamm*, and the rest of the family as they entered for breakfast, about Sylvia and the children.

Her father pointed with his forked bacon. "You mean to say that Luke has been the Rob in the...the thief hereabouts?"

Rose shrugged. "For a cause."

Her *daed* considered. "Well, Bishop Ebersol's a wise man; he'll handle it all right. But you, young lady, had no business out in those woods alone."

Rose was struck by a sudden inspiration. "I did say that your thief might be female, *Daed*. Perhaps I just had to prove my point."

Her *daed* stared at her, then laughed aloud as she'd hoped he would. Her brothers joined in reluctantly. Even her *mamm* and *Aenti* Tabby smiled.

So they went in good spirits to the buggies and on to church, which was being held at the Lamberts' that morning. Joseph Lambert greeted them with a warm smile at the door.

Rose hoped that her marriage might go as well as that of Joseph and Abby. Abby Lambert certainly looked happy as she sat in the married women's section, her stomach rounded with obvious pregnancy. Rose pushed aside the thought of carrying Luke's child and made her way to sit down next to Priscilla. Rose squeezed her friend's hand and decided that Priscilla was looking better, though still too pale, as the wedding loomed.

Then the service began, and Rose was lost in the ancient soothing rhythm of the hymns and the message of Scripture. Then, at last, when she thought Luke must have been mistaken about speaking, the bishop rose to address the community.

"Before we would dismiss, there's a matter of confession that's come to my attention. Young Luke Lantz would ask your patience while he speaks." The bishop sat down, and the crowd rustled with curiosity as Luke made his way forward to the head of the benches.

Rose's heart ached at his pallor, but she knew his eyes were steady and clear. Priscilla now clasped her hand, and Rose was grateful for the support.

Luke began to speak in a strong voice, and the general rustlings of the crowd ceased as his words burned into Rose's heart.

"I have betrayed you all," he began. "All of you, but especially those I love. It's easier to tell what you may

think is the heavier offense—that I've been the one who stole from you these past months."

Rose couldn't ignore the faint gasps of surprise, and swallowed hard.

"Why I took from you doesn't matter. I did it. It was wrong. I confess this wrong and beg your forgiveness. But...there's more..."

Rose felt his gaze rivet to hers across the space of crowded benches.

"I've betrayed you by expecting little from you as a community, as a people. The truth is...the truth is that I've been angry at *Derr Herr* since my mother died. And I've been angry at all of you. I started to believe that if you didn't have the power to save my mother, then you had no power together at all. And that is so wrong. Someone very wise told me that I had judged you, and it's true. I might have asked for your help for a woman and family in need, but I didn't. I believed I could do it alone..."

His voice broke a bit, and silent tears slipped down Rose's cheeks. Priscilla squeezed her hand harder.

"Alone is not what our people are about. Our strength lies in our community. I have wronged the community. I confess this before you all and ask for your forgiveness." He dropped to his knees and bent his dark head.

The bishop rose and placed a hand on Luke's shoulder. "Is it the will of the community, then, to grant Luke Lantz the forgiveness he begs for?"

There was a general assent of *ya*'s, and Rose breathed a sigh of relief.

"Then," the bishop continued, "please come forward following our dismissal to greet Luke Lantz with renewed goodwill and acceptance."

Rose received Priscilla's hug, then wended her way

forward to stand next to Luke. He caught her hand in a fierce grasp, which she returned as people began to come forward.

"Stole my best linens, young man?" Esther Mast inquired with a glint in her faded blue eyes.

"Yes. I'm very sorry," Luke said steadily.

The old woman sniffed. "Well, keep 'em. Probably for a *gut* cause. Would have given 'em to you had you asked."

"I know that now."

"Hmmm," Mrs. Mast mused, ignoring the press of the crowd around her with the distinct dignity of the aged. "Seems like I've got some more linens in a trunk upstairs. They'll make a fine wedding gift to go with what you already got." She gave Rose's hand a squeeze with her bony fingers.

"Danki," Rose whispered.

Joseph Lambert was next. "Hey, anytime you want to talk, friend, I'm here. *Ach*, and keep that old goat of ours too. Kicked me once too often." He shook Luke's hand and winked at Rose.

They came, one after the other, to forgive and to give, telling Luke to keep all that he had taken and offering more should he need it.

Rose thrilled in heart and praised the Lord when Luke turned to her and whispered, "You were right, Rose."

CHAPTER TWENTY-FIVE

WORD OF THE details of Sylvia and the children spread about the community, and Luke was inundated with offers of places to stay, clothes for the children, and a hundred other small kindnesses that made abundance seem too small a word.

In all of the details, he barely had time to talk to Rose and sheepishly asked Joshua one morning if he'd do a favor for him.

"Flowers?" Joshua snorted. "Weeds, you mean? There's nothing much growing now… Why not ride into town and get her something?"

"Just get a bouquet of something pretty. She likes the outdoors, and I want to get over there this evening and see her alone."

"Suit yourself. I'll have it ready."

That evening Joshua thrust a thick bouquet into the darkness of the buggy.

"Danki." Luke sneezed, wondering exactly what his brother had picked. He drove the short distance to the Benders', glad to be rid of his crutches, and went to knock softly on the back door.

Rose opened it with a shy smile, and he produced the bouquet, watching her face light up as she stepped back into the light of several lamps. Then he noticed what she held and dashed the flowers from her arms to the floor.

"Luke? What—are you—"

"*Ach*, that *bruder* of mine! It's poison ivy, Rose."

She gasped and ran to the sink. They both knew that she was badly allergic to the stuff, and somehow Joshua had grabbed a strand as background to the Queen Anne's lace and ragweed. She scrubbed frantically at her wrists and hands.

"I think I got it all. I barely held it."

Luke scraped the would-be bouquet from the floor; he was not allergic to the annoying weed. Then he bundled the stuff together and stalked toward the door. "So much for romance," he muttered.

"It's the thought that counts," Rose called with a smile.

He laughed as he went outside with the offending gift, then returned to wash his hands at the sink. She caught his arm and pulled him to a set of rockers in the living room.

"Everyone's gone to bed, but I wanted to show you the coloring pages Ally's been sending over from the Ebersols' house." She opened several wildly colored scenes, and he nodded.

"Nice."

"You're not getting it." She poked his ribs. "Her clouds aren't crying anymore."

"Oh, I didn't notice—but wait. I thought the clouds were crying for her daddy?"

Rose shrugged. "Maybe. Or maybe just for a sense of home or"—she blinked her green cat's eyes at him—"or community."

He reached over, and with one hand pulled her easily onto his lap. He nuzzled her throat cheerfully until she laughed and tried to push him away.

"Luke!"

He was concentrating on her hair, taking deep breaths of its heady scent. "Hmmm?"

She sighed and relaxed back against him. "Nothing."

THE NEXT DAY was Friday, and Rose woke with her mind set to keep her promise to Priscilla and go and pick up her dress for the wedding. But when she sat up in bed, it was to look with horror at her wrists and inner arms.

"Ach, no," she whispered aloud.

She dressed hurriedly, biting her lip in an effort to make no move to scratch, but the long wool sleeves of her dress were torture against the rash. She made her way to Priscilla's in near tears from the sensation and knocked hurriedly at the back door, shifting her weight from one foot to the other.

"Rose? What's wrong?" Priscilla looked like she was prepared for anything from an ostrich to an airplane landing, and Rose plastered a smile on her face.

"Nothing," she managed. Then she could stand it no longer and burst into a spat of intense itching that made her jump and then wriggle with short-lived satisfaction.

But Priscilla's mother must have recognized the outlandish movements, because she soon rooted in her herbal closet and sent Rose off with her attendant's dress and some salve that she guaranteed would help the affliction.

Rose danced out onto the back porch, then gave in to another fit of intense itching, all the while praying silently that the salve would do something miraculous.

CHAPTER TWENTY-SIX

THE WEATHER HAD taken on a distinct chill, the spiny spindles of tree limbs forming bare arms raised in supplication to the still bright sky.

That afternoon Rose opened the door to Luke, but knew that she probably looked distracted.

"Rose? Are you all right?" Luke took his hat off and stepped aside to reveal a thin *Englisch* man. "Rose, this is Jim. He was released yesterday and made his way out here. He was found not guilty."

Rose snapped herself back from her meditations on not scratching. "*Ach*, that's wonderful. Please come in."

She held the door wider, but Luke shook his head. "We can't. He's got a car and is going to pick up Sylvia and the kids. They're going to Colorado for a new start where his parents live."

Rose bit her lip as the desire to scratch radiated along her arms, but she didn't want Luke to know and feel bad. "That's great," she burst out, reaching to shake Jim's hand.

And then she could stand it no longer and nearly doubled over with her efforts to get at her arms to her satisfaction. Luke groaned.

"What's wrong?" Jim asked.

"Poison ivy," she heard Luke mutter. "Rose, don't scratch."

"Don't scratch!" She rounded on him, then smiled again at Jim, lowering her voice. "Don't scratch? I'll scratch you, Luke Lantz, if you don't…"

Apparently, her betrothed knew when to beat a hasty retreat. She waved good-bye to a bemused Jim.

"Is MRS. KING's salve not working?" *Aenti* Tabby asked from where she sat reading her Bible near her bed.

"I want to believe it's helping." Rose sighed as she maneuvered onto her aunt's bed, rubbing her woolen clad arms against the quilt.

"Well, let's talk about something to distract you then… Tell me if things are better now that you know a little more about Luke."

Rose flopped on her belly and regarded her *aenti*'s merry face. "I have the feeling that there's a lifetime of things for me to learn about Luke."

"That's as it should be—like the Bible says, 'new treasures out of old.'"

Rose gave in to one delightful scratch. "Then I'll pray that we have a lifetime of treasures together, *Aenti* Tabby."

The older woman smiled. "You will, Rose. You will."

ON MONDAY MORNING, Luke's father told him to step into the office. "Just go along and have a hello with our new bookkeeper."

A new bookkeeper? What was his *daed* talking about? Luke shrugged and knocked on the office door with good grace, then, when no one answered, opened it slowly.

The back of a dark head and *kapp* greeted him.

"Rose?" he asked in disbelief.

She spun in a new swivel chair and smiled up at him,

pencil in hand. "*Hiya!* You've always known I have a head for figures."

He smiled slowly. "So you do, but what about…?"

"The house?" she queried. "I can do both, Luke Lantz. Women are great at multitasking."

He had to laugh, then bent close to her. "Is that your secret, Rose? Being able to do two things at once?"

"Maybe. What did you have in mind?" She blinked bright eyes at him, and he lowered his mouth to hers.

"*Ach*, I don't know," he whispered, pressing his lips to hers. "Maybe this…and this…"

"And this," she added, drawing him close again until he had to sigh aloud.

* * * * *

ACKNOWLEDGMENTS

I'd like to acknowledge Beth Wiseman and Kathy Fuller, who were a treat to work with on this novella. These ladies are smart and supportive, as always! Thank you to Natalie Hanemann for her keen insight and to L.B. Norton for her deft editing. A big thanks to my critique partner, Brenda Lott, for her scene insight and to my mother-in-law, Donna Long, for her marketing support. As always, thank you to my Amish readers and especially to my family. I love you, Scott.

ABOUT THE AUTHOR

Kelly Long is the author of the Patch of Heaven series. She was born and raised in the mountains of Northern Pennsylvania. She's been married for twenty-six years and enjoys life with her husband, children, and Bichon. Visit Kelly on Facebook (Fans of Kelly Long) and Twitter: @KellyLongAmish.